Praise for the Blackman Agency Investi{...}

Murder in Rat Alley

"Nicely plotted…intelligent, kind protagonists and an eye-opening historical background help make this one a winner."
—*Publishers Weekly*

"Mark de Castrique fabricates an elaborate, multi-layered mystery that employs espionage elements to deepen the intrigue. The author's skill creating divergent clues that he deftly connects makes for a fascinating read at a compelling pace."
—*Reviewing the Evidence*

"*Murder in Rat Alley* is definitely a very compelling mystery with some surprising twists and unexpected connections!"
—*Fresh Fiction*

"Someone trying to bury the past kills again and threatens Blackman and Robertson before the full, convoluted scheme, involving more decades-old murder and espionage, is revealed."
—*Booklist*

Hidden Scars

2018 Thomas Wolfe Memorial Literary Award nominee

"With its strong sense of place, depiction of racial tension that still lingers in the new South, and appealing sleuths, de Castriqu{...}
—*Library Journal*

"De Castrique combines an examination of the South's troubled racial history with a smart probe of current political-financial shenanigans."

—*Publishers Weekly*

"De Castrique's sixth delivers a vivid gallery of suspects, lively dialogue, and an attractive pair of sleuths."

—*Kirkus Reviews*

A Specter of Justice

"A good choice for anyone who enjoys small-town mysteries and ghost stories."

—*Booklist*

"…an entertaining whodunit with colorful characters, swift-footed plotting, and a confident narrative voice."

—*Kirkus Reviews*

A Murder in Passing

"This solid whodunit offers readers a glimpse into a curious chapter of cultural history."

—*Publishers Weekly*

"This fascinating mystery, merging past and present, brings some little-known history to light and shows that laws change much faster than attitudes, as Sam and Nakayla, an interracial couple themselves, discover."

—*Booklist*

The Sandburg Connection

"Stellar… A missing folk song, a buried treasure from Civil War days, and a pregnant goat all play a part in this marvelous blend of history and mystery seasoned with information about Carl Sandburg's life."

—*Publishers Weekly*, Starred Review

"A suspicious death on top of Glassy Mountain turns two laid-back private sleuths into prime suspects."

—*Kirkus Reviews*

"Folk songs, Sandburg, and Civil War history—what a winning combination!"

—*Library Journal*

The Fitzgerald Ruse

"An excellent regional mystery, full of local color and historical detail."

—*Library Journal*

"The warmth of Sam and Nakayla's relationship and Sam's challenged but determined heart make for a great read."

—*Kirkus Reviews*

"Readers will hope to see a lot more of the books' amiable characters."

—*Publishers Weekly*

Blackman's Coffin

"A wealth of historical detail, an exciting treasure hunt, and credible characters distinguish this fresh, adventurous read."

—*Publishers Weekly*, Starred Review

"Known for his effortless storytelling, de Castrique once again delivers a compelling tale blending fact and fiction."

—*Library Journal*

"In the struggling Sam Blackman, de Castrique has created a compelling hero whose flinty first-person narrative nicely complements Henderson's earnest, measured, and equally involving account."

—*Kirkus Reviews*

Also by Mark de Castrique

The Blackman Agency Investigations
Blackman's Coffin
The Fitzgerald Ruse
The Sandburg Connection
A Murder in Passing
A Specter of Justice
Hidden Scars
Murder in Rat Alley

The Buryin' Barry Mysteries
Dangerous Undertaking
Grave Undertaking
Foolish Undertaking
Final Undertaking
Fatal Undertaking
Risky Undertaking
Secret Undertaking

Standalone Thrillers
The Singularity Race
The 13th Target
Double Cross of Time

Mysteries for Young Adults
A Conspiracy of Genes
Death on a Southern Breeze

FATAL SCORES

FATAL SCORES

A BLACKMAN AGENCY INVESTIGATION

MARK DE CASTRIQUE

Poisoned Pen
PRESS

Published by Poisoned Pen Press, an imprint of Sourcebooks
P.O. Box 4410, Naperville, Illinois 60567-4410
(630) 961-3900
sourcebooks.com

Library of Congress Cataloging-in-Publication Data

Names: De Castrique, Mark, author.
Title: Fatal scores : a Blackman Agency investigation / Mark de Castrique.
Description: Naperville, Illinois : Poisoned Pen Press, [2021] | Series: A
   Blackman Agency investigation
Identifiers: LCCN 2020017181 (trade paperback) | (epub)
Subjects: GSAFD: Mystery fiction.
Classification: LCC PS3604.E124 F36 2021 (print) | DDC 813/.6--dc23
LC record available at https://lccn.loc.gov/2020017181

Printed and bound in the United States of America.
SB 10 9 8 7 6 5 4 3 2 1

For Barbara Peters and Robert Rosenwald,
who made my stories possible

At last he (Béla Bartók) smelled the fresh air again, saw the sky, felt the soil…the constantly tormenting screams of the auto horns and police sirens were drowned in memory by the concert of birds.

—Music publisher Hans Heinsheimer on composer
Béla Bartók's stay in Asheville, North Carolina

I happen to think that computers are the most important thing to happen to musicians since the invention of catgut, which was a long time ago.

—Dr. Robert Moog, inventor of the Moog synthesizer

As we have misused our richest land, we have misused ourselves; as we have wasted our bountiful water, we have wasted ourselves; as we have diminished the lives of one whole segment of our people, we have diminished ourselves.

—Wilma Dykeman, environmentalist
and social activist

If it wasn't for baseball, I'd be in either the penitentiary or the cemetery.

—Babe Ruth

Chapter One

"There's no place where a beer tastes better than at a baseball game." Attorney Hewitt Donaldson made the proclamation over his shoulder as he juggled a hot dog and an oversized plastic cup of brew.

I followed him down the crowded stadium aisle, trying to balance a beer and a hot dog of my own without missing a step. Sliding into home plate is acceptable, sliding into a cluster of unsuspecting fans is not.

The Saturday afternoon in early April offered a cool breeze and clear blue sky, the perfect weather for the opening day of the Asheville Tourists' new season. Attendance at picturesque McCormick Field promised to be a sellout with free T-shirts and half-price beer and hot dogs.

"Excuse us. Excuse us." Hewitt made the apologies as he plowed his way through the feet and knees of those already seated in the front row behind home plate. Without a free hand, he had to collapse into his seat, sloshing beer onto his green-and-orange Hawaiian shirt.

I laid my hot dog across the top of the cup, grabbed the blue armrest to take the weight off my prosthetic leg, and eased myself down.

"Nicely done, young man."

I twisted in my seat to see an older gentleman directly behind Hewitt. He wore a yellow-and-white golf shirt, sharply creased slacks, and a visor that left his bald head exposed. He looked like he'd arrived straight from the country club.

He shifted his gaze to Hewitt. "Unlike your companion, who landed like a beached whale."

"Is that the way to treat your guest?" Hewitt said without bothering to turn around.

The older man laughed. "I apologize. I shouldn't have disparaged a whale like that."

He offered me his hand. The grip was firm. "I'm Ted Kirkpatrick."

"Sam Blackman."

"Ah, the famous private detective."

"Well, I'm far from famous."

Kirkpatrick looked to his left and then his right, surveying the crowd. "Not if we limit it to Asheville."

Hewitt chimed in through a mouthful of hot dog. "He'd still come in behind Nakayla."

"That's your partner, right?"

"Yes," I said. "She gave me Saturday afternoon off."

"To hang out with this hippie troublemaker?" Kirkpatrick patted Hewitt on the shoulder.

The description fit. Hewitt's shoulder-length gray hair, the loud shirt, frayed jeans, and sandals typed him more as an ancient street musician or jewelry artisan than Asheville's premier defense attorney. A little north of seventy, Hewitt was as fierce a trial lawyer as I'd ever known. During my years in the army as a chief warrant officer, I'd not crossed paths with a JAG any tougher.

"And who are you hanging out with?" Hewitt asked. "Or couldn't you get someone to sit beside you?"

Like me, Hewitt had noticed an empty seat on either side of Kirkpatrick.

"Obviously, word got out that I'd given you two free tickets."

I realized Hewitt's invitation to me had come at no cost to himself. Although the banter between the two men was good-natured, I wanted to make sure I thanked my true host.

"These are terrific seats, Mr. Kirkpatrick."

"It's Ted, please. I'm not quite as old as Methuselah here. Hewitt, how was that game in 1925?"

Hewitt swallowed a large gulp of beer without comment.

"What game?" I asked.

"The one Babe Ruth was supposed to play in. That's the tie-in to the Luminaries Festival."

A connection clicked in my brain. "The festival's honorees. Ruth is one of them."

Kirkpatrick nodded. "Ninety-five years ago, Babe was supposed to be in this park for an exhibition game. But he drank so much beer and ate so many hot dogs on the train ride from Knoxville that he collapsed in the Asheville depot." Kirkpatrick lightly knocked Hewitt on the back of the head with his knuckles. "You hear that, Hewitt, too much beer and too many hot dogs."

"No such thing," Hewitt muttered and kept eating.

"What happened?" I asked.

"They managed to get him to the Battery Park Hotel. The rumor spread through the reporters that Ruth had died. For twenty-four hours, Babe Ruth was declared dead in Asheville. The town was suddenly famous around the globe. Then the facts caught up with the furor, and one reporter labeled the whole incident, 'The Bellyache Heard Round the World.'"

"So, it was just indigestion?"

Kirkpatrick shook his head. "No, he had a serious intestinal abscess, no doubt aggravated by the atrocious diet. He didn't return to the team until June."

Hewitt tried to stifle a belch. "Tell him about your balls."

I gave Hewitt a second look to make sure I'd heard correctly.

"Baseballs," Kirkpatrick clarified. "And they're my son's."

"He collects baseballs?"

"Only two. One signed by the Babe and the other by Lou Gehrig. Each one knocked out of this park during Yankee exhibition games in 1931. My son, Luke, has them in a portable display case that will be set up at the festival events."

"They must be valuable."

"A security guard will be standing next to them. One of Babe Ruth's home run balls sold for over eight hundred thousand dollars. Luke had the signatures authenticated by a handwriting expert. As soon as the festival is over, Luke plans to see what kind of offers they might bring, especially since they were home runs."

I glanced at the empty seats. "Is your son joining us?"

"Yes. After the opening announcements. I asked him to kick things off."

"Finally sharing the limelight, Ted?" Hewitt popped the final remains of the bun into his mouth.

"Something that will never cross your mind, Counselor."

Hewitt laughed. "Fair enough. It's hard to share the limelight when everyone's in my shadow." He crumpled up the paper tray that had held his hot dog and then reached for mine. "If you're not going to eat that, I will." He snatched it away before I could object. "I'll buy you two later."

Kirkpatrick gave me a wink. "Hewitt, you keep eating and your shadow's only going to get bigger."

"Remind me how much these free tickets cost me."

"And your generosity is heartily appreciated."

Hewitt leaned toward me and lowered his voice. "I gave him a four-figure donation. Ted's the founder of the inaugural Asheville Luminaries Festival and his company's the underwriting sponsor. I'd rather give my money to remember Babe Ruth's bellyache than to the politicians burning through cash and then begging for more."

A squeal burst from the PA system. Then a booming baritone voice exclaimed, "Are you ready for some baseball?"

The crowd whistled and cheered.

"Then please direct your attention to the pitcher's mound."

"You won't believe the national anthem, Hewitt," Kirkpatrick said.

"Why?"

The players for the Tourists and the visiting Columbia Fireflies stood in front of their respective dugouts. Two men wearing vintage baseball uniforms walked out to the mound, one carrying a small table and the other a wooden box about the size of a footlocker. A long, orange power cord trailed from underneath and disappeared into the Tourists' dugout. At the top of one end of the box rose a silver rod several feet in length. It looked like an old antenna for a car radio. On the other end, a silver rod formed a horseshoe, but if it was a handle, the bearer didn't use it. Instead he cradled the mysterious device in both arms.

As the men positioned the box on the table, the announcer continued, "Please welcome the co-chairs of the Asheville Luminaries Festival, Madison Kirkpatrick and Luke Kirkpatrick."

A man and a woman crossed from the dugout to the mound. They both appeared to be in their late thirties or early forties. He wore a cream linen suit and a red bow tie. Ditch the wireless microphone in his right hand, and all he needed was a straw hat to transport himself back to the 1920s. The woman, a striking blonde in skin-tight black jeans, black high heels, and a gold lamé top, moved like her hips had been set in motion by a Swiss watchmaker. Sun glinted off earrings and bracelets with sparkles so bright you could see them from centerfield. She sported so much bling it would have taken her two days to go through airport security.

I set aside my opinion of women who seem to wear all their jewelry at once and said, "They make a lovely couple, Ted."

Hewitt put his foot on top of my shoe and pressed down. "She's Ted's wife," he whispered.

In terms of a trophy wife, Madison Kirkpatrick rated an Olympic medal.

"Thank you," Ted said, without much enthusiasm.

Hewitt lifted his sandal.

I leaned closer to him. "Next time you try to stop me from saying something stupid, please step on my real foot, not my prosthesis."

He started shaking with silent laughter, and for a second, I was afraid he was choking on my hot dog.

Luke and Madison stepped up onto the mound. She stumbled a bit in the foolish high heels, and he grabbed her around the waist with his free hand.

"Go easy on the beer, Mom," he said into the mic.

The crowd laughed, Ted Kirkpatrick took in a sharp breath, and Madison's cheeks flushed so red she looked like a bejeweled stop sign. Luke ignored the woman's embarrassment and kept talking.

"Hi, everyone, and welcome to the opening home game of the Asheville Tourists' new season, and the opening event of the Asheville Luminaries Festival. Kirkgate Paper, Inc. is proud to be the founding sponsors of this celebration marking important anniversaries of some of those distinguished individuals who are part of Asheville's past. Of course, we've all heard of native son Thomas Wolfe and the Asheville exploits of F. Scott Fitzgerald, and I won't ask how many of you actually read their books, but our history goes beyond these two literary geniuses. Ninety-five years ago, Babe Ruth stepped off a train onto Asheville soil. Seventy-five years ago, Béla Bartók died but not before he'd transformed our most beautiful birdsongs into a piano concerto. And fifteen years ago, we lost longtime resident Dr. Robert Moog, whose invention of the Moog synthesizer changed the sound of music forever.

"The festival not only honors them, but it also brings them together in creative ways. Look in today's program for a list of upcoming lectures, concerts, and ball games that showcase the achievements of these luminaries who once walked the streets of Asheville."

He tilted the microphone toward Madison. She snatched it out of his hand and took a step forward. The tinkling of her bracelets sounded from the speakers.

"And now we are honored to have our national anthem played on the instrument that first captured Bob Moog's imagination."

She and Luke stepped to either side and gestured to the box behind them.

"This is a theremin," Madison continued. "It was invented by Léon Theremin one hundred years ago. The amazing thing is you play it without touching it. Bring your hand to and from the vertical antenna and the pitch changes. Move your other hand farther from or closer to the loop and the volume rises and falls. Music generated solely by electricity. Electricity, I am told that is flowing through the performer's body." She giggled. "Don't ask me to explain it. For all I know the sound could be coming from a smartphone hidden inside."

The crowd laughed. Most, like me, had no idea how the contraption made music when you waved your hands in the empty air.

"Seriously, we have as our guest artist Paul Clarkson. Paul is a native of the region, a graduate of the Department of Music and Music Technology at UNC-Asheville, and a staff member of the Moog factory here. He's also active in the Bob Moog Foundation. But today, he's our thereminist. How many of you have never heard that word before?"

The show of raised hands confirmed my suspicion that thereminist was not a common job posting.

Madison swept her left arm across the arc of the stadium. "Ladies and gentlemen, please stand as Paul Clarkson plays our national anthem."

One of the two men in the vintage uniforms stepped forward and took a position behind the theremin. We rose from our seats, Hewitt having to handle only his beer as the hot dogs were now inside him.

He briefly turned to Kirkpatrick. "Madison gave a nice speech, Ted. No notes. You were smart to stay on the sidelines."

"I agree. When it's my own choosing."

His cryptic comment begged clarification. I was tempted to pursue his meaning, but was saved from inappropriately prying by an eerie vibrato filling the air. Sounding at first like the score of some sci-fi film from the 1950s, the haunting warble became recognizable as the opening measures of "The Star-Spangled Banner." Everyone stood in respectful silence. No one attempted to sing to the strange, oscillating accompaniment. At the concluding note of "and the home of the brave," Clarkson ramped the instrument up to full volume while rapidly moving his right hand in and out to send the pitch swirling up and down the audible range before fading away as a single note echoing off nearby Beaucatcher Mountain.

After a rousing cheer from the fans, Clarkson and his colleague began quickly removing the instrument and table from the field. Madison Kirkpatrick raised the microphone to her lips, but before she could speak, Luke yanked it free.

"I want to remind you to stop by the front of McCormick's Pub by the main entrance, where you can see the theremin up close, and also the two baseballs, one signed by Babe Ruth, the other by Lou Gehrig, that each man knocked out of this park in 1931. And remember, the next two weeks offer lots of opportunities to enjoy the concerts, workshops, lectures, and tours that are all part of the Asheville Luminaries Festival. We at Kirkgate Paper are proud to be the lead sponsor. Now let's play ball!"

The crowd clapped as the Tourists took the field. The mayor threw the customary first ball straight across home plate with only one bounce, and received a round of applause for her effort. Then the game began in earnest.

At the end of the first inning, Madison Kirkpatrick joined her husband. I watched as she maneuvered along Section K, Row B, managing to keep her high heels from spearing the feet of her neighbors. Most of those in the section seemed to know her, and I wondered if Ted Kirkpatrick had purchased the whole block of tickets.

When she reached the empty seat on Ted's right, she flashed a smile of perfectly capped teeth that rivaled the sparkle of her jewelry.

"You know Hewitt Donaldson," her husband told her.

"Of course." She grasped Hewitt's hand and leaned in to give him one of those phony air kisses by his cheek. "So good to see you again." The smile agreed with the words, but the blue eyes held a cold, calculating appraisal of my friend. The eyes shifted to me.

"And this is Sam Blackman," Kirkpatrick said. "He's probably the best private detective in the state. At least he's the one I'd hire, should the need ever arise."

For a split second I detected a break in that penetrating gaze, a look away and then back as if resetting her brain to a new situation.

"How exciting! I believe I've read about you."

We shook hands, but no air kiss for me.

"You know the old saying, 'Don't believe everything you read.'"

She held my hand a little too long. "Thank you for the advice, Mr. Blackman. I'll bear that in mind."

I started to ask her to call me Sam, but in all the P.I. stories I'd read, a buxom blonde usually meant disaster for the detective. Instead, I just smiled and pulled my hand away.

She had to be nearly thirty years younger than her husband, which made me think a story lurked somewhere in the recent past. I'd pump Hewitt for information later.

"Isn't Luke joining us?" Hewitt asked.

Madison shook her head. "Probably not. He's setting up the display for his precious baseballs and that theremin thing. How weird was that? You could have gotten the same sound from a mountaineer playing a handsaw."

Before any of us could respond to her music critique, a voice boomed, "Down in front!"

I turned to see the umpire sweep home plate and then wave the batter into the box. We took our seats.

The game turned into a pitching duel. At the seventh-inning stretch, the score was tied one to one. I decided to make it a true stretch and told Hewitt I needed to walk a little on my leg. My prosthesis felt fine. It was actually my good right leg that was cramped.

"Can I bring anyone anything from the concession stand?"

"Yeah, Hewitt," Ted said. "How about another hot dog?"

Hewitt groaned. "Not unless you want to carry me out on a stretcher."

I started up the aisle to the main concourse, but gave a quick glance over my shoulder. Hewitt and Ted were talking to each other. Madison was watching me. This time she didn't look away. I continued up the aisle, feeling her eyes on my back with each step.

I walked out of the ballpark proper to the cement perimeter that arced around it, providing entries to restrooms, the team store, and McCormick's Pub, a food and drink spot next to the main entrance.

A crowd gathered across from it. As I drew closer, I saw two security guards standing beside a Plexiglas case. Luke Kirkpatrick guided the curious into a stanchioned pathway that passed within a few feet of the display. Beyond, the cordoned-off walkway ended at the theremin. Paul Clarkson, the man who'd played the national anthem, stood behind it, his hands moving in the air like some wizard conjuring up wailing spirits. I recognized the tune as "Somewhere over the Rainbow." Madison had been right—the theremin sounded a lot like a mountaineer playing a handsaw.

I joined the crowd funneling into the stanchion chute and stopped in front of the case where each ball rested upon a small pedestal. The blue-ink autographs of the two icons of baseball appeared as faded as the aged, red-stitched leather on which they'd been penned. Although I wasn't a big sports fan, I appreciated the history embodied in those two artifacts from another era. It was thrilling to think that the Babe and Lou Gehrig played on this spot and sent those balls soaring over the fence.

"Kirkpatrick! What kind of horseshit are you trying to pawn off on us now?"

I pivoted and saw a man pointing his finger at Luke Kirkpatrick. I recognized him. Ken Stokes, a local contractor who happened to be working on a project for my partner, Nakayla Robertson.

The crowd at the exhibit immediately fell silent. "Somewhere over the Rainbow" faded away. Stokes pushed his way closer.

"Don't you ignore me."

Luke Kirkpatrick's face reddened. "What's your problem, Stokes? Too much cheap beer?"

"You're my problem. You, your family, and your company. Asheville Luminaries, my ass." Stokes turned to face the crowd. "Babe Ruth, Béla Bartók, Bob Moog. Nothing wrong with celebrating them. But what about Wilma Dykeman?"

Wilma who?

Stokes saw the puzzled faces of his audience. "She won the first Thomas Wolfe Memorial Literary Award. Her book, *The French Broad*, brought river pollution to national attention. But the Kirkpatricks and Kirkgate Paper don't want the name Wilma Dykeman mentioned. Why not? Because they were the polluters she fought against." He turned around to face Luke, jabbing his finger into the air to underscore his verbal assault. "You're the people who killed the fish and turned the Pigeon River into the Dead River. You created the toxic fields that leach into our creeks and wells, harming humans and animals alike. You dumped the chemicals that gave kids cancer. We'll never know the total score of death and destruction. And now you have the audacity to cloak yourself in the mantel of self-serving, self-aggrandizing civic pride while ignoring the woman who stood up to you and your kind."

Luke Kirkpatrick puffed himself up, his whole body trembling. "These people came for a ball game, not to hear you rant."

A few murmurs of assent arose from the crowd.

"Now get out of here." Luke shoved Ken Stokes hard in the chest.

The bigger man stumbled backwards before catching his balance. His large hands balled into fists and he took a step forward.

Luke shot a quick glance at the two security guards near me. I saw them tense. One gripped the butt of his holstered pistol.

"Leave it, Ken." I shouted the words as I moved toward him. "You've made your point."

Before I could reach Stokes, Paul Clarkson stepped beside him. He whispered something and Stokes relaxed. Then the thereminist looked at Luke and shook his head.

Luke raised his hands, palms out. "I know. I shouldn't have shoved him."

Clarkson led Stokes away.

"I shouldn't have shoved him," Luke muttered under his breath. "I should have slugged the son of a bitch."

Chapter Two

I never did get my hot dogs.

By the time the Asheville Tourists eked out a two-to-one victory, my stomach was making weirder sounds than Bob Moog's theremin. Hewitt offered to treat me to dinner at Pack's Tavern, a pleasant walk from McCormick Field and adjacent to historic Pack Square in the heart of Asheville. He also suggested I invite Nakayla to join us, unless we already had plans for a Saturday night date.

We didn't. Maybe we should have.

Nakayla had cheerfully encouraged me to take Hewitt up on his offer of the baseball game, claiming she could use a little personal time to read her book for next week's book club and then to browse New Morning Gallery for artwork and accent pieces for her new house.

The successful solution to our last case cost her dearly. Nakayla's bungalow in West Asheville had been firebombed, and we'd barely escaped with our lives. During the rebuilding, she'd moved into my one-bedroom apartment that I was happy to share, but which left her feeling adrift. She'd lost everything—the family albums, favorite books, and keepsakes that had been passed down through generations to Nakayla, the sole living descendant. Now all the physical traces of the heritage of her African-American family living in the mountains of Western North Carolina had been reduced to ashes.

We'd met through her older sister Tikima, a Marine veteran who had visited me in the Asheville VA hospital, where I was recuperating from an injury suffered in Iraq. I'd been a chief warrant officer, and my last investigation brought me too close to a military corruption scheme. The perpetrators staged a rocket grenade attack that destroyed my left leg below the knee and left me with a prosthesis. I'd met Tikima only once. She'd lost an arm in the war and was committed to navigating fellow veterans through the trauma of finding their flesh and blood replaced by metal.

She was murdered.

Nakayla and I had worked together to uncover her killer. We'd stayed together and given birth to the Blackman and Robertson Detective Agency.

We'd also fallen in love.

Hewitt and I sat in a booth along the wall of the tavern's expansive dining area. He studied a section of the menu unfamiliar to him. Entree Salads. I didn't have to ask him how the hot dogs were settling. I zeroed in on the burgers but reserved judgment until Nakayla could order. I usually finished her meal as well.

I saw her enter. She wore tight white jeans, a lime-green blouse untucked, and a brown leather bag strapped over her left shoulder. In contrast to the excessive bling of Madison Kirkpatrick, Nakayla's jewelry consisted of a pair of gold hoop earrings that dangled unimpeded by her close-cut hair. She said a few words to the hostess and then scanned the crowd.

I stood and waved. She waved back and then moved gracefully across the room, her slim form gliding like a dancer. As she neared, I sensed the smile on her face belied something else playing beneath the surface. I immediately flashed through the possibilities of what I could have done wrong. I was relatively sober, I'd kissed her goodbye when I left for the game, and I'd texted Hewitt's invitation so that she could discreetly decline without having to do so in an overheard phone call.

Hewitt stood and welcomed her with a hug. I got a quick kiss, and then I stepped back to let her slide into the booth next to me.

She tucked her bag between us. "Sorry I'm late. I got tied up on my phone."

I took the statement as the explanation for her underlying tension. "Anything we need to deal with? We haven't ordered."

Before Nakayla could answer, a waitress arrived bringing her a menu and a glass of water. "Would you like drinks while you're deciding?"

Nakayla didn't bother to look at the beverage page. "Yes, the Chardonnay, please."

"I'll have the draft Porter," I said.

Nakayla laughed. "You must have paced yourself at the game."

"I nursed one beer through seven innings."

The waitress turned to Hewitt. "And you, sir?"

"I'm fine with just water."

Nakayla clicked her tongue in mock sympathy. "Someone must not have paced himself."

Hewitt shrugged. "Let's just say Babe Ruth has nothing on me."

Nakayla opened her menu and started scanning the entrees. "I understand there was some excitement at the game."

"Not really," Hewitt said. "The Tourists won two to one."

"I mean the confrontation between Ken Stokes and Luke Kirkpatrick."

Hewitt gave me a puzzled look. "Do you know what she's talking about?"

I hadn't told Hewitt because we'd been sitting right in front of Luke Kirkpatrick's father. And during our walk to the tavern, I'd decided whatever spurred Ken Stokes's outburst had been personal. He was doing a good job for Nakayla, and I didn't want to spread tales that could reflect badly on him.

"Ken called Luke out for not including Wilma Dykeman in the festival. I don't know who she is, but the two traded some heated words. I got the feeling it's some running feud. I didn't mention it in front of Ted." I turned to Nakayla. "How'd you hear about it?"

"Ken called me about the construction. He said he saw you at the game and wanted to apologize for his behavior."

"No blood, no foul. It was over as soon as it began. What's up with the construction?"

"The door came in from Virginia this morning. The weather's supposed to be good tomorrow so he's going to hang it. He said they should be done around three, if we want to swing by and take a look."

Hewitt laughed. "I'm impressed. He's working Sunday afternoon. Of course, it's neither deer nor football season, so what else is he going to do?"

Nakayla set her menu aside. "Knowing Ken, he'd prefer to be out on the river in his kayak."

Our waitress returned with my beer and Nakayla's wine. "Are we ready to order?" she asked.

"Are we?" Nakayla asked.

Hewitt closed his menu. "Yes. Go ahead, Nakayla."

"I'll have the Thai salad with the vinaigrette."

The waitress made a quick scribble and then turned to me. "And you, sir?"

"I'll take the Southern, medium, with mustard on the side." The burger more than made up for my missed hot dogs, and the layer of pimento cheese and fried pickles promised a cardiologist in my future.

"That sounds wonderful," Hewitt muttered.

"And will you have the same?" The waitress held her pencil poised over the pad.

Hewitt sighed. "No, the spinach salad."

Nakayla arched an eyebrow. "You do know that's good for you?"

"Don't remind me."

The waitress left.

"So, what's so special about a door from Virginia?" Hewitt asked.

"An indulgence," Nakayla explained. "Ken Stokes knew of a company that salvages vintage and unique architectural pieces. Windows, doors, banisters, finials. He found a front door of chestnut and beveled glass."

"Ken's all about recycling," Hewitt said. "Does he have you putting solar panels on the roof?"

Nakayla laughed. "He tried. We compromised on a high-efficiency heat pump."

Hewitt took a sip of water and cleared his throat. "And this confrontation between Ken and Luke Kirkpatrick, was it just about Wilma Dykeman?"

"No," I said. "Ken accused Luke and his company of being polluters. Of being the kind of people this Wilma Dykeman challenged."

Hewitt nodded. "Stokes is correct. I knew Wilma Dykeman. She was an amazing woman. As an outspoken critic of racial discrimination and environmental abuses, she used her fiction and nonfiction to champion her causes. This is back in the fifties and sixties."

"She also fought gender inequalities," Nakayla said. "My book club read her novel, *The Tall Woman*, a story honoring the strength and courage of mountaineer women. She was a prophet as much as a successful author."

Hewitt gave a humorless laugh. "Well, that wasn't going to happen. Not if her antipollution book's the connection. Ted got pulled into a series of lawsuits back in the 1990s. His company was small potatoes compared to Pisgah Valley Paper, the largest company dumping toxic waste in the Pigeon River. But Ted was also targeted. This wasn't just a group of do-gooders. Tennessee and several of its counties sued. You see, the pollution flowed across the state border and created an environmental disaster downstream. Tennessee won, but not before violence broke out."

"Did the companies use strong-arm tactics?" I asked.

"No. Residents from Tennessee made a surprise march on PVP."

"PVP?"

"Pisgah Valley Paper. They targeted the administrative offices, not the plant and workers. One of the protesters confronted an executive trying to escape to his car. The protester evidently lost toddler twin sons to cancer and held the paper company responsible. He took a baseball bat to the car, and then to the executive."

"Good God." I looked at Nakayla. "Did you know this?"

"I was in grade school. I remember the trouble but not the specifics."

"It's not the kind of thing your parents would have talked about," Hewitt said. "At least not in front of you. The executive was beaten to death."

I took a deep breath. "What happened to his killer?"

"He got life. His lawyer petitioned for manslaughter but the guy came to the scene with the bat, not something he grabbed on-site. And it was clearly used as a deadly weapon."

"What about Ted's company? Was there violence there?"

"Not directly. His plant was down the river about a mile. But PVP had a minority share of his company, so Ted's operation was targeted in the overall suit. Ted made specialty paper and then moved into recycling. He bought out PVP years ago. Old pizza boxes alone have made him a millionaire many times over."

"And the lawsuits?"

"Settled with undisclosed damages and North Carolina promising to enforce its clean water laws. The discharge into the river has been significantly reduced and most toxic waste is buried in sealed landfills. The river has come back from being a dead zone. Fly fishermen can venture into the water without their waders dissolving. But, with the administration in Washington foolishly rolling back environmental protection regulations, who knows how long that will last? People like Ken Stokes are taking up the mantle because, God bless him, someone has to."

"You think Ted's company is relaxing their standards?"

"No, I don't. And PVP now has new ownership that's demonstrated more concern for minimizing their environmental impact. Ken Stokes is right to champion the accomplishments of Wilma Dykeman and to work to safeguard our rivers, but he's wrong to think that Ted Kirkpatrick will choose greed over green. He lives here. I find it hard to believe he'd soil his own nest."

I remembered Luke Kirkpatrick shoving Ken Stokes away. "And Ted's son?"

"Spoiled. He'll have a trust fund and Ted's board of directors would never approve giving Luke real responsibility."

"And Madison?"

A sly smile played across Hewitt's lips. "A prenup. She's well cared for. As long as she doesn't stray from the nest while Ted's alive. When you've got a trophy wife, you make sure she doesn't become a trophy for someone else."

"What about Luke's mother?" I asked.

"Cancer took her. Five years ago. Ted was a faithful husband. Do I think Madison's a gold digger?" He shrugged. "Doesn't matter. It's what Ted thinks that counts. I just try to minimize the potential damages."

I got the message. Although Hewitt was a defense attorney, the trust, the prenup, and probably Ted Kirkpatrick's will itself, had all been reviewed by him. If Luke or Madison tried to circumvent the estate plan, they'd have to go through Hewitt Donaldson.

They'd have a better chance of convincing the devil to air-condition Hell.

Chapter Three

I surprised Nakayla the next morning by offering to attend her church. Since the fire six months earlier, she'd returned to the congregation of her youth, Mt. Zion Missionary Baptist, a gothic, redbrick, historic structure a block off Pack Square. I guessed her close brush with death had kindled the need for a spiritual community. I hadn't been in the sanctuary since her sister's funeral several years ago, but I knew the primarily African-American membership would be welcoming.

I didn't anticipate my Sunday morning announcement would create a traffic jam in my apartment's one bathroom.

"If you'd told me last night you wanted to go to church, I would have gotten up earlier." Nakayla made the statement before and after I took my shower. "Now the bathroom is steamed up and I can't put on my makeup. You know the service begins at ten forty-five, not eleven."

I made the mistake of offering my theological advice. "I know God's more interested in what's in your heart than what's on your face."

"And obviously God forgot to put a brain in your head. Make yourself useful and take Blue out."

Our bluetick coonhound heard his name, stood from his

cushion, and padded to the front door. I grabbed his leash from a hook on the wall. Sometimes walking the dog is the best response to an argument.

Nakayla and I rode to the church in silence and entered the sanctuary as the opening chords sounded for the first hymn. Once in the pew, she calmed down. The sermon couldn't have been better. The preacher spoke on how anger destroys the bearer, not the target. I risked reaching over to hold her hand. She gave me a squeeze in return. I dropped a twenty in the offering plate.

After the service, Nakayla and I were mobbed by her friends. The older folks made a point to talk to me about her parents, now both deceased. Gentlemen with white hair and ladies with magnificent hats told how Nakayla and her sister, Tikima, grew up in the church and what a wonderful family they'd been. I wondered if they saw me as the prodigal son. Was I to be celebrated, or was I a white man who might separate Nakayla from her roots? Probably a mixture of both perspectives, although I felt no trace of hostility from anyone.

We returned to the apartment close to one o'clock. Since breakfast had fallen by the wayside in the morning's chaos, I offered to make my famous pecan pancakes. Famous because it was one of the two or three things I could make from scratch. While Nakayla ran Blue out for his second constitutional of the day, I whipped up enough batter to feed the five thousand. Add Irish butter and real maple syrup, and no one would have touched the loaves and fishes.

At two thirty, with full stomachs and mended hearts, we loaded Blue in the back of my Honda CR-V and headed for West Asheville about fifteen minutes away.

As we turned down Nakayla's street, Blue began a mournful howl.

"It's all right, boy." Nakayla reached to the rear seat and stroked the big dog on his muzzle.

"We'd better leave him in the car," I said. "It's still too stressful for him."

"Well, he's going to have to get used to the new house sometime."

Blue and me both. The coonhound had nearly perished in the blaze. And I'd gotten used to Nakayla being my full-time house-mate, even if the bathroom was disputed territory.

I parked behind Ken Stokes's white Ford F-150 pickup. You must not be a real contractor unless you drive that model. An old, rusty brown Bronco was in front of Ken's truck. The newest thing about it was the "I'd Rather Be Fishing" bumper sticker. No, as Hewitt had pointed out, it wasn't deer or football season, but I'd heard trout fishing on the hatchery-stocked streams had opened this weekend. Ken must have enlisted the aid of a good friend if the man passed up a nice afternoon on one of the nearby rivers.

We left Blue whimpering in the car. The pitiful sound was quickly overwhelmed by the sharp whine of a power saw cutting through wood. Nakayla had elected to rebuild her house in the original Arts and Crafts style of a hundred years ago. All on one level, the floor plan expanded the size to include a third bedroom and second bathroom. She'd also increased the front porch to accommodate a few rocking chairs and a glider. On either side of slate front steps, dry-stack stonework formed the base for timber pillars that supported the porch roof.

Horizontal siding, still unpainted, enclosed the exterior so that inside work now could progress, rain or shine. Windows sported stickers on their panes, and with the hanging of the antique front door, the house could be properly locked.

Except, as we neared the porch, we saw the door leaning against the porch railing. A pair of sawhorses held two-by-fours laid across them. Ken Stokes was measuring the length for another cut. An older man stood in the open doorframe, sanding the edges of the siding that had been cut away. He wore carpenter's overalls, the kind with a loop on a leg for hanging a hammer. One dangled by his knee. I'd never seen that feature in actual use before.

Stretching a tape measure, Ken concentrated on marking a cut point with a broad lead pencil. Then he rechecked it for accuracy.

"Measure twice, cut once," I said.

He looked up and smiled. "Hi. Sorry it's not done yet. We ran into a little problem."

"Oh?" Nakayla voiced concern as we stepped up on the porch.

The man with the hand sander turned around. Flecks of sawdust speckled a short gray beard. "Nothing we can't fix. In fact, I told Kenny the mistake was a good thing." He pointed to the door on the railing. "That chestnut is heavy and could settle on you."

Ken Stokes pulled a red bandanna from his hip pocket and wiped his hands. "This is my dad. Walt Stokes. I sort of drafted him to help."

"He'd rather be fishing," Nakayla said.

Both men laughed.

Walt set the sander on the board his son was measuring. "Yep. Where do you think all Kenny's friends are? He had to have his old man come to the rescue."

Nakayla looked at the boards and the fresh cuts to the siding. "Is something wrong?"

"Richmond told me the wrong measurements," Ken said. "The door's actually four inches wider than described."

"And that's a blessing," Walt added. He stepped closer to his son.

I saw the family resemblance. Although the father had gray hair and a beard while Ken was dark-haired and clean-shaven, they both had the same thin face and lanky build. But it was the piercing blue eyes that marked their kinship. Each man stared at us with the crystal-clear gaze of a Siberian husky.

"A blessing," I repeated.

"Yep," Walt said. "We have to reframe the doorjamb, and feeling the weight of the chestnut wood and heavy beveled glass, we're doubling the boards in the jamb and bolting them to the crossbeams. A tornado could knock the house down, but the door would still be standing."

I walked to the door. The designs carved into the old chestnut wood and the inlaid prismatic glass represented the craftsmanship of a bygone era. "If it's that heavy, you're going to need more than two people to hang this."

Ken shrugged. "Maybe."

"Well, I'm willing to help if it's just muscle power."

"Yes," Nakayla said. "Don't let Sam touch a hammer or a saw."

Walt turned to his son. "What do you think? Another hour?"

Ken nodded. "More or less."

"You don't have to do this today," Nakayla said.

"It's the baby," Walt said. "Kenny's wife is due any day."

"What?" Nakayla exclaimed. "Lynne's expecting?"

Ken blushed. "I thought I'd told you. We found out about the time we started on your house."

"Well, that's great news. Do you know the gender?"

"A little boy."

"And they have a name," Walt said, "but they won't tell anyone."

"We want to wait until the baby arrives," Ken explained. "Then the name is attached to a real little person, not just a word people will judge in isolation."

"Walt's a word with a nice ring," Walt said.

"Don't worry if you need to reschedule something," Nakayla said. "A baby takes precedence."

"Thanks." Ken looked back at the altered doorframe. "That's why I wanted to get this hung today. My subcontractors laying the hardwood floors and finishing the sheetrock can work whether I'm here or not. They can leave their equipment and lock up."

"Then consider me your number one volunteer," I said.

Nakayla pulled her cell phone from her hip pocket. "And I'll be ready to call 911 when Sam drops the door on his foot."

She and I watched as Ken and his father made the precise cuts and hardware installations in preparation for the door to be mounted on its three oiled hinges. Walt and I managed to wrestle it into position and Ken dropped the lynchpins, securing the door in place. He pushed it closed and the latch clicked. He reached in his pocket and pulled out a set of keys. The deadbolt turned smoothly. He yanked on the handle and the door didn't budge. It couldn't have been any sturdier than if it were mounted in granite.

He unlocked it and offered the keys to Nakayla on his open palm. "The keys to your castle."

Nakayla beamed. "This is so exciting."

Ken's smile faded. He bit his lower lip with nervous agitation. "I do have some bad news."

"What?"

"I got word Friday that the kitchen cabinets you wanted are on backorder. Six to eight weeks minimum. I know you've told me how anxious you are to move in, but this was totally unexpected. The manufacturer should have given us more warning."

Nakayla reddened. Ken's statement made it sound like she'd been pushing him to get her out of my apartment and into her home as soon as possible. I suspected she had.

"I do have another option," Ken said. "There's a cabinetmaker in Weaverville I've worked with before. I've talked to him about stepping up. He has an opening in his schedule if you like any of his designs. He could start tomorrow."

I looked to Nakayla. "Could he copy the ones Nakayla wanted?"

"Possibly. Those might be more expensive. More labor-intensive than some other designs."

"That's fine," Nakayla said. "I'd like to talk to him."

"Great. I'll call him later today and let you know. Could you meet here in the morning?"

"Name the time." She pulled the keys from her pocket. "Do you need these back?"

Ken waved them away. "I've got a spare set. I'll give them to you after our final walk-through."

"Sounds good," Nakayla said. "I'll wait for your call."

Walt Stokes looked at his watch. "Well, Kenny, we might have time to hit a stream." He looked at Nakayla and me. "Want to go fishing? I've got some extra gear."

"No thanks," I said. "We've got our coonhound in the car. He's not much for retrieving trout."

"And I've got some errands to run," Ken said.

Walt winked at us. "Errands. He's just afraid to be fishing in a dead zone and miss the cell call from Lynne. I'll be glad when this baby shows up and life gets back to normal."

Ken laughed. "Like when I was born?"

Walt pretended to ponder the question. "You're right. Neither your dear mother nor I ever recovered from that momentous event. Now, thank God, I'll get to see you go through the same ordeal."

Nakayla and I left them teasing each other.

We had a light supper of scrambled eggs and bacon, the second breakfast of the day. Around eight thirty, I took Blue out for his final walk while Nakayla scoured through more catalogues for items to furnish the house.

When I returned, I found her standing and staring out the front window of the apartment.

"He hasn't called," she said.

"You mean Ken?"

"Yes. Do you think he forgot?"

"No. He might not have been able to reach the cabinetmaker. Everybody and his brother seem to be fishing today."

"Maybe I should call Ken and tell him it's fine to phone as late as he needs to."

"Or we could be there at a moment's notice if he can't reach the man till tomorrow."

Nakayla sighed. "I realize I'm coming across as ungrateful for your generosity in giving me a place to live."

I walked closer to her. "I think no such thing. I want you here. And I guess I'm being selfish about it."

She turned to me. "It's not that I don't love you."

"Then you don't have to say anything else." I kissed her on the lips.

She wrapped her arms around my neck and laid her head against my chest.

I heard her cell phone vibrate in her pocket. "And there's Ken now."

We broke apart.

She glanced at the number on the screen and frowned. "It's not his cell." She accepted the call and pressed the phone to her ear.

"Oh, hi, Lynne. Ken told us about the baby. Congratulations."

A long pause, and I saw Nakayla's brow furrow.

"No, we haven't seen him since this afternoon at the house."

A longer stretch of silence as Nakayla listened.

"Yes, Ken told me about the incident at the ballpark. You think that might be where he went?"

Nakayla looked at me and gave a slight shake of her head. "No, but I think we could find it. Have you heard from your father-in-law?

"I see. No sense alarming him. No, Sam and I are happy to help. Don't worry. I'm sure there's a simple explanation."

She disconnected.

"Simple explanation for what?" I asked.

"That was Lynne Stokes. She hasn't heard from Ken, and he should have been home by now."

"And she thinks he went to the ballpark?"

"No. She thinks he might have gone to the river below the landfills for Kirkgate Paper."

"The Pigeon River?"

"Yes. Ken's part of a volunteer group that measures contaminants in the water. Toxins are in the sludge and coal ash buried in adjacent landfills. The state's so lax it basically cedes self-monitoring to the paper companies. Ken and his team check for leaching. Like Hewitt said, the Pigeon River once was classified by the state as good for only one thing—dumping toxic waste. That's how bad things had gotten. It took the Tennessee suit, the courts, and the environmentalists to reverse that condition."

"Environmentalists like Wilma Dykeman."

"Like Wilma Dykeman and Ken Stokes. Lynne says Ken was vigilant that the river still be protected. It's a minor miracle that it recovered the first time. He wasn't going to risk a second."

"So, Ken's incident with Luke Kirkpatrick might have prompted him to take new samples?"

"That's what Lynne thinks. He told her he was going to pull some quick water checks, but he didn't say where."

"And when you said you thought we could find it, you meant the spot on the river?"

"Yes, it's just a quarter mile downstream from Kirkgate's old landfill. Lynne had been with him a couple times. Ken would walk upstream closer to the site, but without trespassing on their property. He'd park at a launch site for canoes and kayakers."

"Did Lynne give you directions?"

"Yes. A turnoff from Highway 215. It's just beyond Grace Baptist Church. Should we bring Blue?"

"No. I don't want him pulling us through the dark if he picks up the scent of a raccoon. Put him in his little house while I change my prosthesis."

Blue's ears perked up at the euphemism "little house," a name much more charming than "the crate."

Nakayla clapped her hands. "Okay, Blue. Little house."

The dog trotted to the wire cage, nudged the door open with his nose, and waited inside for his cookie.

I went to the bedroom, put a fresh sleeve over the stump of my leg and attached my Range Rover. That was the name I tagged the device designed for more strenuous physical activity like running and hiking. I also put on shoes with nonskid soles. There was a chance I might do a little river wading, and trying to balance on slick rocks where I had no direct feeling would be a disaster waiting to happen.

Finally, I engaged myself in a brief debate on what kind of situation we could be facing. The worst scenario won out. I tucked my Kimber 45 semiautomatic in a holster in the small of my back.

The drive took about forty minutes. Traffic was light on Sunday night with most day-trippers having safely returned home. The parking lot of Grace Baptist Church was empty without even an echo of an Amen or Hallelujah left from the evening service. We found the dirt side road to the river penetrating a forest of pines and hardwoods. Branches arched over the single lane, cutting off any light from the moon and stars. Our headlights raked across a DO NOT LITTER sign, then created sparkles on the ripples of flowing water before bouncing back off the side of a white F-150 pickup.

Nakayla clutched my hand. "This isn't good."

"Do you want to wait here?"

"No. But let's stay together. Maybe there's a path along the riverbank."

There wasn't. Each of us held a halogen flashlight as we pushed through the undergrowth near the water. Nakayla played her beam in front and to the left through the trees. I focused mine on the river, looking into the shadows behind downed limbs or rocks rising out of shallower depths.

"How far do you think we've come?" Nakayla asked.

"Close to a quarter mile, I guess. We must be getting near the landfill."

I wasn't too far off. A few minutes later, the tree line broke at the boundary of an open meadow. The ground was covered in rough pasture grass, uncultivated but green with new spring growth. A sign on a pole read POSTED: NO TRESPASSING. VIOLATORS WILL BE PROSECUTED.

"It doesn't say anything about toxic waste," Nakayla remarked.

"They probably worded it to meet the minimum legal requirements."

"Should we turn around?"

I reached behind my back to make sure the Kimber was snuggly in place. "No. Let's go a little farther."

Without the tree covering, the moonlight made visibility greater. Although the unkempt field stretched out in a square several hundred yards in dimension, we still stayed close to the river. The sound of rippling water was broken only by our breathing and the distant hoot of an owl.

Nakayla stopped. "Maybe Ken left his truck door cracked and the courtesy lights drained the battery. He might have been walking out while we were coming in."

"Maybe," I agreed. I swung my beam farther up the bank of the river. Several spots of bare earth marked where someone had dug out the grass in clumps.

"This looks fresh," I said.

We advanced slowly, Nakayla close to my side.

I shone the light into two narrow holes at least a yard deep. "Looks like someone used posthole diggers or a spade with a long, narrow blade."

"Ken?"

I said nothing and walked closer to the water's edge. The current had eaten away at the bank, creating an overhang of dirt and grass roots. I angled the flashlight beam beneath me.

A patch of dark-blue denim protruded out of the water. I bent over for a better look and felt the earth break free. I tumbled into the river, cracking my elbow on a flat rock and dropping the flashlight. The waterproof casing kept the bulb burning, kept the beam shining up through the clear water and onto the pale face of Ken Stokes.

The once-crystal blue eyes were now dull and lifeless.

Chapter Four

I stayed beside the body, standing in the knee-deep river with a wet flashlight and wetter clothes. I protected the potential crime scene, which meant leaving Ken where I found him. But it didn't seem right to leave him in the water alone.

Asheville lay in Buncombe County. We'd crossed into Haywood County and the jurisdiction of Sheriff Cliff Hudson. He'd been sheriff for at least ten years and had a good reputation for running a professional operation. We'd met at a fundraiser for the Haywood County youth program that he and his deputies sponsored. Nakayla and I had made a sizable contribution so I didn't expect to be hassled for being on private property.

Nakayla had placed the call to the Haywood County Sheriff's Department, identified who and where we were, and that we had found a body. She went back to the parking area to lead the responding officers to the scene.

While I waited, I tried to reconstruct what might have happened. Had Ken come to the site for soil as well as water samples? If so, where were the tools he used or the samples he extracted? One possibility was he'd stepped back from his dig to the river's edge and a section of the overhanging bank had collapsed underneath him as it had beneath me. His samples and tools might have gone into the river with him. They could be a few feet downstream but not visible in the dark shadows.

I scanned the water with my flashlight and saw only rocks. If Ken had tumbled backwards, he would have had no way to break his fall. Even though the drop was no more than a yard, his head smacking a river rock could have been enough to kill him outright or at least knock him unconscious so that he drowned. The medical examiner would make that call.

But if we found no tools or samples, then someone else must have taken them. Whether accident or murder, whoever was involved might have been afraid that fingerprints or other evidence would be discovered. Better to take everything that might have been touched.

One thing was certain. In Asheville, a baby was about to be born who would never know his father. A tightness spread across my chest as the weight of the tragedy settled on me. I didn't know Ken very well, but he'd been honest and straightforward in his dealings with Nakayla. He'd been so conscientious about the door, and I'd witnessed the close relationship he had with his father. I looked down at the body. Not just a person but a world had been destroyed. I wouldn't want to be the one bringing his wife and father the news.

Lights twinkled through the trees. I counted four. Three deputies must have responded. I swept my beam across the figures as they emerged into the open pasture. A tall man in jeans and a windbreaker walked beside Nakayla with two uniformed officers trailing a few steps behind. Evidently, Sheriff Hudson had come from his home to investigate. In the backwash of his flashlight, his distinctive brown handlebar mustache identified him as clearly as if he'd worn his nameplate.

I aimed my beam at the holes in the soil. "You might want to stay off that area. Our footprints are there, but others might be as well. Ken Stokes's body is at my feet where I found him."

Without hesitating, Sheriff Hudson arced toward the river,

keeping clear of the area I illuminated. He stepped down into the water and waded toward me. I moved away to give him free access.

Hudson bent over and ran his light up and down the body. "No marks other than the gash on the back of his head?"

"None visible in a cursory exam. Once I determined he was dead, I took no further action."

Hudson grunted approval. "You were what? Military police?"

"A chief warrant officer."

"And you know this Ken Stokes how?"

"He's a contractor. He's rebuilding my partner's house. Nakayla Robertson." I looked up to where Nakayla stood with the two deputies. "She phoned it in."

"And why are you and your partner out here?"

"His wife called Nakayla. He hadn't come home when she expected him. His wife's expecting their first child any day."

"Ah, hell." Hudson said nothing further for a few seconds. Then he shouted, "Jack, radio for the medical examiner and the mobile crime lab. Wake up whoever you have to and get things rolling PDQ. And tell them we need a generator."

One of the deputies peeled off to return to his vehicle. Hudson directed additional orders. "Graham, phone dispatch to find a number for Ted Kirkpatrick. There's a gated road to this field. I want it unlocked or we'll break it down to get access. I don't want to haul all the crap from the launch site." He turned to me. "How did you know Stokes would be here?"

"He's part of a group that monitors pollution in the rivers."

"River Watchers," Hudson interjected. "I'm familiar with them."

"His wife thought he'd come to take water samples."

"Not soil?"

"No. She made a point of saying he kept downstream of the old Kirkgate landfill."

Sheriff Hudson looked down at the body. "Obviously, this time he didn't."

"But if he took those samples, where are they? And what did he dig with?"

Hudson stepped back. He swept his flashlight beam downstream over the rippling surface. Nothing but water and rocks. "Did you check in his truck?"

"No. Good point. Maybe Ken carried his samples and tools back but left something behind. It was on that final trip that he fell into the river."

"Graham," Hudson yelled. "When you finish that call, go to the white pickup and see what's in the cab and bed."

The deputy was on the phone but raised his left hand to signal he heard.

Another cell phone rang. Nakayla pulled hers out of her jacket pocket. The lit screen shone on her face, illuminating the pain for all of us to see. "Oh, Sam, it's Lynne."

"Send her to voicemail."

"Is that the wife?" Hudson asked.

"Yes. We can't break the news over the phone."

Hudson lowered his flashlight to his side. "It's not much better having two strange deputies show up on your front porch."

I knew what he was asking. "You want Nakayla and me to tell her?"

"I'd be obliged. That way I can keep all my available men focused on the investigation. We'll arrange to get a statement from Mrs. Stokes tomorrow, but it would help to get that initial shock out of the way."

"That shock's not going away overnight," I snapped.

"I know it's not. But there's a difference between being shocked and being in shock. Grief so profound you can hardly breathe let alone talk."

The sheriff was right. Lynne Stokes had asked us to find her husband. We couldn't hide behind an impersonal protocol. Although they were no longer close, Nakayla and Lynne had known each other since elementary school. The woman needed someone she could cry with, not be forced to welcome badges and guns into her home.

"And our statements?" I asked.

"We can take those tomorrow as well. Let me know how Mrs. Stokes is doing and we'll prioritize her. Maybe you two can come by the department in the afternoon."

Hudson's request wasn't unreasonable.

"What do you think, Nakayla?"

"We shouldn't delay. I'll drive. With the heater going all out, maybe you'll dry off before we get there."

"Again, I really appreciate it," Hudson said.

I stepped up out of the river onto a solid patch of ground. I turned to look down at the sheriff, catching him full face in my flashlight. "Before I make an official statement, you need to know Ken Stokes and Luke Kirkpatrick had heated words at the Asheville Tourists game yesterday."

The sheriff squinted against the light. "About what?"

"About this Asheville Luminaries Festival that Luke and his father are promoting." I described the altercation including the shove and Luke's muttered words that he'd like to slug Ken.

"And you think that's why Stokes came here? To prove they were polluting?"

"I don't know. I'm more interested to know where Luke was this evening."

Sheriff Hudson nodded. "Then so am I."

Lynne called twice more as Nakayla and I raced back to Asheville. Both went to voicemail. The sheriff had agreed to keep Ken Stokes's name off the police radio to delay the onslaught of media for as long as possible.

Ken and Lynne lived on the east side of Asheville. I'd been to his house once to drop off a check so that he could purchase construction materials. The tree-lined street contained a mixture of bungalows and two stories, some renovated, others in need of repairs that elderly residents or renters left unaddressed.

Given Asheville's booming housing market, it was only a matter of time, a short time, before neighborhoods like the Stokes's would become totally gentrified.

Nakayla turned onto their street. I glanced at my watch. Half past midnight. The houses were dark. Except for one. Light shone from every window as if the inhabitants attempted to keep the night at bay.

"This is it," I said.

Nakayla slowed and parked in front of the house next door. We got out of the CR-V, closing the doors as quietly as possible. Although my pants were no longer soaked, they were still damp and beginning to create the itches that you can't scratch in mixed company. As we walked up the sidewalk, Nakayla took my hand.

The front door, not unlike the one Ken had installed for Nakayla only hours earlier, swung open before we could knock. Lynne stood wrapped in the glow of the living room lights. She wore loose gray sweatpants and a burgundy maternity blouse that looked like it was covering a beach ball. Her blond hair was tightly pulled into a ponytail. Perspiration glistened on her pale face. Time seemed to stop.

Lynne's green eyes searched ours and read everything she feared. Her hands cradled her distended abdomen, rubbing the curve as if trying to protect her unborn child from what was bearing down on both of them.

Nakayla started to speak, but Lynne wailed, "No. Don't say it. Please don't say it." Then her knees buckled, and she collapsed onto the threshold, pent-up tears flowing even as she lost consciousness.

Chapter Five

"I don't want to go to the hospital. I don't need to go to the hospital." Lynne Stokes shook her head violently in case her vocal protests weren't strong enough. "I need to see my husband."

The distraught woman sat propped in a corner of the living room sofa, revived after Nakayla had soaked a dishcloth in cold water and then patted Lynne's forehead and cheeks until the fainting spell passed.

We'd carefully helped her off the floor. I had my phone out, ready to dial 911 for an ambulance when she started pleading and then demanding to be taken to the site of Ken's death. That wasn't going to happen.

"The sheriff is investigating," Nakayla explained. "He wants to rule out anything other than an accident. We can't interfere. Think of the baby. Ken would want your child's wellbeing to be your priority."

"I want my husband." Lynne's words collapsed into muffled sobs as she buried her face in her hands. Nakayla sat down beside her and gently placed her hand on Lynne's knee. At that slight touch, the grieving woman leaned closer, wrapping her arms around Nakayla's neck and weeping into her shoulder.

Nakayla looked up at me, her own eyes overflowing with

tears. "Water," she silently mouthed and nodded toward the kitchen.

The lighting in the kitchen was modern and bright. The appliances appeared to be state of the art and the hardwood plank flooring had been refinished to a spotless sheen. Ken must have done the remodeling himself, as I could see some of the touches he'd recommended to Nakayla. A selfish thought flashed through my mind. *Who was going to finish her house now?*

I brought the water glasses into the living room. Nakayla still hugged Lynne but the sobs had reduced to staggered breaths. Nakayla nodded to a table at the other end of the sofa. A set of coasters were stacked next to a silver-framed photograph. I recognized Ken and his dad each holding a brown trout. A happy time on a river. I nudged the frame to the rear of the table and placed the glasses on coasters in front of it. Then I crossed the room to a bentwood rocker, sat, and waited.

A few minutes later, Lynne raised her head. "Walt. Who's told Walt?"

"I don't believe he knows," Nakayla whispered. "Would you like us to call him?"

Lynne's eyes widened. "No, not over the phone."

Nakayla looked at me.

I stood. "Give me his address."

———

"Make a suspect sweat" had been embraced by Sheriff Cliff Hudson. I sat alone in an interview room for nearly half an hour with the temperature seeming to rise a degree a minute.

Nakayla and I had arrived at the department a little after one the afternoon following the discovery of Ken Stokes's body. We were told that the sheriff was in Asheville but had left instructions for Nakayla and me to write out statements describing what had happened the previous night. We'd been placed in separate rooms to avoid collaboration, although if we were fabricating a story, we would have had plenty of time. Neither of us had slept a wink.

Walt Stokes had been devastated by the news. A widower, he had no living relatives other than his son and daughter-in-law. The prospect of a grandchild had promised to be one of the most joyful events of his life. Now that joy crumbled beneath the weight of those awful words I couldn't soften, couldn't make less painful, couldn't make less forever.

He'd immediately wanted to go to the river, but when I told him Lynne had collapsed, his backbone stiffened and the tears dried.

I offered to drive, but he insisted on taking his Bronco. He lived on a small farm north of Asheville, and I feared he might make a run to the river. I tailgated him all the way into town. Nakayla and I sat with the two of them for another hour, assuring them Sheriff Hudson would contact them soon. Then we left them with their combined sorrow.

I signed my statement and pushed the pen and papers away. Assuming I hadn't been locked in, I could at least find cooler air outside.

The door opened before I reached it. Sheriff Hudson entered and nodded for me to return to the table.

He sat across from me and glanced at the handwritten pages. "Thanks for coming in and sorry to hold you up." He sighed the words as much as he spoke them.

For a moment, we just looked at each other. My eyes were probably as bloodshot as his, his energy as depleted as mine.

"I spoke with your partner first," he said. "She told me about your night. I saw Mrs. Stokes and her father-in-law late this morning."

"What did you tell them?"

"That we didn't know what happened. The most probable cause was accidental. The riverbank gave way and he hit his head on the rocks."

"And the digging with no tools? The missing water samples?"

"I'm holding that back for now. There's the possibility of no connection at all. The soil samples, if that's what they are, could have been taken earlier. Before Stokes ever got there. Maybe the holes caught his eye."

"What about Luke Kirkpatrick?"

"He came to the scene last night. He and his father."

"Alibis?"

"The father had a late dinner with some piano player. Luke was at his home alone."

"One of your deputies reached them?"

Hudson shook his head. "One of my deputies reached the father and then Mr. Kirkpatrick called his son."

"They drive together?"

The sheriff cocked his head. "What difference does that make?"

"If Ted Kirkpatrick called his son's mobile and not a landline, then Luke could have been anywhere. But if they arrived together, I'd be interested to know who picked up whom and where. You might pull cell tower records on both of them."

Hudson considered the suggestion. "All right, but Ted Kirkpatrick's alibi checked out. The piano player was almost an hour late. They were to meet at some restaurant called Rhubarb."

"I know it well. It's in my office building."

Hudson collected the sheets of my statement. "I'll have this typed up. Your partner's is being done now." He got up from the table.

I stayed seated. "What's your next step?"

He smiled. "It's an ongoing investigation."

I stood and stepped close to him. "The wife and father deserve an explanation."

Hudson's lips drew into a tight, thin line nearly disappearing into his thick mustache. "And they'll get an explanation." The tired eyes suddenly ignited. "When I'm satisfied it's the correct one."

He pivoted, walked to the door, and held it open for me to precede him. We found Nakayla waiting in the lobby. The sheriff's grim expression brightened when he saw her. Evidently, I was the only one who had managed to piss him off.

"Thank you again for coming in." Hudson pulled a business card from his pocket and handed it to Nakayla. "If you think of anything else beyond what's in your statements, here's my direct number."

I didn't get a card, but I did get a handshake.

"When do you expect the medical examiner's report?" I asked.

"Around four." He hesitated and then added, "I'll have someone give you a call." A smile broke beneath the mustache. "But, as you know—"

"It's an ongoing investigation."

When we were in the car, Nakayla said, "You realize it's to our benefit to play nice with a sheriff."

"I did play nice. But there are rules to the game, and I just want to make sure he understands that Ken's family needs to be informed of the progress. I guess he thought I was telling him how to do his job."

"Your reputation precedes you."

I remembered Ted Kirkpatrick calling me the famous detective. "Yes, it's difficult being the Sherlock Holmes of Asheville."

"Especially when you're Inspector Clouseau."

I laughed for the first time since finding Ken's body.

We decided to stop at the office with the hope that Sheriff Hudson would make good on his promise to share the autopsy report. The message light was flashing on the phones.

"I'll check them." Nakayla punched in the retrieval code and activated the speaker.

"Hi. This is Sonny Jenkins. I'm trying to find a Nakayla Robertson." The voice came through with a high-pitched mountain twang. "I'm down from Weaverville and was supposed to meet Ken Stokes this morning in West Asheville to talk about some cabinet work. He never showed and he ain't answering his mobile. I'm a sittin' here at the house in my pickup but nobody's here. I'll hang here another twenty minutes or so. Please call as soon as you get this message. Maybe I got the day wrong."

The time stamp was eleven thirty-five. Sonny Jenkins had long since returned to Weaverville.

Nakayla wiped her eyes with the back of her hand, visibly upset that the horrible news would have to be repeated.

"I'll call him," I volunteered. "You want me to tell him you're interested but we will just have to reschedule?"

"Yes, thank you. At some point soon, we need to find a new contractor."

I didn't want to say "no rush" since it had become clear that Nakayla was anxious to get back in her own home. "Well, maybe this Sonny Jenkins will have a suggestion. Ken recommended him so he must be a skilled craftsman who's worked for other contractors."

"Good idea," Nakayla said without enthusiasm. "But not on this call. Ken's death is bound to be a shock."

I went into my office, read the number off the phone ID, and used our landline, anticipating he would recognize the same number he'd dialed earlier.

He answered on the first ring. "Jenkins here."

"Mr. Jenkins, I'm Sam Blackman. I work with Nakayla Robertson."

"Yeah. Did you get my message? Did I screw up somehow?"

"Yes, I got your message. No, you didn't screw up. Mr. Jenkins, I'm so sorry to tell you that Ken Stokes died last night."

Silence, except for the distant bark of a dog.

"Mr. Jenkins?"

A heavy breath sounded in my ear. Then a hoarse whisper: "Well, hell, he was a young fella. What happened? Car wreck?"

"No, sir. He was found in the Pigeon River. They think he

was taking water samples and might have slipped." I decided not to speculate any further. I certainly didn't want to spread the word "murder" around.

"I'm sorry to hear that. I truly am."

"I apologize that we didn't show up. We've been with his wife and father all night."

"Don't give it another thought."

I cleared my throat. "Nakayla would still like to talk to you about the cabinets. Maybe toward the end of the week. Can we reach you at this number?"

"Yeah, that'll be fine. Whatever suits you." He paused. "Listen, are you calling his friends?"

"No, sir. Do you need me to get in touch with someone?"

"I just wanted you to know a young man came looking for Ken at the house this morning. It was after I left the message. He said he was hoping to catch him."

"Did it have to do with the construction?"

"Maybe. He said something about samples. Would I tell Ken that Paul Clarkson had been by. Like me, he'd tried to reach him on his mobile but got no answer. Now I know why, but he doesn't. If you know this Clarkson, you might want to give him the bad news."

I thanked Jenkins and promised to be in touch. Then I headed across our conversation area for Nakayla's office. We had a three-room suite with the hallway door opening into the larger, middle room where we met clients. A leather sofa, matching armchairs, and Persian carpet were designed to create a relaxed environment, as much for us as for those hiring our services.

Nakayla looked up from her desk, but before I could speak, there was a knock and the hallway door opened. Walt Stokes leaned in, keeping his body on the other side of the threshold.

"Can we come in?"

He'd changed clothes, but exhaustion still ruled his gaunt face.

"Certainly." I pulled the door open wider and stepped to one side.

Nakayla joined me as Walt entered, followed by Lynne. She walked as if her shoes were made of concrete. The cheerful colors of her maternity outfit belied the staggering grief visible in her haunted eyes. Nakayla caught her arm and led her to the sofa.

"I told Lynne we should call for an appointment," Walt said. "But we were at the funeral home and she thought you might have a few moments."

Nakayla sat beside Lynne and patted her hand. Walt and I each took a chair.

"Sheriff Hudson and a deputy came by this morning," Walt said. "He didn't tell us much. Just asked a bunch of questions."

"That's the way it works," I said. "He won't say much till he gets a report from the medical examiner."

"That's what he told us. He claimed it was most likely an accident, but he wanted to know if Kenny had any recent run-ins, you know, with customers or subcontractors."

"Did he?"

"No. I mean in the building trade there's always the chance for miscommunication, but Kenny never wanted to surprise a customer. He'd been building for ten years and not one lawsuit against him."

I thought about how concerned and conscientious he'd been when the front door came with the wrong measurements.

"What about his volunteer work with River Watchers?"

"He was serious about that. He'd take on the paper companies, the state environmental people, anybody he thought wasn't protecting our waterways."

Lynne leaned forward. "He had a run-in last Saturday with Luke Kirkpatrick. He said you were there."

"I was. He was upset that the Kirkpatricks hadn't included Wilma Dykeman as an honoree. He didn't accuse them of any new pollution."

"But then he winds up in the river by their old landfill," Walt said. "I saw it. Drove out after the sheriff left us. Waded upstream till I saw the crime tape on the bank. Hell, Kenny could walk a riverbed as surefooted as if walking on a sidewalk. Been fishing since he could hold a rod. And if he was taking water samples, where were they? Sheriff Hudson didn't have no answer for that. So much for his accident theory."

Lynne and her father-in-law exchanged a glance as she clutched the fabric of her maternity blouse. She looked at me and then turned to Nakayla. "We want to hire you to investigate."

Nakayla's mouth dropped open. She was as surprised as I was.

"But at this point there's no need," Nakayla said. "The official investigation is just starting."

Walt stood, too agitated to stay in the chair. "Which means the truth could be nipped in the bud. I don't know this sheriff. Maybe he's bent, maybe he's as honest as the day is long. But I do know Ted Kirkpatrick is one of the richest men in Asheville. If he can't buy a county sheriff, he'll bribe whoever can put pressure on the sheriff. Lynne and I want someone we can trust. Y'all were on the scene, you're the best detectives in North Carolina, and you knew Kenny. Now, we'll pay you. We ain't expecting no charity."

I shook my head. "Nakayla's right. It's too early to second-guess Sheriff Hudson."

Walt walked so close to me I had to look straight up at him. He bent down. "Then tell me this. From what you saw, do you think it was an accident?"

I couldn't say no, so I didn't say anything.

"That's what I thought." Walt stepped back.

I got to my feet. "We're not taking your money."

"Then do me a favor. Let me finish Kenny's job." He focused on Nakayla. "Your home is my son's last project. I should be the one to finish it. I'm still a licensed contractor. It will be a trade. My time for yours."

Lynne grabbed Nakayla's arm. "Please."

Chapter Six

"What else could I say?" Nakayla stood at the window, gazing out at Pack Square below.

I wasn't sure whether she wanted an answer to her question. We'd returned to the office after escorting Lynne and Walt to the elevator and agreeing to look into Ken's death.

Nakayla turned around and collapsed onto the sofa. "I mean, how do you say no to a woman who's just lost her husband?"

"You don't." I bypassed my customary chair and sat beside her. "We do what we can, and that might be nothing more than validating Sheriff Hudson's work so that Lynne and Walt have confidence in his findings."

"Hudson won't react well to our second-guessing him."

"Yes," I agreed. "He's made that abundantly clear, but would he rather have us working discreetly? Or Lynne and Walt going to the press with accusations of a cover-up?"

"Word will soon get back to him."

"I know. I'm going to tell him. Where's that card he gave you?"

Nakayla folded her arms across her chest as if to keep her hands from carrying out my request. "Don't you think I should tell him?"

"He likes you. Why ruin that? Me, on the other hand, not. It's our own version of good cop/bad cop."

Nakayla laughed. "You mean nice human being/total jerk."

"I don't know about the total part. Blue seems to like me."

Nakayla rose from the sofa with renewed energy. "The card's in my office. Maybe you can offer Hudson an olive branch."

"An olive branch?" Her comment triggered something I'd meant to explore.

"Sonny Jenkins saying Paul Clarkson came by the house asking about samples."

"Brilliant. I bet they weren't samples for the house but water samples. Clarkson might be the only person who knows what Ken was up to."

I remembered how Clarkson had intervened to calm the air between Ken and Luke Kirkpatrick at the ball game. He obviously knew both men. "So, we give Hudson that lead, our lead?"

"Which we can follow up later. In the meantime, we stay in the sheriff's good graces, even if we are conducting a parallel investigation."

She retrieved Hudson's card, followed me into my office and sat on the corner of my desk. I used the landline to dial the mobile number Hudson had written on the back.

"Listen to a master at work," I told Nakayla as the first ring sounded.

"Hello."

I recognized the voice although he gave no identification that he was Hudson or a sheriff.

"It's Sam Blackman. Can you talk a few minutes?"

"I was just getting ready to call you."

The medical examiner's report. I definitely wanted to keep on his good side until he gave me that information.

"Nakayla and I learned something you might find interesting and wanted to get it to you right away."

"I'm listening."

I gave him the summary of our conversation with Sonny Jenkins and his encounter with Paul Clarkson.

Hudson was quiet a moment as he assessed the implications. "So, Clarkson not only witnessed this confrontation, he kept it from escalating."

"Yes. I'm not sure what his connection is to Ken, but he's involved in the Asheville Luminaries Festival. He works at the Moog factory and is evidently an accomplished musician."

"Do you know how to reach him?"

"No. But the factory should have a number and an address for him."

"Thanks." Hudson rattled some papers. "Afraid I don't have much for you from the autopsy report. Stokes was clean as far as any alcohol or drugs in his system. No water in his lungs, so he didn't drown."

"He was killed on land and dumped in the river?"

"I wish it was that definitive. The ME says Stokes died from a single blow to the back of his head and neck. His spinal cord was severed. But the wound's shape was consistent with the rounded edge of a jutting river rock. Under the gashed skin were traces of mica particles consistent with the riverbed. The ME also states the position of the body and the collapsed river bank indicate he fell backwards, making it unlikely someone could have struck him from behind."

"In other words, he could have fallen, been pushed, or even struck with a rock from behind."

"That's about the size of it," Hudson said. "Which brings us back to the missing samples. If that was indeed his purpose for being there, then who took them? I'll be interested to hear from this Paul Clarkson."

I sensed the sheriff was wrapping up.

"Listen, Stokes's wife and father came by our office this afternoon."

"Oh. Did they have any complaints about the way we treated them?"

"No. Nothing like that."

Hudson spoke the words before I could. "They asked you to investigate."

I couldn't deny the guy was sharp. "Yes. And we agreed, not for lack of faith in your capabilities, but to try to bring some comfort to Lynne Stokes. We have no intention of getting in your way."

Nakayla rolled her eyes at my assurance.

"What a relief." Hudson was probably rolling his eyes as well. His voice rose by at least ten decibels. "Because I'd hate to petition for the revocation of your P.I. license. So, we have an understanding, right?"

"Yes, Sheriff. And thank you for being so understanding." I hung up before he could say something like "stay out of my county."

I leaned back in my desk chair, its squeal reminding me to drop a few pounds. "That went better than I hoped."

Nakayla nodded. "You and he have an understanding."

"He welcomes our help."

"Was that before or after he threatened your license?"

"You heard?"

"Of course I heard. He was nearly shouting. What I didn't hear was everything else." Nakayla slid off the edge of the desk. "I'll get a fresh legal pad and you can give me the details."

We settled into our customary places, she in a corner of the leather sofa, shoes off, feet tucked under her thighs. I sat in the nearer armchair and tried to provide a verbatim account of Sheriff Hudson's side of the phone call.

When I'd finished, Nakayla took a few minutes to read back over her notes.

"How do you want to start?" I asked.

Nakayla flipped to a clean sheet. "Paul Clarkson's top of the list. Then Walt and Lynne separately. Clarkson might create some lines of inquiry for Walt and Lynne that we don't know about."

"Good point. They in turn might say something that circles back to Clarkson."

"Ted and Luke Kirkpatrick are obviously persons of interest," Nakayla said.

"But Ted has an alibi. Dinner with a piano player."

"That piano player goes on the list." Nakayla scribbled on the pad. "Ted says he was an hour late. Was Ted waiting at the restaurant all that time or had they been in touch by phone?"

"Easy enough to check on," I said. "I think that's enough to start with."

Nakayla touched the point of her pencil to the tip of her tongue and frowned at the anemic list of interviewees. "What about the River Watchers?"

"What about them?"

"If Ken Stokes was a member, maybe someone in the group would know if he specifically targeted the Kirkpatricks, or this was simply a routine monitoring."

"I was just about to say the same thing. I'm so pleased my detective skills are rubbing off on you."

"Sam Blackman, a legend in his own mind. The only thing rubbing off on me is Blue's hair. And we'd better go to the apartment and let him out. We'll track down Clarkson tomorrow." She slipped on her shoes and headed for her office.

A knock sounded and then Hewitt opened the hallway door. "Good. You're both here. Can we talk a moment?"

It became apparent that the "we" meant more than just the three of us. Ted Kirkpatrick followed Hewitt to the sofa where they remained standing. Instead of his country club attire, the executive wore a dark blue suit, white shirt, and red tie. Someone entering the room would think he was the lawyer and not the guy beside him with a ponytail and cabana shirt.

Nakayla and I exchanged a glance that conveyed the same question: *What the hell's going on?*

"Would either of you like coffee?" Nakayla asked. "I could put on a fresh pot."

Hewitt looked to Kirkpatrick.

"No, thank you."

"None for me either," Hewitt said.

I gestured to the sofa. "Then please sit down."

As they sat, I saw Nakayla's legal pad on the coffee table in front of them. The visible sheet revealed the penciled list of interviewees and potential lines of questioning. Kirkpatrick hadn't noticed it, but Hewitt's eagle eyes swept down the names. He picked it up and handed it to Nakayla, cutting his eyes between us.

When we were settled, Kirkpatrick looked to Hewitt to begin, but the defense attorney appeared to be studying the backs of his hands.

"Should I start, Hewitt?"

"Yes. Sorry. You know Sam, but I should have introduced you to Nakayla Robertson, the brains of the agency. Nakayla, Ted Kirkpatrick."

Kirkpatrick leaned across the coffee table to shake her hand.

"Thanks for seeing me on such short...well, actually no notice. As you know, Ken Stokes's body was found in the Pigeon River." He stopped and appeared flustered. "What am I saying? Hell, you found him. My son, Luke, and I went to the scene after I got the call from the Haywood County Sheriff's Department. The property adjacent to the river was one of our containment sites for disposal of chemical byproducts from our manufacturing process."

Chemical byproducts. So much more benign than toxic waste.

"The sheriff and one of his deputies spoke with us today wanting to know our relationship with Stokes. I told them what I'm telling you. We don't have a relationship. Yes, at one time in our history we discharged waste into the river, but we were small potatoes compared to Pisgah Valley Paper. And once the research demonstrated the undesirable consequences of the practice, we were the first to take action."

He paused, as if allowing time for applause.

"That happened before the settlement?" I asked.

A flash of anger, and then he forced a smile. "Once we had clear instructions as to the requirements and standards agreed upon, we quickly responded."

Hewitt gave me a hard stare like I was cross-examining one of his witnesses. The translation of Kirkpatrick's statement— "We complied because we were compelled."

I ignored Hewitt and pressed on. "So, the confrontation I saw between your son and Ken Stokes was all about history?"

"Yes. Some people can't move on." Kirkpatrick moistened his lips and looked at Hewitt. "We were never cited for any violations."

"That's correct," Hewitt confirmed. "But I believe Sam heard the argument differently. Ken's dispute was over the Luminaries Festival and his perception Wilma Dykeman's work was being slighted."

Kirkpatrick nodded. "I'll concede if I had it to do over, I would include her." He gave a humorless laugh. "She was a thorn in my side alive, and now she is again."

Nakayla shifted in her chair, holding her pencil at the ready. "Then you had nothing to fear from whatever water or soil samples Ken might have taken?"

"Nothing whatsoever. He shouldn't have been on our property. We monitor the site regularly, so I have no doubt we'd pass any evaluation."

I looked at Hewitt. Time for someone to explain why they were here.

Hewitt leaned forward. "Ted is concerned that he and his family are considered suspects in Ken Stokes's death."

"But they haven't been charged."

"No, but we're talking about optics. There's an adversarial history and the argument at the ballpark. Top it off with your discovery of the body by their property and the court of public opinion will render a guilty verdict. And it couldn't come at a worse time than when Ted and Kirkgate Paper are highly visible because of the festival."

"We feel the Luminary Festival is a real tribute to Asheville's past," Kirkpatrick said. "It's a way of giving back to a city that's been so good to me. Now we risk being tainted by a tragic event, an event we had no part of. If it was more than an accident, then we want the guilty party found as much as anyone. In fact, on Hewitt's advice, we're offering a twenty-thousand-dollar reward to whoever provides information leading to an arrest and conviction."

Defense attorney Hewitt Donaldson going on the offensive. He wasn't one to react to events.

"That should help sway public opinion," I said.

"That's one action," Hewitt agreed. "There's another with a greater chance of succeeding. That's why we're here."

Ted Kirkpatrick pointed a finger at me so that there was no mistaking the target of his words. "Sam, I said at the ball game that if I ever needed a detective, you would be the one." He nodded toward Nakayla. "You and your partner. I want you to investigate Ken Stokes's death. We are innocent, so I have no fear of what you might find. No one in Asheville has heard of this Sheriff Hudson, but you are a different story. The public will have confidence in whatever you conclude. It's the surest way to dispel the cloud of suspicion hanging over us."

He smiled and leaned back into the cushions, confident that his proposition was irresistible.

Hewitt pursed his lips, looked at me and then at the legal pad in Nakayla's lap. He knew what was coming.

I cleared my throat. "Thank you, Ted, but I'm afraid we can't accept your case. We're already working it for another client."

Kirkpatrick flinched like I'd slapped him. "Another client? I'll pay you double."

"We have a contract," I lied.

"Then who is it? Someone paying you to find something incriminating on me and my company?"

Nakayla bristled. "We find the truth, and whether that's helpful or harmful to you isn't the point. You're the one who said you have nothing to fear."

Hewitt patted his client's knee. "Don't look a gift horse in the mouth, Ted. You're getting what you want without having to pay for it."

"But I won't get any progress reports, will I?"

"No," I said. "Although your cooperation will make that progress go faster. Our findings won't be buried. We'll share our conclusions with Sheriff Hudson. Our client only wants the truth."

Kirkpatrick nodded. "It's the Stokes family, isn't it?"

"Our client wishes to remain anonymous."

"The Stokes family," he repeated, no longer a question. "I understand Ken's wife is expecting."

"Any day," Nakayla said.

His eyes moistened. "I feel for them. I really do." He was either genuinely moved or a hell of an actor. He turned to Hewitt. "I guess we're done here."

Hewitt stood and the rest of us followed suit.

"You asked for my cooperation," Kirkpatrick said. "What do you need?"

"A chance to interview you," I said. "We can set a time here, or in Hewitt's office, or any other place you choose."

"Now?"

"No. We've got some other sources to check first. We'll be in touch." I offered my hand.

He shook it and did the same with Nakayla's. "Good hunting." He and Hewitt closed the door behind them.

Chapter Seven

"Sorry about the legal pad." Nakayla made the apology as she locked it in her desk drawer.

"Not your fault. How could you know that Hewitt would bring Kirkpatrick by so late in the day? And it might have been for the best. Hewitt figured out we were already working the case and wasn't blindsided when we turned Kirkpatrick down."

Nakayla grabbed her purse. "Well, I'm glad to call it a day."

"Me too. But we should still wait a few minutes."

Nakayla dropped her purse on her desk. "Hewitt?"

"Yeah. He'll want to ask some questions without his client present."

She looked at her wristwatch. "Let's wait ten minutes. If he comes, then limit the conversation to fifteen minutes. Otherwise, I'll leave you with him and take care of Blue. You can call an Uber or hitch a ride with Hewitt."

"Forget it. We'll talk to him tomorrow." I opened the door to leave.

There stood Hewitt.

"I won't take more than fifteen minutes. Promise."

I looked at Nakayla. She blushed.

"That's consecutive minutes," I said. "No loopholes."

"Yes. You can set a timer. I'll use the first minute to apologize." He returned to his spot on the sofa. Nakayla and I took the chairs.

"I shouldn't have just dropped by with Ted. I didn't mean to put you on the spot."

"It was awkward," I said. "But if he's serious about wanting the truth, then whether we're working for him or someone else, the result will be the same."

"I reiterated that. Ted would like to be in control as your client, but he's reluctantly accepted the situation. How are you and Sheriff Hudson?"

"We've reached an understanding."

Hewitt laughed. "You give him what you discover, and he keeps what he discovers."

"He's given us the preliminary autopsy," Nakayla said.

Hewitt arched his bushy eyebrows. "Oh? What does it conclude?"

"That Ken most likely struck his head on the edge of a jutting river rock," I said. "But with no determination whether he accidentally fell or was deliberately pushed."

"Or pushed and then accidentally fell into the river," Hewitt said.

I pictured Luke Kirkpatrick shoving Ken at the ball game. "And Ted has a dinner alibi for last night, but his guest was late. So, what time does this alibi begin?"

"The pianist playing Bartók's concerto was supposed to meet him at Rhubarb at seven thirty. He didn't get there till nearly eight thirty."

"Did Ted know he was running late?" I asked.

"Yes. He'd phoned from the road. But Ted was in the restaurant early. I'm his alibi. We had a drink at the bar."

"And Luke?"

"Luke was home alone. He's divorced. No kids. Ex-wife moved back to her hometown in Michigan two months ago.

Luke picked Ted up and they drove to the containment field together."

"Luke has no alibi before meeting his father," Nakayla observed.

"That's right. It's one of two reasons he wants the Stokes case wrapped up quickly."

"What's the other one?" I asked.

"They're in the process of applying for county and state permits to increase the plant's capacity. Ted's running three shifts, seven days a week, but the public's insatiable appetite for online shopping has exploded the need for shipping cartons that use the corrugated paper he manufactures. In turn, recycling has created an unending source for extracting the necessary raw materials. He has both supply and demand, and he needs to physically expand his facilities."

"And is that increase in production increasing the waste?"

"Yes," Hewitt admitted. "And Ted's incorporating new technologies to counteract that. But bad press could delay or even sink those plans. If he doubles capacity, he doubles jobs."

"Careful, Hewitt," I chided, "you're sounding like a politician."

He threw up his hands. "I know. But I've known Ted since high school. Yeah, he's got his faults and he had to be pressured into cleaning up his operation, but I believe he's trying to do the right thing now. He's willing to talk to you and give you access to anything at the plant that might be relevant."

"When's this announcement of a twenty-thousand-dollar reward happening?"

"A press conference at ten tomorrow." He turned on the sofa and peered out the window. "At the base of the Vance Memorial. You'll have a bird's-eye view."

The Vance Memorial was a tall granite obelisk honoring Zebulon Vance, the North Carolina governor during the Civil War and then a United States Senator. It stood on the edge of Pack Square closest to our office.

"And Ted's working tonight to expand his Luminaries Festival events," Hewitt added.

"Don't tell me," Nakayla said, "he's suddenly seen the light about Wilma Dykeman."

"Yes. He's working with UNC-Asheville to have a professor give a lecture on Dykeman at the auditorium in Lipinsky Hall. It's the university's music building. He hopes to have it Saturday night, which will allow for at least a little publicity. And he's adding a brief reading of her works at the Bartók concert."

"When can we interview him?" I asked.

"Whenever you want. He's happy to come to my office or yours."

"You want to be there?"

Hewitt smiled. "Yes, so my office. It will save me the trouble of bugging yours."

————

The next morning, Nakayla, Blue, and I arrived at the office at nine thirty. The first priority was to track down Paul Clarkson and find out what he knew about Ken Stokes. I checked the internet and learned the Moog factory opened to the public at ten. At precisely ten, I called and asked for Clarkson.

"Speaking. How can I help you?"

"This is Sam Blackman. I'm a private detective here in Ashe—"

"I hope you're looking into what happened to Ken Stokes," he interjected.

"That's why we'd like to talk to you. Do you have time to meet this morning?"

"Hold on a sec."

I heard the background sound muffle as Clarkson must have put his hand over the phone. There were some garbled words, and then he was back.

"I'm leading a tour at ten thirty. We could talk after that."

"How long's the tour?"

"It runs about forty-five minutes. We have a few spaces available."

I'd driven by the factory thousands of times. Located at the end of Lexington Avenue, the brick structure had an exterior mural of a giant synthesizer that covered a wall of windows. Colorful, eye-catching, the painting had the pop feel of the 1960s. I'd never been inside. Like so many residents, I didn't take advantage of all the attractions in my own city.

"Sure," I said. "Ten thirty."

"Be here about five minutes early. Feel free to play some of the instruments in the showroom."

"Not if you want anyone else to stay for the tour."

Nakayla elected to remain in the office and compile backgrounds for our other potential interviewees. She also wanted to connect with Sonny Jenkins about the kitchen cabinets so that construction could resume as soon as Walt Stokes was ready take over his son's role as general contractor.

On the clear, spring morning with the temperature hovering in the midsixties, I decided to walk the roughly half a mile to the Moog factory. The route along Lexington was mostly downhill so I was hardly winded when I opened the door and entered the Moog showroom.

A young woman stood behind a checkout counter on the left. "Welcome," she said. "Are you here for the tour?"

"Yes. The one with Paul Clarkson."

"He'll be out in a few minutes. Feel free to look at the exhibits and try the synthesizers." She gestured to the rear of the large room. "Or better yet, check out the books and T-shirts."

I noticed that the Moog keyboards all had headphones attached. Maybe I could test them without driving my fellow tour-goers away after all. Six other people were spread out among the instruments and merchandise. Four young men in black jeans and matching windbreakers gathered around one of the synthesizers. They looked like members of a band. One played the keyboard while the other three passed the headphones around. An older couple, who had the relaxed look of retirees, studied a mural covering the back wall. Bob Moog's head against a backdrop of electrical schematic diagrams and keyboards rose ten or fifteen feet above the floor. The couple stood beneath a quote incorporated into the artwork.

To be human, to be fully human, is to need music and to derive nourishment from the music you hear. What you do with our instruments helps us to be more human, too, and I want to thank you all for that.—Bob Moog

I nodded to the gray-haired couple as they turned away and moved to the largest exhibit in the room. This synthesizer was approximately five feet high but without the preponderance of knobs and switches. Instead, multicolored cables entwined like renegade spaghetti as they were patched into sockets that must have routed electric signals into numerous loops. The device looked more like an old-time telephone switchboard minus the operator.

I overheard the man say, "Moog's first synthesizer. You couldn't have played it live."

"If you're part of the tour, please step this way." The voice came from behind me, and I turned to see Paul Clarkson enter through a rear door. I caught a glimpse of technicians busy at workbenches before he closed the door and walked over to what I recognized as a theremin.

The others joined me as we formed a semicircle around him. The only other time I'd seen Clarkson, he'd been dressed in the vintage baseball uniform. Today he wore slacks and a shirt with the Moog logo. His black hair was almost to his shoulders, and I realized on Saturday he must have had it pulled up in a man bun beneath his cap. I pegged him for late twenties or early thirties. A contemporary of Ken Stokes.

"I'll first tell you a little bit about Dr. Robert Moog," Clarkson said. "Then about this instrument in front of me." He patted the wooden case of the theremin. "And then we'll go onto the factory floor." He smiled. "Any questions so far?"

The older lady raised her hand like we were a class on a field trip.

"Yes, ma'am," Clarkson said politely.

"I've heard the name pronounced two ways, Moog with a long O, and Moog like mood." She spoke with a British accent making her own pronunciation sound different. "Is one for the man and one for the machine?"

Clarkson laughed. "I've heard the same. My feeling is if you buy a synthesizer, you can pronounce it however you want. Now Bob would have felt differently. He had a little sign on his desk saying, '*Moog rhymes with rogue, not Moog rhymes with fugue.*'" Clarkson winked at the musicians. "Although we did use the 'mood' pronunciation for a line of guitar pedals called Moogerfoogers."

"I know," the tallest band member said. "I own a Cluster Flux."

That stopped conversation for a moment.

"Well," Clarkson said, "let me tell you about the man behind the name."

He gave a brief biography. How Moog earned his doctorate in engineering physics from Cornell. How he'd been fascinated by the theremin since he built one as a kid. Clarkson's explanation of how it worked was more detailed and I'm sure more accurate than what Madison Kirkpatrick had said on the pitcher's mound. Inductors in the theremin generate the electric field and your body and the theremin create a capacitor that changes the voltage as you move your hands, which corresponds to volume and pitch. I wondered if my metal prosthesis would be an issue if I ever decided to take up the instrument. That point was moot, or should I say, *mote.*

Although Bob Moog wasn't a musician himself, he loved music and wanted to make a new tool for musicians to play. His synthesizer tied to a keyboard hit the music world at the same time as the psychedelic sound. George Harrison brought his new Moog into the studio for four of the tracks on the *Abbey Road* album. Keith Emerson of Emerson, Lake, and Palmer wanted to play it in live concerts, so Moog developed preset modules for fast changes that could be made on the spot.

Moog wasn't a good businessman and had to sell his Moog Music company. He moved to Asheville, became a professor in music research at UNC-Asheville, and then managed to start a new company here and buy back the Moog Music name.

Clarkson led us through the door to the factory floor. Synthesizers were being assembled by hand. Some workers seemed to be calibrating instruments. There were Minimoogs and large Moogs. Technicians worked on modules that looked like they would be installed as interchangeable components. We went upstairs to a black-walled studio with monolith-sized towers of knobs and lights. This was the laboratory for new product development. Even though the technology was proudly analog, using waves, low-pass filters, and noise instead of digital bytes and bits, Moog Music was striving to bring new tools to feed the creative drive of a new generation of musicians.

We returned to the showroom and gave Clarkson a polite round of applause. During the course of the tour, the retired couple said they were on vacation from England. The man mentioned he'd been a sound engineer for Pink Floyd, which immediately impressed the musicians. The six of them headed off to a pub to swap musical war stories.

Clarkson looked at me. "Why don't we go up to the studio where we can speak in private?"

I followed him back to the second floor where he rolled two

chairs into the center of the electronics-filled room. We sat and he leaned forward, elbows on knees, hands clasped tightly together.

"I couldn't say this in front of the tour, but after you phoned me, I got a call from the Haywood County Sheriff's Department."

"Did you tell them you were meeting me?"

"No. They weren't chatty. They just wanted to know where I'd be this afternoon. Two deputies are coming by to talk to me."

I was surprised Sheriff Hudson hadn't talked to Clarkson already. Maybe he was waiting on a more complete forensic report. As an investigator, I liked to know as much as I could about the cause of death and any peculiarities of the crime scene before conducting more than a superficial interview.

"If they ask if you've spoken with anyone else, don't lie," I said. "But if it doesn't come up, then it might be best not to mention me."

"You mean if they know you're asking questions, they'll feel intimidated?"

I laughed. "Hardly. They just don't want someone else treading on their turf. I get it."

"But you're working for Lynne, right?"

"I'm working to find out what happened. Now, why don't you tell me how you knew Ken."

Clarkson appeared to relax. He took a deep breath and then slowly exhaled. "I really got to know him through River Watchers, the organization that works to protect our rivers and streams. Ken had been monitoring pollution levels since high school. I joined after I graduated from UNC-Asheville and started my job here. I never had time before."

"What was your major?"

"I took advantage of both music performance and music technology. I'm a decent keyboardist. Not in the same league as William Ormandy." He gestured to the equipment around us. "But I can build it and play it."

"Who's Ormandy?"

"The concert pianist coming to perform Bartók's Third Piano Concerto, the one they call the Asheville Concerto."

Ted Kirkpatrick's alibi for the night of Ken Stokes's death.

I gave a sheepish grin. "I'm afraid I don't know much about classical music. Is Ormandy a big deal?"

"Yes. And he's got roots here. William and I started college together, but after a year he transferred to the North Carolina School of the Arts. He teaches at the University of Cincinnati College Conservatory of Music. Ted Kirkpatrick's paying him a boatload of money to perform two pieces, one's Bartók's Asheville Concerto and the other's the premiere of a commissioned work that William's composed especially for the festival. I'm supposed to play in both of them."

I caught the sarcastic inflection on the word *supposed.* "You don't sound so sure."

Clarkson shrugged. "William Ormandy's no longer a mountain boy like the rest of us. Ted's insisting the commissioned piece be a tribute to Asheville. Sort of bookending the Bartók. Ted wants the Moog sound infused into the work, which is why he hired me. Let's just say William's not keen on being told how to orchestrate his composition."

"Have you rehearsed?" I asked.

"Not with William. I got the score last Friday. Tonight we're gathering at a recital hall on the university campus. Just William and me, although Ted will probably show up." Clarkson lifted both hands and wiggled his fingers. "I must admit I'm looking forward to seeing how I stack up to the great William Ormandy. He knows his snooty persona won't fly with me. I knew him when he was a pimply-faced kid named Willie from East Tennessee."

One didn't need to be a famous detective to hear the jealousy underpinning his words.

It was time to focus on the real purpose of my interview. "To get back to Ken, what can you tell me about his relationship with Luke Kirkpatrick?"

"That's easy. They can't stand each other."

"Is it tied to the River Watchers?"

Clarkson shook his head. "It's more personal. There was a chemical spill about five years ago. Nothing major, but Ken was the one who caught the jump in the river's toxic levels. He reported it to Raleigh and then organized a picket line at Kirkgate Paper until the Kirkpatricks admitted there had been an accident and publicly committed to addressing the problem. Luke's a hothead and he ratcheted up the rhetoric against Ken, saying he'd falsified the data. His father calmed him down because his father had been through the turmoil of the nineties."

"When that Pisgah Valley Paper executive was killed," I said.

"Yes, and back then Kirkgate was just as culpable as PVP for the pollution."

"What did you say to Ken after Luke shoved him at the ball game?"

"That he'd won the argument because Luke's physical action made him look like an ass. Escalating the confrontation would cost Ken sympathy. I reminded him our goal was to keep the waterways pure."

"Why did you come by the construction site yesterday morning?"

"Ken had told me he was going to pull some samples Sunday afternoon."

"When was this?"

"Sunday afternoon. I told him I had to work on William Ormandy's score for the concert, but I offered to pick up the samples the next morning and send them to the state lab in Raleigh. He said thanks and that it depended upon when he finished. I tried his cell phone again late Sunday, but he didn't answer. I thought maybe Lynne had gone into labor, so I dropped by his jobsite yesterday." His eyes narrowed. "Tell me, does Luke have an alibi?"

"I don't know," I lied. "You're the first person I've spoken with. As for alibis, it may have been a tragic accident involving only Ken."

"Well, whatever happened, I feel guilty I didn't go with him. I was studying the damn score for tonight's rehearsal. Maybe if I'd been there, he'd be alive now."

"Maybe," I agreed. "But don't beat yourself up. Life is full of maybes." And, I thought, if Ken Stokes had been murdered in that river, maybe Paul Clarkson would now be dead as well.

Chapter Eight

Nakayla waited until I'd briefed her on my conversation with Clarkson before sharing the fruits of her internet research.

"Let's start with Ted Kirkpatrick." She opened her notepad. "He was born in Asheville in 1948. He graduated from NC State with a double major in chemical and mechanical engineering."

"Well suited for his career," I observed.

"Yes. He won a scholarship funded by Pisgah Valley Paper and had a job waiting for him when he finished. After six years at PVP, he saw the coming boom in recycling, took his savings and what funds he could raise from private investors, leased land from PVP, and started Kirkgate Paper. The business prospered, he prospered, and aside from the stigma of toxic waste, he's been a model corporate citizen."

"A citizen whose cleanup was compelled by a lawsuit, not to mention a fellow executive beaten to death with a baseball bat."

Nakayla's lips drew into a tight line, signaling there was more to the story than my flippant remark. "Oscar Weld, the executive vice president of PVP, was the victim. Ted Kirkpatrick was at their offices that day to discuss the industry's pollution problems. When the protestors arrived and the one went ballistic, Ted tried to intervene. He was knocked unconscious for his efforts."

"So, he's not easily intimidated."

"No. He wound up testifying for the prosecution at Mock's trial, even though he'd received death threats from the accused protestor's sympathizers."

"Who's Mock?"

"Leroy Mock. The man with the baseball bat. The man whose twins died of cancer believed to have been caused by dioxins that got into the groundwater and wells near the Pigeon River."

I shuddered. As heinous as the attack was, the rage fueling it had been stoked by grief and loss. How do you get justice when you know the culprit is protected by a phalanx of lawyers?

"Are dioxins definitely in the paper mills' toxic waste?" My knowledge of chemistry equaled my knowledge of Italian fashion designers.

"Yes. The term covers a whole group of related compounds. They most commonly get into the food chain and collect in the body. But drinking the stuff is like drinking poison. I guess the dioxins in the Pigeon River came from the process of bleaching pulp and paper. You've also got acids and other nasty stuff in the sludge flowing across the state line into Tennessee."

"And the River Watchers are self-appointed monitors?"

"They take their responsibilities seriously. Ken was one of their instructors. He taught others, like Boy Scouts or new recruits, how to collect the samples, fill out the paperwork, and get it to the testing lab in Raleigh. River Watchers also raises funds as a legitimate nonprofit to pay for shipping and testing. Since the major cleanup, the relationship between them and the industries along the waterways has been less adversarial."

"But there are still problems?"

Nakayla nodded. "The old landfills pose threats of leaking or leaching. The mills are liable for those past dumping grounds, but with minimal state inspections and reliance on the mills to self-police, you understand how activists like Ken Stokes would turn their passion into a crusade."

"What about Luke Kirkpatrick?"

Nakayla shrugged. "Not much more than what we learned from Hewitt. Divorced, no children. A couple of DUIs, and I suspect there might be others that were expunged when he was younger. He flunked out of Carolina his sophomore year and took some courses at the community college in Charlotte to get an associate's degree."

"Why there and not here at A-B Tech?"

Nakayla laughed. "Charlotte has pro football and basketball. I looked at his Facebook and Twitter posts. He's got season tickets for both teams."

"Anything about his work?"

"His Facebook profile reads, 'works at Kirkgate Paper.' The Kirkgate web page has him listed as Vice President for Public Affairs, but he rarely shows up in any media coverage."

I thought about the job title. If Luke Kirkpatrick were serious about his public affairs responsibilities, the last thing he'd want would be another toxic waste scandal. "Ted and Luke won't like it, but we need to start with the status of Kirkgate's landfills. I'll ask Hewitt to see if they can meet with us tomorrow afternoon."

"Separately," Nakayla said.

"Definitely. Ted might be a stand-up guy, but he's likely to protect his son. Blood's thicker than water."

Nakayla closed her notepad. "Especially if the water's toxic."

My conversation with Paul Clarkson spurred Nakayla to find more information about the River Watchers. The group's website gave their address as being in Asheville's River Arts District, known locally as RAD. RAD was a successful renovation of abandoned factories and warehouses on the flood plain adjacent to the French Broad River.

Nakayla printed out the home page and handed it to me. "Want to run by there this afternoon?"

I studied the sheet. An Eli Patterson was listed as executive director. "Unannounced?" I asked. "As a drop-in?"

"Sure. We live by the river. Drop in."

I groaned, disappointed that Nakayla had gotten the line in before me. "I thought RAD was only for artists and artisans." In our last case, I'd interviewed an artist who worked in mosaics. Every studio I saw was for some kind of craft: painting, pottery, metal sculpture, leather goods, jewelry. All the artistic talents that eluded me.

Nakayla took back the sheet. "But what better tenant for the River Arts District than someone monitoring the river?"

She had a point. And if we dropped in and no one was there, we could innocently ask the neighbors about the group.

Gossip was often the best source of information.

We parked in front of an old brick warehouse. Much of the exterior had been the canvas for a splash of bright colors and intricate designs that popped off the walls. This art was a far cry from gang tags and amateur graffiti.

The door to River Watchers was a painted waterfall cascading from top to bottom. A pair of binoculars with magnified brown eyes stared out from above the transom. That image didn't capture my attention as much as the steel chest with a combination lock sitting to the right of the entrance. Stenciled on its lid was the word "Samples."

Nakayla rang the buzzer. We heard the electronic latch click and she pushed the door open.

"Come in," a man's voice called from somewhere farther in the office.

The front room was dark. Boxes lined one wall. A large map of the area's rivers and streams hung from another. Pins in assorted colors dotted the meandering blue lines signifying some kind of code.

"I'm in the back."

We stepped through a doorless archway into a smaller room lighted only by the glow of a desktop computer monitor with a kayaker and rushing whitewater frozen on the screen.

A gray-haired man swiveled in his chair and peered at us through thick, owlish glasses. His lined face hadn't seen a razor in a couple of days, but I doubted he was intentionally growing a beard. A headset was draped around his neck, and he was clearly in the middle of a video edit.

"Sorry to bother you," Nakayla said. "We're looking for Eli Patterson."

"You're not looking for him, you're looking at him." He pulled off the headset and stood. "What can I do for you folks?"

Nakayla offered her hand. "I'm Nakayla Robertson. This is my partner, Sam Blackman."

Patterson's hands were rough and callused, probably from years of clutching a paddle.

"We're looking into Ken Stokes's death," Nakayla said.

"What a tragedy. Ken was the heart and soul of River Watchers." His voice dropped to a whisper as the words caught in his throat. He turned back to the screen. "That's Ken in his kayak. I'm putting a little tribute video together. We're going to have a gathering at my house Friday night."

"That sounds nice," Nakayla said.

I studied the freeze-frame. The action had been shot from behind and, in the life jacket and helmet, the paddler could have been anyone. If only Ken had worn his helmet Sunday night. The thought brought me back to the purpose of our visit.

"I couldn't help but notice the box labeled Samples outside your door. Is that where volunteers pick up collection materials?"

Patterson shook his head. "That's where they can drop off their specimens. We work the first weekend of every month. Some watchers go out on Saturday, some on Sunday. I come by both evenings and pack the vials for shipment to the Raleigh lab Monday morning."

"So, Ken would have brought his samples here Sunday night?"

Patterson nodded. "Yes, but later than usual. And I have no idea why he went back to the river."

Nakayla and I exchanged glances.

The back of my neck tingled. "What do you mean?"

"I was here Sunday evening till a little after eight thirty. Ken hadn't dropped anything off. Yet yesterday morning, when I came to take the weekend's samples to UPS, I found Ken's report and vials packaged, labeled rush, and sitting on top of the chest. I don't know why he didn't put it inside. It was empty. He knew the combination. Then I learned later Monday that his body had been found in the Pigeon River. He must have forgotten something to go back there."

"Where's that package now?"

Patterson shrugged. "On the way to the lab. I'd already sent it."

"It's not there yet?"

He gave us a rue smile. "We can't afford overnight. Not even second-day delivery. It should arrive by the end of the week."

"And you're sure you were here till after eight thirty?"

"Yes, definitely. I must have just missed Ken."

"Anyone else here with you?"

"No. I locked up." Eli Patterson eyed me suspiciously. "Am I in some kind of trouble?"

Not unless you're lying and were with Ken at the river. "No, Mr. Patterson. It's just that Ken couldn't have brought those water samples here. He was already dead."

Chapter Nine

"Answer me why someone would bring samples to Eli Patterson after Ken Stokes's death?" I posed the question to Nakayla as we drove back to the office.

"I can think of two reasons," she said. "Ken could have been on the river with someone else who left with the samples while Ken stayed behind. That person dropped them at River Watchers later that night."

"And hasn't come forward when news broke of Ken's death?"

"You asked for an answer, you didn't say it had to be a good answer. I assume Sheriff Hudson is going through the list of Ken's potential companions. Maybe he already knows who was with him."

"Maybe," I conceded. "But I would have thought he'd have started with Eli Patterson."

"And if this companion had been a fellow River Watcher, why not put the package of samples in the box, rather than leave it on top? My second, more ominous reason, is someone confronted Ken and took the samples from him. Whether Ken fell in the river during their scuffle or slipped accidentally will be hard to determine."

"That's already conjecture, but it doesn't answer why bother to turn in the samples."

"How do we know they're the samples from the Kirkgate landfill?" she asked. "Someone could have substituted clean soil and water, but labeled it from the Kirkgate site."

I took my eyes off the road long enough to flash an appreciative smile. "Now that's a good answer. Like swapping urine for a drug test."

She shifted in the passenger's seat to better face me. "Seriously, when those samples generate a clean bill of health, we should ask Eli Patterson to repeat an identical test."

"And if that test comes back clean?"

She sighed. "Then we'll just have to come up with reason number three."

As soon as we were in the office, I telephoned Sheriff Hudson's mobile.

"What's up, Sam?"

Either he recognized my number or I'd been honored with my own name in his list of important contacts.

"Any sign of tools or sample containers show up at the river?"

"No. I told you I'd let you know if they do." His tone conveyed my inquiries weren't welcome.

"Then I know where the samples are."

A few seconds of silence. "Well, are you going to tell me or do I have to guess?"

"Eli Patterson shipped them to Raleigh yesterday."

"The River Watchers director? He's next on my interview list."

So, the sheriff wasn't missing an investigative avenue. Nakayla and I were just ahead of him. I related what Patterson had said about the package of samples being left overnight.

"Did Patterson offer any explanation as to why the package wasn't locked up?"

"Nothing other than the person didn't know the combination."

The sheriff sighed. "And we have no way of knowing whether the samples were tampered with."

I jumped to the real reason I'd called him. "What time did Luke and Ted Kirkpatrick get there and what time did they leave?"

"We've already gone over this," Hudson stressed. "You know Ted's alibi is Hewitt Donaldson, of all people. Luke doesn't have one."

"But neither Luke nor Ted have an alibi for after they left the site."

"That wasn't until two in the morning."

"Which gave one or both of them plenty of time to take those samples to River Watchers."

I heard Hudson take a deep breath.

"All right, we'll look into it. I also want to see the paperwork that shipped with the samples."

"Handwriting analysis?"

"That and fingerprints," he said. "I'll get word to the test lab not to open the package without someone there who can dust. I'll enlist the aid of the Wake County Sheriff's Department."

"Then can you put a rush on the testing?"

"That goes without saying."

I figured my information had earned me the right to push the sheriff one more time. "Anything new you care to share with us?"

Hudson cleared his throat and lowered his voice. Evidently, giving information to a private detective wasn't something he wanted overheard in the department.

"Footprints. Impressions in the soft dirt that spread from the dig sites"

"Not Ken's or ours?"

"No. You wear a ten, Ken was an eleven. These are a little smaller. Nines. Maybe nine and a half. No distinctive tread, and the sizes are so common as to be good only for ruling people out. But it shows someone else was at the scene during or after the earth was turned over."

"An innocent man would come forward."

"Yep. And that hasn't happened. I was a young deputy back when the violence flared between the mills and the river people. I know how things can escalate. We're going to get to the bottom of this quickly because I won't have a damned river war on my watch."

"I hear you."

But he didn't hear me. He'd punctuated his dramatic pronouncement by hanging up.

Nakayla had been standing by my desk throughout the call. "If I heard correctly, Hudson's setting the right things in motion."

"Yeah. Between the footprints and the samples, he's moved from *possibly accident* to *probably murder*. I think we do our due diligence and talk to the Kirkpatricks as planned. Then if we don't uncover anything new, we hold back while the sheriff moves forward."

"Should I make a preemptive call to Lynne?"

I thought about what we'd learned. "Let's wait a few days till we have something more conclusive. They've got a funeral to get through."

"The service is Saturday. Lynne's made arrangements for Ken's interment in her family's plot at a Methodist church in Canton. Make sure your good suit is cleaned and pressed."

"Canton. A paper mill town."

"And a river town," Nakayla added. "I hope those two factors didn't get Ken killed."

A knock on our door and Hewitt opened it enough to lean in. "Got a few minutes?"

I rose from my desk. "As long as you're not billing us for the time."

He answered by walking to the sofa. "Make yourselves at home."

Nakayla and I laughed at the audacity of the man hijacking our own office. She took the other end of the sofa. I eased into a chair.

"Should we take notes?"

He grinned. "Do that, Sam, and I will bill you. I just wanted you to know I've got Luke coming in at ten tomorrow and then Ted at two. Since I assume Luke is a person of interest for Sheriff Hudson, I'd prefer you interview him first. If there are contradictions or discrepancies, I'd like those out in the open before you see Ted."

"So he has time to clear them up?"

Hewitt scowled. "No. So Ted can't hear your line of questioning and prep his son. Ted's my friend, Luke's a waste of space. It's simple. If Luke's guilty, I don't want him dragging his father down with him. Unless you have a compelling reason for changing the order."

I looked to Nakayla. She shrugged. Like me, she must not have seen much difference. If Ted and Luke were going to collude, they were going to collude. I guessed Hewitt was thinking ahead to the courtroom and whatever spin he might devise.

"That will be fine," I said. "Although I assume you'll be more than a bystander tomorrow."

"If you mean I'll let Luke's arrogance and self-importance incriminate him, then yes, more than a bystander. But, as you know, there's no attorney-client privilege in that meeting, so whatever he blurts out," Hewitt threw up his hands in surrender, "will be yours to do with as you want."

The defense attorney's mission to protect his old friend triggered a question I'd forgotten to ask. "Have you purposely held back information about Ted?"

Hewitt's eyes narrowed. "You mean that has a bearing on your investigation?"

"Yes. The fact that Ted Kirkpatrick was knocked unconscious by the same man who killed the other executive."

"You just answered it yourself. It has no bearing on the investigation." He gave me a hard stare, challenging me to refute his assertion.

I wasn't ready to give up. "Was that because we might think the attack caused Ted to bear a grudge against activists?"

Hewitt waved a hand dismissing the idea. "While you're researching my client, check the charitable gifts made by his foundation. He's the single largest donor to River Watchers. Why would he do that if he held a grudge?"

I didn't have an answer.

"But I understand. You had to ask." Hewitt relaxed and leaned back into the sofa cushion. "Now, I have a question for you. Why did Sheriff Hudson ask for Ted's and Luke's shoe sizes?"

I answered without looking at Nakayla. "Probably for the reason you think."

Hewitt slapped his palms on his thighs. "Fair enough. And have you talked to William Ormandy yet?"

"No," Nakayla said.

"You might want to check that box. He was Ted's alibi after I left."

"He's on our list," I said. "Do you know where he's staying?"

"The Albemarle Inn. The same room where Béla Bartók stayed. If you'd like to cross paths before your interview with the Kirkpatricks, he's rehearsing tonight at the university's music department."

"Is that his only connection?"

"That and the fact he went to high school with Ken Stokes."

———

The campus of the University of North Carolina at Asheville lies on the north side of the city. One of the smaller universities in the state's system, it takes pride in being the only dedicated liberal arts institution. From what I understood, the academic programs catered to the curious who wanted a wide range of options—from engineering to philosophy with multiple disciplines and electives in between.

Hewitt told us William Ormandy would be in one of the rehearsal rooms in Lipinsky Hall. At a few minutes after seven, a light rain began falling as we looped around the main quad. As on most college campuses, the difficult challenge was finding a place to park. I pulled into Lot P17 that was close to the main quad and the music building. I didn't have a permit, but no evening public program was being offered so spaces were as plentiful as I'd ever seen them. Nakayla and I each grabbed a small umbrella and hoofed it around to the main entrance.

A campus security guard stood just inside the door. Hewitt had told us Ted Kirkpatrick arranged for the extra manpower because Ormandy didn't want his rehearsal to turn into a free concert. The words "High Maintenance" popped into my mind.

The man held up his hand as if we were about to cross against the light. "I'm sorry. The building is closed this evening."

"We are guests of the Luminaries Festival," Nakayla said. "I suggest you check with Mr. Kirkpatrick."

The guard looked at me and then back to Nakayla. It was clear whom he thought more likely to be at home in a fine arts building.

"Names please."

"Nakayla Robertson. This is Sam Blackman."

I gave a winning smile, prepared to be recognized as the brilliant detective I am.

"Are you folks from in town?"

So much for my celebrity status.

"Yes," Nakayla said. "I've been here for concerts before, but I'm not sure which rehearsal studio they're in."

The guard rolled his eyes. "Well, they're not where they started. Mr. Ormandy insisted on playing in the auditorium. Claimed he needed open acoustical space."

"Are there accompanists?"

"Just a guy with some synthesizers. Everything had been set up and then Ormandy said he wouldn't rehearse under those conditions. I was outside the door. You'd think he was about to be waterboarded. Artists."

"Thanks for the warning," Nakayla said. "I know the way from here and we'll tread lightly."

I followed Nakayla to a set of double doors. I went to open the left one, but Nakayla put her hand on my forearm.

"Wait," she whispered. "Listen."

At first, I didn't hear anything and then soft trills of high piano notes became audible.

"That's the second movement of Bartók's Third Piano Concerto," Nakayla said. "The part supposedly based on Asheville birdsongs. This is not a good time to go in."

We stood still for a few minutes as the playing continued.

"How long are these birds going to chirp?" I asked. "It's after dark."

The piano notes were augmented by what I took at first to be strings, but since the guard had said there was only the piano and synthesizers, I knew the Moog had been set up to emulate violins, violas, and cellos. Then the piano took over again, trilling notes up and down the high treble range. I could hear birds, a whole chorus of them. The Moog returned, swelling underneath. Suddenly, the light piano notes became crashing, discordant chords. A man screamed, "No! No!" and every other sound faded away.

I grabbed the door handle. "Well, I'd say the rehearsal is going splendidly."

We stepped inside the auditorium. A grand piano occupied center stage. To the left, Clarkson sat in the middle of a semicircle of three Minimoogs I recognized from my tour of the factory. A small amplifier sat on the floor facing the empty audience seats. Empty except for one man in the front row. Ted Kirkpatrick.

"This is the dumbest thing I've ever been involved with." A man in black jeans, a maroon pullover, and white trainers jumped up from the piano bench. He had to be William Ormandy. His long, brown hair flew in all directions, matching his gesticulating arms. "We've got the damned symphony on stage with us. Why laden the piece with this electronic trash pile? Strings bring warmth. The Moog sounds are so cold and brittle Bartók's birds would fly north for the winter."

Ted Kirkpatrick stood up from his seat. "We're not replacing the strings, we're showing the versatility of Bob Moog's creation. I've already been through this with the conductor, and he's blessed the score. Paul and his Minimoogs will briefly join each orchestral section. They'll blend."

Before Ormandy could respond, Clarkson ran up a musical scale with what sounded like chimes. Then he bowed to the pianist. "Except, of course, for the beloved piano score, in deference to the majestic talent of William Ormandy, the greatest thing to come out of East Tennessee since Dolly Parton and I-40."

Ormandy visibly trembled. He looked like he wanted to throw the piano, or at least its bench, at his accompanist.

Ted Kirkpatrick stepped toward the stage. "You knew what we were doing when you signed the contract. However, I will, as a show of good faith and an acknowledgment of your artistic prerogative, relinquish my request that the Moog be included in your composition."

Ormandy stood motionless, apparently weighing his options. Then he threw up his hands. "All right, let's just get this disaster over with." He shot a scornful glance at Clarkson. "And try and play the right notes this time."

As he turned toward the piano, he noticed Nakayla and me at the back of the room. "Hey! This is a private rehearsal. You'll have to leave."

Ted Kirkpatrick spun around and was clearly surprised to see us. "They're with me."

Ormandy reddened. "But…but…"

"They have nothing to do with music." Kirkpatrick started down the aisle toward us. "Sorry, I can't talk now."

I looked beyond him. "It's Mr. Ormandy we need a word with. We can wait."

Ormandy straightened. "Me? I'm sorry, I'm way too busy for an interview this evening. Some other time."

"They're detectives," Clarkson said with undisguised glee. "So you'd better abandoned that pompous persona and hear what they have to say."

Ormandy looked to Kirkpatrick for an explanation. The older man simply nodded without clarifying that we were private and not police detectives.

"Fine," Ormandy said in a tone declaring the situation was anything but. "Let's just run the second movement again and call it a night."

Nakayla and I sat in the back row, away from Ormandy's eyeline. I have an untrained ear, but to me the pianist sounded like a virtuoso. Clarkson, on the other hand, performed as much for the eye as for the ear. Seated with the three Minimoogs, he often played two keyboards at once. And whenever he had a free hand, he was throwing switches and turning knobs. I knew from our tour of the factory that published sound charts showed the proper settings for tonal variations. They ranged from the hard, brittle, electric feedback fervor of heavy metal bands to the sweeter sound of flutes and strings. As Clarkson mixed and varied the three synthesizers, I understood how he could blend with the orchestral instruments, demonstrating the versatility of both his playing and Bob Moog's invention.

When the piece was over, Ormandy stood and rubbed his hands together like he needed to brush off some contamination. He turned to Clarkson and uttered one word—"Better."

Clarkson shrugged. "We'll both be at the mercy of the sound mixer."

"Which is why he'll be at the dress rehearsal," Kirkpatrick said. "Tomorrow we'll work here with a small ensemble from the symphony. We'll go over some of the other selections as well as William's Blue Ridge Concerto."

"The one I'm now not a part of," Clarkson said.

"Right," Ormandy interjected.

"Then I'm out of here." Clarkson switched off the synthesizers and stepped down from the stage. "You coming, Ted? I assume our detectives want to talk to Willie alone."

Kirkpatrick looked at me. I nodded. The whole point of our conversation was to confirm Kirkpatrick's alibi.

"Yes," he said. "I'll tell the guard to lock up after you leave."

Clarkson and Kirkpatrick walked past us. Clarkson said, "Have fun," and rolled his eyes. Kirkpatrick said, "See you tomorrow afternoon."

Ormandy walked to the front edge of the stage. "Who are you and why do you need to talk with me?"

We walked from the back of the auditorium and didn't answer until we reached the first row.

"My name is Nakayla Robertson. This is Sam Blackman. We're looking into the death of Ken Stokes. I believe you know him and his wife, Lynne."

"Yes. I was in high school with Ken."

I gestured to the seats beside us. "Why don't you come down where we can sit together. This won't take very long."

He sat next to Nakayla with me on her other side. It seemed natural that she should take the lead with the temperamental musician.

"Where was home?" she asked.

"Hartford, Tennessee. Although I went to high school in Cosby. That's where Ken lived. Hartford only had an elementary school. Cosby was the closest community with a high school."

"I thought Ken grew up in Asheville," Nakayla said.

"No. His mother died his senior year. His father moved him to Asheville where there was a greater demand for good carpenters. Ken followed in his footsteps." Ormandy paused and looked at me. "What's this about? Ken and I didn't have much in common. I was in college here my freshman year. Ken was working. We saw each other a few times."

I kept silent. He wasn't going to dismiss Nakayla as irrelevant to our discussion.

"And you didn't keep up with each other after you transferred to the School of the Arts?" Nakayla asked.

"I'd come to Asheville or Brevard for workshops in the summer. We'd grab a beer. I liked Ken but we saw each other a couple of times a year at most."

"And you know Lynne?"

"Yes. Actually they asked me to play at their wedding. That's three or four years ago. I don't think I've seen them since then."

"You know they're expecting their first child."

He nodded. "It's a real tragedy. I'll be at the funeral, of course."

I moved out of my seat and sat on the edge of the stage. "Mr. Ormandy, we understand you were with Ted Kirkpatrick Sunday night."

"Yes. At Rhubarb. And I was running late."

"That's what Ted said. Did you stop off somewhere beforehand?"

Ormandy scowled. "That's really none of your business. But, no, I just got a late start from Cincinnati. And traffic was heavy. People returning from the weekend."

"And Ted waited for you?"

"Yes. Some friend was with him. Guy looked like he stepped out of the 1960s. He left as soon as I arrived."

"And what time was that?"

"I guess around eight fifteen. I apologized, and then we ordered dinner and talked about the concert."

"Had you tried to reach Ted before then?"

"Yes. When I realized I was going to be almost an hour late, I phoned. He was very understanding."

Very understanding. I wanted to say, "And yet you were acting like a horse's ass during the rehearsal."

Instead, I looked to Nakayla to pick up the questioning.

"Did you know much about Ken's work with River Watchers?"

"Some. But he got into that after high school."

Nakayla stared at him, waiting for the silence to pressure him into saying more.

"But I wasn't surprised. We'd both grown up with the stories."

"Stories?"

Ormandy shifted his gaze back and forth between us. "The pollution. The dioxins. The cancers and other illnesses created by the toxins dumped into the Pigeon River. I suspect that's what killed his mother. It got in our water, in the fish we caught, in the tissue of the livestock we ate." He grew more animated. "Hartford was in the dead zone. You know what people called our town?"

"What?" I asked.

"Widowville. That's also the name of the second movement of my Blue Ridge Concerto. You'll hear traditional Appalachian melodies descend into discord and chaos." He gave a humorless laugh. "Maybe I should reconsider using the Minimoog. Have Clarkson dial in the harshest, most brittle sound he can generate."

His eyes focused beyond us. I knew he was serious.

"That could be quite effective," I ventured. "I doubt there are many composers bold enough to write for the Minimoog with such passion and authority."

Nakayla covered her mouth with her hand to hide an involuntary smile at my blatant sycophancy. But Ormandy turned into a six-year-old who'd just been handed cotton candy.

"Yes," he said. "You get it. I'll have to talk to Ted." Then his forehead creased in a frown. "It was my idea, but I appreciate the encouragement."

"Hey, we're just happy to be here when your inspiration struck. It must be similar to Bartók and his birds."

He jumped up and started pacing between the stage and seats. "Exactly. A great parallel for the concert's program notes."

"There's another thing you could add to those notes," Nakayla said. "Ken was upset that Wilma Dykeman wasn't originally celebrated by the festival. A paragraph about her might be a nice tribute to Ken."

Ormandy's eyes widened. "Yes, but better than that, why not dedicate the whole second movement to Ken? Treat it as part of the score so his name will be linked to it forever."

Nakayla stood and offered her hand. "Mr. Ormandy, I think that would be wonderful."

I too piled on the praise. After establishing that we might need to talk with him again, we left the pianist beaming and promising us reserved front row seats at the concert.

As soon as we were outside the auditorium doors, Nakayla said, "You laid it on so thick I thought I was going to gag."

"But you have to admit I had him eating out of my hand. Flattery will get you everywhere."

"I know, World's Greatest Detective. I've used it often enough on you."

"It's not flattery when it's true."

We found the guard at the front door. Outside, the rain fell harder than when we'd arrived.

"It won't be letting up for a while," he informed us. Then he looked at my empty hands. "Didn't you have an umbrella, sir?"

Nakayla waved hers in the air. "It looks like this. Remember?"

I ignored her jab and addressed the guard. "I left it on the floor of the back row. Be right back. Watch her for me."

The guard laughed. "She's the one with the umbrella, sir."

I heard the sound of their high five as I returned to the auditorium.

"You're a damned thief. A despicable fraud. You know this is my work." The voice penetrated the closed doors. A man's voice. An angry voice.

"You're jealous. How can I plagiarize folk melodies that have been in the public domain for years? How many composers were influenced by the musical traditions of the common people? Liszt, Copland, just to name two. And that's the point of my Blue Ridge Concerto, to weave in Appalachian melodies in a new way."

The second voice clearly belonged to William Ormandy. I cracked the door enough to see Ormandy at the foot of the stage facing another man. His silver hair pegged him as at least in his early fifties.

He held a sheaf of papers in his right hand and waved them in Ormandy's face. "Don't lecture me! I'm not talking about the damned melodies; I'm talking about the transitions and modulations. Straight out of the piece I've been working on for years. The unifying theme is practically stolen note for note."

Ormandy put his hands on his hips in a pose more petulant than powerful. "Really, Professor Slocum? For years? Since I was in your freshman composition class? How many times has this masterpiece of yours been performed? Tell me where can I buy the score? Meanwhile, I've actually accomplished something. And you're the one holding stolen property. Where did you get that copy of my score?"

"From someone who obviously knows you're a fraud. We'll see what Ted Kirkpatrick thinks when he has to appear in court and learns he's funded a charlatan."

"And we'll see what the university thinks when one of their largest donors is harassed by a frivolous lawsuit brought by one of their professors. Inscribe that tune on your musical staff and play it."

The two men glared at each other, unaware of anything else around them. I glanced down and saw my umbrella lying beside the end seat of the last row. I didn't want to be confronted by either Ormandy or Slocum, so I darted inside, grabbed my umbrella, and exited before the door could swing shut.

Chapter Ten

"Do you think we should tell Ted Kirkpatrick what you saw?" Nakayla raised her voice to be heard over the noise of the rain and wipers.

I kept my eyes on the taillights in front of me as we headed home. "Tell him what? That I saw a professor and former student arguing? Even if the charge of plagiarism is true, how does that involve Ted or the festival?"

"Well, for one thing, Ted has the deepest pockets."

I had to admit she made a good point. If a lawyer's working for Professor Slocum on contingency, where would he focus his efforts for the biggest payday? I thought of the famous line attributed to the criminal Willie Sutton. When asked by a reporter why he robbed banks, Willie answered, "Because that's where the money is." Yogi Berra couldn't have said it any better.

"What if we tell Hewitt?" I suggested. "He'll have a clearer understanding of the legal ramifications."

"And you don't see any way it affects our investigation?"

"I don't understand. How could it?"

"Ormandy knew Ken. Ormandy was late getting to a business dinner at the same time Ken was probably killed. Ken and Ormandy go back to childhood together. Ormandy played at

Ken's wedding but acts as if they hardly kept in touch. Maybe that's the case, maybe not."

I saw where she was heading. "And since we're working for Lynne and Walt, we should verify what Ormandy told us before bringing it up elsewhere."

"That's my take."

"But you're the one who wanted to tell Ted?"

"No. I asked if *you* thought we should tell him. I didn't think so."

"And if I'd said we should?"

She laughed. "Then I'd know for sure that we shouldn't."

———

The rain ceased sometime during the night but soaked the ground so thoroughly that after Blue's morning walk, I had to dry his paws with an old towel.

Nakayla had showered and left to meet the cabinetmaker Sonny Jenkins. I made a pot of coffee and a bowl of granola and sat at the kitchen counter with a pencil and legal pad as my breakfast companions.

I compiled a list of questions for Luke Kirkpatrick and then started a second list for his father. Some questions were the same, but I didn't overthink Ted's. I figured Luke's answers would generate additional questions for Ted.

At nine thirty, Blue and I headed for the office only ten minutes away. Nakayla texted me that she was already there and we'd wait to be summoned to Hewitt's conference room.

Blue flopped down on his cushion, and I walked into Nakayla's office.

"How'd things go with Sonny Jenkins?"

She swiveled away from her computer. "Fine. I gave him the job. His cost wasn't that much more than the original order."

"And can he fit you in?"

"He took measurements. We'll use the cabinet hardware already ordered. Walt Stokes showed up. He had Ken's key and was assessing the status of the construction. He and Sonny mapped out a timeline. Meanwhile the flooring will go in."

"Did Walt give you a completion date?"

"Six weeks. June first at the latest."

"Good," I forced myself to say.

Further discussion was curtailed by a soft knock as the door opened. A wisp of a woman entered. Her curly black hair looked like it had been styled by the hand dryer in a public restroom. Where most women applied a little color to their faces, a layer of what could have been chalk dust covered her cheeks. The gaunt, skeletal effect was enhanced by dark-blue eye shadow and long black lashes. Her slim body was clothed in a black dress that could have been a monk's robe minus the cowl.

Despite the dour appearance, she flashed a smile filled with white teeth.

"Hi, Shirley," Nakayla said. "Is it time?"

Hewitt Donaldson's office manager shook her head. "His royal lowness wants you to hold up ten minutes. He needs some AA time with his client."

Nakayla and I looked at each other, wondering what she meant.

I took a guess. "Alcoholics Anonymous?"

"Attitude Adjustment. Luke Kirkpatrick's arrogance level needed realignment."

Luke must have shown up protesting the need to talk with us.

"That's one good thing about Hewitt," I said. "He doesn't suffer fools, even his own clients."

"Except for himself," Shirley added. "And that's my job, to keep him humble."

Shirley didn't exaggerate. She told Hewitt straight to his face when he was wrong. He tolerated her insubordination because she was the smartest person in the three-person firm. The second-smartest person was his paralegal, Cory DeMille. And to Hewitt's credit, he had no hesitancy in hiring and keeping strong-minded women.

Shirley glanced at her large Mickey Mouse wristwatch. "It's ten now. I didn't call because I didn't want to risk Luke over-hearing my instructions." She backed out the door. "See you in ten."

"Sounds like we're about to face a hostile witness," Nakayla said.

"Maybe, but Hewitt won't put up with any foolishness. He'll report that back to Ted in a heartbeat."

"You want to take the lead?"

I held up my legal pad. "I made a list of questions. You're welcome to use them or chart your own course."

She reached for the pad. "Do you mind?"

I watched as she read the top sheet. My questions weren't numbered, but I guessed there were around ten. She flipped the page to the next where I'd prepared a few questions for Ted.

She nodded her approval. "You take the lead, but I do have a suggestion."

"What?"

"We still have a few minutes. I'd like to print Luke's questions on our letterhead and put that sheet in a leather portfolio. It will give Luke the impression that this is more than a conversation instituted by his daddy. It could reinforce whatever AA Hewitt managed."

"Not a bad approach," I agreed. "Do you mind taking notes?"

"Using the Tascam might be better. Then I can concentrate on listening and being ready with follow-up questions."

The Tascam was a small audio recorder that could be placed in the center of Hewitt's conference table.

At ten after ten, we locked the office, leaving Blue asleep beside a bowl of fresh water. I'd liberated a spare tie from my desk drawer, and with the portfolio under my arm and Nakayla carrying the Tascam, we made the short walk down the hall to Hewitt's suite.

Shirley sat at her desk and peered around a computer monitor. At the sight of my tie, she clutched her throat like she was being strangled.

"What?" I whispered. "Surprised to see a real professional come calling?"

"Surprised to see you in a tie without food stains on it." She rose from her chair. "Let me escort you to the conference room like you're important."

I gave a half bow. "Don't put yourself out."

"The person I'd like to put out is the client."

She knocked on the conference room door, opened it and announced, "Nakayla Robertson and Sam Blackman are here."

Hewitt's conference room was unlike any other lawyer's. Instead of walls of leather-bound legal tomes meant to impress, Hewitt surrounded himself with classic covers of vinyl albums from the 1960s. Beatles, Stones, Dylan, Iron Butterfly, the Incredible String Band, and the Grateful Dead to name just a few. Track lighting illuminated each cover as if it was an exhibit in an art gallery.

The round conference table meant no one sat at the head, and Hewitt had never shown a preference for any particular seat. As we entered, he stood up from the chair farthest from the door.

Luke Kirkpatrick sat diametrically opposite with his back to us, forcing him to swivel around to see us. He wore a light-blue collared shirt that looked like a dress shirt except it was designed to be untucked. Khaki slacks, no socks, and tassel loafers created the epitome of prep, if that was still a style.

Hewitt, on the other hand, had ditched his customary Hawaiian shirt for a subdued tan one that could have come off the rack at a safari outfitters. He'd pulled his long gray hair into a ponytail. His profile could have been swapped onto the Jefferson nickel without anyone noticing.

Luke made no effort either to get up or fake a smile.

"Please join us." Hewitt pointed to two chairs that placed Nakayla and me on either side of Luke so that he'd have to bounce his gaze back and forth.

We sat, and Nakayla lifted the recorder. "Do either of you mind?"

"What's the purpose?" Hewitt asked.

"To insure neither Sam nor I misremember any aspect of the interview. I believe that's in everyone's best interest."

Hewitt looked at his client. "I have none if you don't."

Luke shrugged. "The sooner we get on with this charade the sooner I'm out of here."

So much for the attitude adjustment.

"We'll be quick." I flipped open the portfolio so that Luke saw a page filled with text. "Quick, but thorough."

From the corner of my eye, I saw Hewitt suppress a smile. I nodded to Nakayla. She activated the recorder and laid it on the table with the dual built-in microphones pointed at Luke.

She folded her hands in front of her. "It's ten fifteen on Wednesday, April 8th. The location is the conference room of defense attorney Hewitt Donaldson."

She emphasized the word *defense*. A nice touch.

"Present are Hewitt Donaldson, Sam Blackman, Luke Kirkpatrick, and Nakayla Robertson. The topic is the murder of Ken Stokes."

"Wait a minute," Luke objected. "Is this a conversation or an interrogation?"

"Questions and answers," Nakayla said. "Nothing more."

"I've already gone over everything with the police. Is this some perjury trap? Do I need a lawyer?"

Hewitt leaned forward. "Remember me? I'm a lawyer. Now if you feel like you need your own counselor instead of sharing one with your father, then, by all means, we'll end this. Oh, and there's no perjury trap when you haven't said anything under oath."

Luke's cheeks blazed crimson as he realized how foolish he sounded. "I just wanted clarity."

"Of course," Hewitt said, helping his client to save some of his red face. "Don't hesitate to speak up if something isn't clear."

Luke turned his hands palm up on the table. "Okay. What do you want to know?"

I made a point to study my questions for a moment. "How did you know Ken Stokes?"

"I really didn't. I'd seen his name listed on reports he generated through river monitoring."

"Did you know him well enough to speak to him?"

"Not so as we ever had a conversation. That's what I told the police."

"Did you tell the police you called him by name at last Saturday's ball game?"

Luke glanced at Hewitt.

"Sam was present at the argument between you and Ken," Hewitt explained.

"Then he knows Ken started it." Luke turned to me. "Unprovoked, I might add. He started yelling at me."

I nodded. "You're right. But you also called him by name. He wasn't a stranger."

Luke bristled. "I never said he was a stranger. Look, I'm in public affairs for our company. Ken would show up at hearings and community meetings from time to time."

"Had he shown up at recent hearings as Kirkgate Paper proposed to increase size and capacity?"

"Yes, but he only asked some technical questions about water treatment. His behavior on Saturday came completely out of the blue."

"So, as far as you know, it was all about omitting Wilma Dykeman from the festival?"

"Yes. And now my father's rectifying that."

I returned to my notes, and then looked up to catch an encouraging nod from Nakayla.

I tapped my page of printed questions like it was holy scripture. "Five years ago, there was an incident that was more than technical questions. You had an actual spill."

Luke's Adam's apple bobbed as he swallowed. I suspected his throat was getting dry.

"A minor incident. Ironically, it happened as we were constructing a circulatory system to treat wastewater without it ever flowing back into the Pigeon River. A valve broke before the new system went online."

"This new waste treatment system, is that to be extended along with the new manufacturing facilities?"

"We can't expand without it."

"Your system is like Lang Paper in Brevard?"

Luke's eyes widened. "You're familiar with them?"

"Yes. I toured their plant. I believe their toxic waste is down to zero." I didn't tell him my introduction to the world of recycled paper had been in the course of another murder investigation, one that didn't have a happy ending for the company executives.

"Then you appreciate the technology," Luke said. "It's the same as they use but on a grander scale. And pollutants in the Pigeon River have been lowered by ninety-nine percent."

"From the paper-making process?"

"Yes."

I decided to hold off on the natural follow-up and said, "Back to the spill five years ago. What was Ken's reaction?"

Luke expelled a puff of air as if blowing away a pesky gnat. "You mean overreaction. We notified EPA and state officials, but the next day Ken had picketers at our front gate, demanding the mill be shut down until the system was installed."

"How was it resolved?"

"Sheriff Hudson ran them off. Our land extended a good fifty yards beyond our perimeter fence. The land for our expansion. Ken and his minions were clearly trespassing." Luke smiled. "And then it rained. Nothing soaks a picketer and his cardboard sign better than a mountain thunderstorm."

I ignored his sarcasm. "No violence? They moved peacefully?"

"They did," he conceded.

"How old were you when your father was attacked?"

"What's that have to do with anything?"

"It happens to do with the relationship between your family's company and the environmentalists."

"That attack was on Pisgah Valley Paper. My father just happened to be there."

"And you were how old?"

"Six."

"So, you don't remember much about it?"

Luke paused, as if time-traveling back thirty years to the event. "I remember my mother crying while we were in a hospital waiting room. I remember seeing my father bandaged like an Egyptian mummy. Blood had oozed through several spots on the white wrappings."

I could envision the scene and the trauma such a sight might have engendered in a six-year-old kid. "Did you notice any difference in your father's attitude afterwards?"

"What do you mean?"

"Did he speak more critically of the protestors? Did he put up more resistance to their demands?"

Luke threw up his hands. "I was a kid, for Christ's sake."

I stared at him, letting silence fill the room. Neither Hewitt nor Nakayla broke it.

Luke sighed. "My father and I have talked since then. He did what he had to do, testifying against Leroy Mock. The man was a killer. But the fight against the lawsuit went out of him. I heard my mother tell him, 'their children are dying.' When you're six, you remember your mother crying over dying children."

"He settled separately?"

"Yes. A manageable financial penalty, since back then we were only a small part of the waste discharge. Our commitment was to clean up our process. And we've done that."

I glanced at my notes. "How did you learn of Ken's death?"

"My father called me. I was at home."

"And what time was this?"

"About eleven. Sheriff Hudson had just informed him that Ken Stokes had been found in the river. He also wanted us to open the gate to the access road."

"The one to the landfill," I clarified.

"Yes."

"And you went straight there?"

"I went to pick up my father first."

"Because he was along the route?"

"Because he was upset, and I didn't want him driving at night."

"That makes sense," I said. "Or maybe your stepmother could have driven him."

"Madison? The very idea of a dead body would have been too much for her to handle. Besides, she plays in a Sunday night bridge club. She was still out."

Which gives her an alibi.

"And when did you and your father leave the site?"

"Two. Maybe two thirty. Sheriff Hudson made us stand away from the scene. We could have left earlier, but my father wanted to be available."

"And afterwards, did you take your father straight home and then return to your house?"

"No. I stayed with my father. He was very upset. Neither of us felt like sleeping."

"Was your stepmother up as well?"

"She'd come in and gone to bed. My father checked on her. We decided not to wake her. We told her in the morning."

Nakayla and I would confirm this timetable when we interviewed Ted. I was ready to shift the line of questioning. "How do you know Paul Clarkson?"

"Clarkson? Why?"

"He's part of the River Watchers. He evidently knew Ken Stokes was collecting samples Sunday night."

"He plays the theremin and Minimoog. My father found him through the Moog Foundation. He's helping us plan the Luminaries Festival, and he put us in contact with William Ormandy. So, I've only gotten to know him over the past six months."

"And no friction because he's a River Watcher?"

Luke shot an exasperated look to Hewitt, but the attorney said nothing.

"I'm fine with the River Watchers," Luke stated. "Our company gives them donations. I'm fine that Ken Stokes was a member. I wasn't fine that he dragged up ancient history at the ball game and tried to embarrass me. Yes, I lost my temper, but I didn't kill him."

I nodded to Nakayla, hoping she was ready to follow up because Luke was obviously tired of hearing my voice.

She smiled warmly and said softly, "Your advanced papermaking process keeps dioxins and other harmful chemicals out of the Pigeon River?"

Luke relaxed. "Correct. It's state of the art and we have no negative impact on the environment."

"Very commendable," Nakayla said. "You know samples were sent for testing Monday morning that we believe Ken took Sunday night."

Luke seemed genuinely puzzled. "You mean Ken shipped samples and then came back to the river?"

"We don't know exactly what happened. But we expect the lab in Raleigh to run an analysis as soon as the package arrives. We'll definitely know by the end of the week."

"I don't understand. If he'd already prepped the samples for shipment, why would he return to the collection site?"

"Why, indeed?" Nakayla posed. "The probable answer is he didn't ever leave the site. The package was left at River Watchers by someone else after the time of Ken's death."

"But how does that involve me?" Luke asked the question not of Nakayla or me but of his lawyer.

"Right now, it doesn't," Hewitt said. "And I don't think Sam and Nakayla will go so far as to make any accusations to the contrary. But it leads to some theories that not only they might be postulating but also Sheriff Hudson." Hewitt looked first at Nakayla and then at me. "Mind if I add a comment or two?"

I waved my hand toward him.

Hewitt stood, a sure sign he was seeking to impress his views upon his client. "Nakayla was asking about the new eco-friendly process because it's not nor will be relevant. She wanted to get it out of the way. What's relevant is that Ken Stokes or someone else was taking soil samples from the old landfill. That's the relevant contamination source, not your current manufacturing."

"But those landfills are clean," Luke protested.

Hewitt started walking slowly around the table. "When's the last time they were checked?"

Luke shrugged. "I don't know. That's not my area of responsibility."

"Well, I've done some research, as I'm sure our detectives have, and learned the state is woefully behind in its monitoring. River Watchers test water purity but the leaking or rupturing of a sealed landfill would mostly likely show up first in the soil. Maybe Ken found a little spike in his last water tests. Maybe he thought he was zeroing in on the source. That's what drew him to your property."

"And maybe he wasn't there alone," Luke said. "The other person left first with the samples, and then Ken fell into the river accidentally."

"That would be the simplest and least adverse circumstance for Kirkgate Paper," Hewitt said. "However, no one has come forward. Ironically, if the samples get a clean report, then the greater the suspicion that someone swapped out the originals."

"So, we're screwed either way?"

"Not if Sheriff Hudson or Sam and Nakayla get to the bottom of it. That's why your father wanted two respected detectives to interview you. That's why I agreed to facilitate this meeting. You get the picture now? If you're innocent, then the truth is your friend. Anything you do or say that looks like obfuscation just raises suspicions."

"In the mind of the public?"

Hewitt completed his circular pacing around the table and gripped the back of his chair with both hands. "No, Luke. In the mind of the jury."

Chapter Eleven

"Regardless of the lab report, the tests will need to be run again." Nakayla made the pronouncement before biting into her Avogoddess sandwich, her favorite combination of avocado, mozzarella, and greens on multigrain bread.

After our interview with Luke, we'd respectfully declined Hewitt's offer of lunch and I'd walked half a block to City Bakery for food we could eat in the office. I countered Nakayla's vegan special with a pastrami Reuben, the sandwich I could eat three times a day.

I swallowed my first bite and checked to make sure Thousand Island dressing wasn't dribbling down my shirt. So far, so good. "Then I wonder if Sheriff Hudson has requested new tests. No use waiting."

"Think you should call him?" Nakayla asked.

"Not yet. Let's wait till after we talk with Ted Kirkpatrick."

Nakayla took another bite of her sandwich, a signal she didn't disagree.

"What stood out with Luke?"

She held up a finger and continued to chew. Unlike me, she wouldn't talk with a mouthful of food. She took a swallow of iced tea before answering.

"His reaction when you told him the samples had been sent to Raleigh. I think he was genuinely surprised."

"If so, that makes it unlikely either he or his father took those samples to Eli Patterson."

Nakayla set her sandwich on the coffee table. "You know, we only have Eli Patterson's word that he found that sample shipment Monday morning."

"Meaning what?"

"Meaning maybe he was collecting with Ken."

"Then why wouldn't he say so?"

Nakayla steepled her fingers beneath her chin. "Why, indeed?"

I pondered the question as we ate our sandwiches in silence.

Ted Kirkpatrick must not have needed an attitude adjustment. Shirley phoned at exactly two and said Hewitt and Ted were ready. We went to the conference room unescorted and found Ted and Hewitt sitting beside each other at the far end of the table. Both men rose to greet us.

As we shook hands, Ted kept his face all business. The meeting would be cordial, but it was clear he saw no levity in the situation.

After Nakayla received permission to start the Tascam recorder, she looked to me to begin.

Before I could open my mouth, Ted said, "I understand you gave Luke a thorough interrogation."

"Interview," I interjected. "We weren't treating him as a suspect."

"Interview," Ted repeated. "And that's not a criticism. No matter how old he gets, he's still my child and I'm his parent. Some things never change and that includes children not listening to their parents. But between the sheriff and the questions you put to him, I think he's viewing the potential consequences of Ken Stokes's death with a more enlightened eye. That the sometimes cavalier manner with which he treats situations has no place in this investigation. So, for that I thank you.

"Now let me assure you Luke and I haven't concocted any story. Nor do I have any reason to believe that Luke has told me or you anything less than the truth. I recognize that should discrepancies arise between our answers, you will not hesitate to dig further or confer with Sheriff Hudson." He looked at Hewitt. "And I understand there is no attorney-client privilege about this meeting." He leaned back in his chair. "So let's get started."

I hadn't bothered with the leather portfolio or typed questions on letterhead, just a legal pad with a few questions scrawled in my barely legible handwriting.

"Very well. The night Ken died you were scheduled to meet the pianist, William Ormandy."

"That's right. We'd agreed to meet downstairs at Rhubarb. I'd gotten there early and saw Hewitt leaving the building and invited him for a drink. A few minutes later, Ormandy called to say he was running late."

I glanced at Hewitt for confirmation.

"That's right," Hewitt said. "I heard Ted's side of the conversation. He told Ormandy to drive safely and let him know if he'd be later than eight thirty."

"Why?" I asked.

"Because the restaurant closes at nine thirty," Ted said. "I didn't want to be rushed. We would have gone somewhere else."

"What time was he supposed to meet you?"

"Seven thirty."

"And he waited till six thirty to let you know he'd be late. Did he call again?"

"Yes. At eight fifteen to say he was parking. Hewitt waited, exchanged a few words with Ormandy and left. We moved from the bar to a table. By then, diners were thinning out."

"How did you choose Ormandy to be part of the festival?"

"Madison had heard him in concert. And I thought his local roots would be a neat connection for the festival."

"That he was from East Tennessee," I said.

"And attended UNC-Asheville. I was also impressed that he was a composer and so I commissioned the piece he's calling the Blue Ridge Concerto."

I was tempted to say, "Yes, the one you'll be sued over," but I held my tongue. Instead, I said, "Just in my brief exposure to him last night, he seems rather temperamental."

For the first time, Ted Kirkpatrick laughed. "You mean he can be an ass. Or the more appropriate musical term, a prima donna."

"In a word, yes."

Ted waved his hand dismissively. "This is a big deal for him. He knows it. I'm playing to his ego—putting him up at the Albemarle Inn in Bartók's room, allowing for leisurely rehearsal time, arranging interviews on local radio and TV, and, most importantly, writing a check for the second half of a big payday. I believe that will be sufficient to keep him in line."

"You say you heard about him through Madison. Luke told us he got Ormandy's name from Paul Clarkson."

Ted shrugged. "We had multiple avenues at work when we were conceiving the festival. This was eight months ago. Luke had found Clarkson, so maybe he got Ormandy's name there. But I heard of him from Madison. She's the one who drags me to the symphony."

"You're not fond of the symphony?"

"It's fine. Though it would be more interesting if it involved a ball and a net."

I flipped the top sheet of my legal pad to the questions I'd prepared for Ted. "What time did you leave Rhubarb?"

"Nine thirty, as they were closing. We'd had coffee, which I needed after three drinks with Hewitt. I got home a little after ten. I was awake but in bed when Sheriff Hudson phoned with the bad news."

"And you called Luke?"

"Immediately. I offered to pick him up, but he insisted on driving. Said he was dressed and could leave right then."

"What happened when you got to the landfill?"

"Sheriff Hudson met us at the gate. It was still locked, so he knew no one had come in or out by the access road."

"No one without a key," I corrected.

"Right. Then he separated us. Luke went with one of the deputies. We were asked where we'd been that evening, did we know Ken Stokes, did we know why he would have been on the property. We had no clue and weren't any help."

"You know we believe the samples Ken took are en route to Raleigh."

"Luke told me you said that."

"When was the last time you or the state took soil and water samples?"

Ted leaned forward, elbows on the table. "Look. I'm confident there is no pollution coming from either the plant or any of our landfills. Still, we run tests once a quarter, on the river by the plant and at our landfills."

"How many landfills do you have?"

"Three. The one where Ken died is the oldest, and it's the one closest to the river. But I'm confident if I took those samples today, we'd pass with flying colors."

"And the state?" I pressed.

"I send them our results. To be honest, I don't know how often they conduct their own monitoring. That's why I'm not opposed to the River Watchers. Hell, we make sizable donations to them. Clean water is in everyone's interest. And if old landfills—most of them are Pisgah Valley Paper sites—start leaking or leaching, then we're all in trouble. The public doesn't distinguish between one company or another."

I nodded. "Which, unfortunately, you learned firsthand."

Ted's jaw tensed. "You're talking about the attack with the baseball bat."

"Yes."

"Leroy Mock was a distraught, dangerous man. I couldn't condone or excuse what he did. But he'd gone through hell, and I hope to God we never see that situation occur again. That's why I take those readings, whether the state does or not; that's why I support River Watchers; that's why I readily admit it was a mistake not to celebrate Wilma Dykeman in the festival; and that's why I want to find out who killed Ken Stokes, even if it was someone in my own company."

"You have suspects?"

"No. If I did, I would tell you. You have my word."

His voice rang with undisguised passion, an authenticity Hewitt would love in a witness. I looked to Nakayla to pick up the questioning.

"Five years ago, I understand there was a problem and Ken Stokes led a group of protesters picketing your plant."

"Yes. We had an accidental spill. It occurred while we were converting our water treatment system. Frankly, Ken and his fellow activists jumped the gun. By the time they showed up, the spill had been contained and the new system was functioning that prevented such incidents from ever happening again."

"You'd called the sheriff?"

"I called the sheriff because they were trespassing, blocking a key gate into the plant."

"That was Sheriff Hudson?"

"Yes."

"How did the protesters respond?"

"They mouthed some objections. Accused Hudson of being in my pocket. But they retreated to the shoulder of the road about a hundred yards away. In another hour or two, they'd all left."

"And Ken backed off?"

"I never saw him on our property again, which is why Sunday night is so strange. I thought we'd established a tolerance for one another. I'd offered to have him tour our new upgrades, but he declined. I guess he didn't want to appear too cozy with a company he considered an adversary. I didn't feel that way."

"And Hudson?" Nakayla asked. "Were you cozy with him?"

Ted scowled. "You mean am I paying him off?"

"No. Just that if push came to shove, would he take your side?"

"No. But that's why I tried to hire you because Hewitt said you'd tell it like you found it. Hudson and I might appear to be too close, even though I assure you we're not." He took a deep breath and moistened his lips. "May I ask you a question?"

"Yes," I said. "Anything at all."

His eyes narrowed. "What do you think happened?"

"I think my partner summed it up very well, Ted. Push came to shove."

Chapter Twelve

I decided to risk the wrath of Sheriff Hudson and phoned him as soon as Nakayla and I returned to the office.

Instead of hello, I got a cranky "What is it now?" spoken like a beleaguered doctor cornered by a hypochondriac.

"Don't feel like you have to curb your enthusiasm on my account."

Hudson snorted. "I answered your call, didn't I? You're getting all the enthusiasm I can muster."

"Then I'll be brief. Nakayla and I just had a conversation with Ted Kirkpatrick. He assures us there's no toxic discharge from either the paper mill or the landfills. He admits the state is very lax in their oversight so he's been monitoring on his own and supporting River Watchers."

"That's consistent with what he told me. So, what's the problem?"

"Not so much a problem as a looming need to retest. I wondered if you had ordered that?"

Hudson paused a moment, probably trying to decipher the reason for my question. "I plan on doing that after we get the report from Raleigh."

"But if it comes back clean, what assurances do you have that those were even samples from the Kirkgate site? And if they're dirty, the state will step in. But by the time the wheels of bureaucracy turn, we might be too far removed from the initial spill for an accurate reading."

A longer pause this time. "You may have a point. I'll request Eli Patterson collect new samples no later than tomorrow afternoon."

"Under your supervision," I insisted. "Sealed and shipped overnight."

He grunted his approval. "Chain of custody?"

"That and the fact we have only Patterson's word that he found the package on the collection chest."

"You're starting to piss me off, Blackman."

I didn't rise to the bait but kept quiet.

"Too many good suggestions." The ice in his voice melted. "If you call again, bring me a motive." He hung up.

Nakayla hopped off the corner of my desk where she'd perched during the call. "Nicely done. Sounds like you and the sheriff are still on speaking terms."

"He's coming to appreciate my superior sleuthing skills."

"He's that desperate?"

"That's another way of putting it."

"Are we ready to talk to Lynne now?"

I mulled over the question. Lynne Stokes was our client, and I had no doubt she was prejudiced against the Kirkpatricks and their mill. How objective would her comments be? On the other hand, who better to speak for her husband?

"Why don't you call her," I said. "You'll probably get voicemail anyway. Let her know that Sheriff Hudson is mounting a thorough investigation."

"And if she wants to meet?"

"Unless she has information for us, I'd rather wait till after her husband's funeral Saturday. Say, no earlier than Sunday afternoon. We should have the lab report by then, plus maybe fingerprints or DNA from the person that prepared the package."

Nakayla headed for her office. "What will you do in the meantime?"

"What I do best. I'll—"

"Take Blue and a poop bag outside," she interjected.

"Exactly."

Hearing his name, Blue rose from his cushion, shook himself from the tip of his nose to the tip of his tail, and ambled over to where we kept his leash.

"And I'll be thinking deep thoughts about the case," I said, closing the door behind me.

"Don't hurt yourself," came the muffled reply.

God, I loved that woman, even though she always managed to get the last word.

We walked around the perimeter of Pack Square. Blue sniffed, peed, and did his more serious business. I ran through what we knew and what we didn't know. What we didn't know was who killed Ken Stokes, or if anyone had killed him at all. The simplest solution was that Ken Stokes and Luke Kirkpatrick crossed paths Sunday evening at the riverside landfill. Their Saturday argument picked up where it left off. Either by accident or a shove from Luke, Ken tumbled backwards from the bank and broke his neck on a river rock. Luke panicked, took the samples Ken had been collecting, substituted untainted replacements and left them at the River Watchers office. He wouldn't have known the combination to the storage chest, so he left the package sitting on top.

Luke had the motive: avoid any bad publicity regarding potential pollution from the mill while Kirkgate Paper was acquiring the permits for expansion. And Luke was the one without an alibi.

But, this theory ran into problems. How did Luke and Ken wind up at the site together? That was a huge coincidence. Had Ken called Luke asking permission to take the soil samples? Had someone seen Ken by the river and phoned Luke? And rather than leave with the samples, why didn't Luke concoct a story that Ken had slipped and fallen? Why send samples at all? Simply destroy them. That he didn't, supported the conclusion that Luke was afraid of what the samples might reveal. Better to have clean tests on the record. But Luke had seemed genuinely surprised when we told him samples had been sent.

It was clear to me that the case was at a standstill until Sheriff Hudson's law enforcement colleagues in Raleigh made a thorough forensic examination of the package and the lab conducted its tests. Till then we could only wait.

My cell rang. The screen flashed Nakayla.

"Everything okay with Lynne?" I asked.

"Yes. Where are you?"

"Just walking past French Broad Chocolate Lounge, resisting the urge to go in for ice cream. Want to join us?"

"Get back here. Ted Kirkpatrick just called. He's asked us to come to the Albemarle Inn. William Ormandy's received a death threat."

Fifteen minutes later, we were headed out Charlotte Street to the inn. While I drove, Nakayla filled me in.

"A package came to the Albemarle Inn addressed to Ormandy. The owners set it beside the door to his room."

"Was he there?"

"Yes. He'd asked not to be disturbed. Said he needed to work on his score."

"What was in the package?"

"A letter. A letter jammed in the beak of a dead crow."

"You're kidding. Did he call Ted?"

"He saw the bird, the letter, and freaked out. Questioned the owners on their security. Wanted them to call the police."

I flashed back to the previous night's temper tantrum and could imagine the scene. "Did they?"

"No. They called Ted instead. He was the one paying for the room. Ted asked them to put Ormandy on the phone. Evidently, he talked him off his emotional cliff and promised that we would be a better resource than the police."

I risked a quick glance at Nakayla. "Ted doesn't want the publicity."

"That's right. He freely admitted it."

"Might not be possible to keep it quiet. If we take the threat seriously, the letter and package should be dusted for prints. That requires the police and their database. I doubt if there's anything to be gained off the crow. Ormandy's prints will need to be taken to rule him out, as will anyone else's at the inn who might have touched the package. The exterior will be pretty useless, as it must have been handled by multiple postal workers."

"If it came through the mail," Nakayla said. "I didn't question Ted that far. And I only committed us to come to the inn. Nothing more."

I'd never been to the Albemarle Inn, but Nakayla had attended several weddings there. She navigated our route along the foot of Sunset Mountain, the site of the historic Grove Park Inn and Spa.

"How far out Charlotte Street?" I asked as we drove past the turn to Grove Park.

"Almost to the golf course. That's where Charlotte Street ends."

"So, how old is this inn?"

"It predates the Grove Park. I believe it was built in 1909 and the Grove Park opened in 1913. It was the private residence of Dr. Carl Reynolds, a prominent physician from an old Asheville family. He specialized in treating tuberculosis, but had a broad interest in public health. Quite progressive for the time."

"And owned a mansion."

"That too. This was the area where the rich and well-to-do hobnobbed together. There was a trolley that ran to connect the movers and shakers out here to the town. Reynolds sold the house to a school for girls, and then later it became a rooming house and finally a bed-and-breakfast. The current owners have had it a while."

"Bet this is their first death threat."

"Probably," Nakayla agreed. "But that's not the kind of thing you'd put on your brochure."

We turned off Charlotte Street into a neighborhood of nice homes. In a few hundred yards, the road veered left but a driveway marked THE ALBEMARLE INN guided us to continue straight. Between the trees, I could see a large, white three-story home with four classic columns rising to the roof and a balcony protruding from the second level.

I gave a soft whistle. "Nice. What do you call that architecture?"

"What it looks like. Neoclassical Revival. Classic Greco-Roman design. Very popular in the eighteenth and nineteenth centuries."

"But this was built in 1909. A little late to the party."

Nakayla undid her seat belt as we parked along the side of the house. "Why don't you point that out to them? I'm sure they'll want to remodel."

Several sedans and SUVs were also in the gravel lot. A white Lexus had an ASHEVILLE LUMINARIES FESTIVAL bumper sticker. I pegged that for Ted Kirkpatrick's car. Next to it a black Subaru Forester bore an Ohio vanity plate reading PIANOMAN.

I caught Nakayla by the arm and turned her to face the vehicle. "That car either belongs to Ormandy or Billy Joel's dropped by to pay his respects to Béla Bartók."

"Ormandy. Billy Joel probably has more humility."

The entrance was not on the expansive front but on the side adjacent to the parking area. Beside the door hung two bronze plaques, one proclaiming the house to be on the list of the National Register of Historic Places and the other designating it a Distinguished Inn of North Carolina.

"Should we knock?" I asked.

"No. Let's go in quietly. You never know what you'll overhear."

"Sneaky," I said with honest approval. I opened the door and allowed Nakayla to enter first. We stepped into a large room with high ceilings, area oriental rugs, and a wide, sweeping staircase ascending to the upper levels. What struck me was the beauty of the wood in the house. Massive hand-carved finials atop the banister posts, wainscoting of lighter grain complementing muted yellow plaster walls, and beautifully finished hardwood floors. Seated in a central conversation area of wingback chairs were two men, Ted Kirkpatrick facing us, and William Ormandy in profile.

Ormandy was talking a mile a minute. "I mean, do I need to go into hiding? How about bodyguards or police protection? What about when I'm on stage? I'm a sitting duck. Will this maniac know you don't shoot the piano player?"

Kirkpatrick saw us. "Here they are," he interrupted. "Sam, Nakayla, come, join us."

The older man seemed relieved to see us. Ormandy watched us cross the room and take the two remaining chairs.

"Ted says you can help me." The pianist didn't bother to hide his skepticism.

"We need to know what we're dealing with first," Nakayla exclaimed.

"We're dealing with some nut job who's got me in his crosshairs."

Nakayla looked at Kirkpatrick. "Where's the package?"

"I had William leave it in his room like you told me. No one's touched it since he opened it."

"Then we should see it."

Ormandy started to rise. "Do you want me to fetch it?"

Fetch it. The man still had East Tennessee flowing in his veins.

"No," Nakayla said. "We'd prefer you not to handle it anymore."

"Then I guess we'll hike up two flights of stairs."

We all stood. As Ormandy headed for his room, I caught Kirkpatrick by the elbow. "Ted, a quick word?" Then to Nakayla. "Be right behind you."

I steered Kirkpatrick a few yards farther away and whispered, "It's better if just Nakayla and I talk to him."

He frowned. "Why? He's my responsibility while he's here."

"Because we need to question him about potential enemies. He might not be forthcoming if you're with us."

He nodded slowly. "That's a fair point."

"Of course, you can wait down here, or I can phone you with a verbal update when we're finished."

Kirkpatrick checked the time on a wristwatch that looked more expensive than my car. "It's four now. I've got a meeting in thirty minutes with the professor at UNC-Asheville who's giving the Wilma Dykeman talk. The phone update might be the best plan."

"Good."

"What would you and Nakayla say to staying here while Ormandy's in town? I've checked with the innkeeper and they've got a room on the third floor near Bartók's or on this floor by the base of the stairs. I'll cover the cost and your fee."

"Let's just see how the afternoon unfolds."

"All right," Kirkpatrick agreed, "but it'll be worth it to keep him from calling me every five minutes. I'm starting to wish Madison had never met him."

I hurried up the stairs and found Nakayla and Ormandy waiting on the third floor landing.

"Where's Ted?" Ormandy asked.

"He has a festival meeting. I'll update him later."

"Look, before we go in, I've got a lot of papers and score sheets scattered around. They may look unorganized, but there's a method to my chaos. I'd appreciate if you tried not to disturb anything."

"Sounds like Sam's office," Nakayla said.

If anyone broke into the inn looking for Ormandy, they'd have no trouble finding his room. A brass plaque on the door identified the Bartók Retreat and a photograph of the composer hung on an adjacent wall. The room itself was bright and cheery with a triple window providing late afternoon sunlight. It was framed by dark-green drapes tied back on either side. A queen-sized bed with a light-green comforter folded across its foot angled from one corner. The lamps and accent pieces seemed appropriate for the inn's history, and there was a single twin bed in an alcove to the left. But as Ormandy had forewarned, sheets of paper were spread across the larger bed, and the period furniture had been invaded by a card table and folding chair.

Ormandy waved his hand across the bed and table. "One thing the room's lacking is an adequate work desk. Bartók must have had one since he was here for four or five months. I have to make-do with what could be rounded up."

Nakayla pointed to the window. "Do you hear the birds?"

For a moment, Ormandy forgot about the received threat. "Yes. Just listen."

He put a finger to his lips.

At first I didn't hear anything but the room's air conditioner. Then my brain sought other sounds, and chirps and tweets rose above the mechanical hum. Once my ears were attuned, I realized how noisy the little creatures were.

"I can hear the corresponding trills Bartók wove into his concerto," Ormandy said. "More importantly, I can play the piece with a more authentic interpretation. You'll hear these sounds again at the concert. And get this."

I tried in vain to force my face into a display of unbridled enthusiasm.

"I'm introducing these birdsongs into my own Blue Ridge Concerto. It's only natural to infuse them into an Appalachian composition, blending new melodies and harmonies with the timeless traditional."

The phrase "Good artists copy, great artists steal" popped into my head.

"I think the birdsongs would make nice transitions," I said.

Nakayla shook her head in disbelief at the audacity I would express a musical suggestion when I couldn't carry a tune if it were sealed in a bucket.

Ormandy cocked his head and stared at me like a bird studying a worm. Then he looked to the pages of the handwritten score as if they were in danger. "You read music?"

"Only if it's spelled M U S I C."

He gave a nervous laugh.

"Certainly not enough to plagiarize your work."

His face went red, and I prepared for a full-scale outburst.

The storm never broke. "It happens," he said. "Sometimes inadvertently. Once, while driving, I started composing a melody in my head. A slow but gentle tune that might be developed into a theme. I stopped for a red light and grew impatient at the delay. I took it out on the tune, speeding it up four-fold. I was stunned to hear the notes reveal themselves as the finale of Rossini's *William Tell Overture*. You know, 'Hi, Ho, Silver' from the old *Lone Ranger* TV show." He shrugged. "It happens." He looked out the window. "Even with birdsongs."

"Birds don't have lawyers," I said.

"No, they don't," he agreed. "And they don't write death threats."

He walked to the far side of the bed and lifted a box from the floor. "I was so startled I just dropped it. A crow, for God's sake. My grandma said crows and ravens are harbingers of death. Ted came up and saw it, but neither of us touched it again. We thought we might destroy a clue."

"Set it on the foot of the bed," I said.

The box had once been an Amazon delivery as shown by the company logo. It had been recycled and sent through U.S. Mail by metered postage. The flaps were partially open. Printed on one were the words, "William Ormandy, c/o The Albemarle Inn." There was no return address. The box was about a foot square and six inches deep. I took a handkerchief from my pocket and bent the flaps back. Nakayla and I peered inside.

In the center lay a crow, its feathers ink-black with a sheen of deep purple on the wings. The eyes, beady and brittle in life, were now covered with a milky film. A plain white envelope had been wedged in its beak.

"You didn't open the envelope?" I asked.

"Hell, no. The damn bird was disturbing enough."

Using the handkerchief, I pulled the envelope free. It hadn't been sealed. No DNA from saliva. Nakayla stepped to my side as I slid the letter free.

The paper appeared to be a generic, standard-sized computer sheet folded lengthwise into thirds. I held it by the top edge and shook it open. In the center panel of the folds were two words: "no birdsongs." The printing, like the address on the box, was simple with no telltale swirls or other distinguishing characteristics. The jet-black ink had not flowed beyond what must have been the diameter of the ballpoint. In other words, if you were looking for a clue, you would be hard-pressed to find something more useless than computer paper and a ballpoint pen.

I turned and showed the note to Ormandy. He rocked back and forth anxiously. "'No birdsongs.' It's a threat not to play the Bartók concerto. What can you tell? Man? Woman? Would a handwriting analyst help?"

I refolded the letter, slipped it back into the envelope, and laid it on the crow. "We'll take it with us. We also need something with your prints on it."

"My prints are on the package already."

"Yes. That's why we need to know which are yours and which might be someone else's. We'll also get prints from the innkeeper before we leave."

"On a sheet of paper?"

"No. Paper can be difficult to make a print visible. A nonporous surface like a glass would be better."

"There's one in the bathroom. I'll get it for you."

I held up my hand. "In a moment. Could we ask a few questions first?"

"Sure." He looked around the room, but the only chair uncluttered was the folding one. "Do you want to go downstairs?"

"We can stand. Privacy is more important than comfort. The obvious question is who would want to threaten you?"

He stepped away and began pacing in a small circle. "Don't you think I'd tell you if I knew? I've been racking my brain."

"Anybody threaten you before? Or maybe not threaten but strongly advise you not to come to Asheville?"

He stopped and shifted his gaze between Nakayla and me. "No. I was invited here. The symphony, the Kirkpatricks, the media, everyone has been very welcoming. This is like a bolt out of the blue."

"And there's no one, no one who's not pleased that you're performing? The note doesn't say get out of town; it basically says don't play."

"Everyone seems excited. That's why this is so scary. It could be anybody."

He started pacing again.

"Anybody?" I repeated. "Anybody like Paul Clarkson, who didn't seem pleased that you called his synthesizer an electronic trash pile?"

"I was just frustrated. Things got better. I spoke with Paul this morning and we're fine."

"Did you also speak with Professor Slocum this morning?"

Ormandy gave me a hard stare. Before he could say anything, I gestured back to the music. "As that might explain why you're reworking your transitions, birdsongs included."

"No. I haven't talked to him." He pointed a shaking finger at the music on the table. "This work is mine."

"Slocum didn't seem to think that last night."

"You were spying on us?" His voice constricted with rage.

"I came back for an umbrella. I heard enough to know what Slocum thinks. I'm not saying he's right, but he sure was angry."

"Well, he's not right," Ormandy snapped. "Sometimes people hear what they want to hear. And I'm reworking the score because I want to, not because I plagiarized anything."

"At least not intentionally."

He glowered at me.

"And you don't think Professor Slocum could have sent this letter?" The tone of Nakayla's voice was more sympathetic.

"No. It had to have been mailed yesterday. Before Slocum's big scene."

"And did you play part or all of your Blue Ridge Concerto last night?" she asked.

"Paul Clarkson and I just rehearsed Bartók."

"So, what was the basis for Slocum's accusation?"

"Some detectives," he huffed. "Duh, he obviously got a copy of the score."

"Before your confrontation."

"Yes."

"Before it was too late to mail this yesterday."

I could see the light bulb go on in his head.

"Yes," he whispered. "He could have posted it before he ran into me at Lipinsky Hall."

"Is he the kind of person who would kill you?" Nakayla asked.

"No. He wouldn't have the guts. Just like he didn't have the guts to sign this letter."

"He killed this crow," I said.

"He lives out in the country. A shotgun and ten minutes would be enough." Ormandy headed for the bathroom. "I'll get you that glass. Then you'll find any extra prints are his."

He returned with a small glass. Nakayla pulled a tissue from her purse and grabbed it by the rim.

"What next?" Ormandy asked.

"We'll see if we can get any prints," I said. "But the most direct step is to ask Slocum if he sent the package."

Ormandy nodded eagerly. "Should I go with you?"

"No. That would only escalate things. Let Nakayla and me hear what he has to say first. Then we'll see where that leads us."

"You'll let me know. If it's not him, then I could be in real danger."

I could see his anxiety resurfacing. "One thing you might consider is moving out of the Bartók room. The festival has touted your accommodations as part of its publicity. You could still work here but sleep in another room. Ted said two were available."

"Ted said those were for you."

"Well, I don't know that we really need to stay here. It's likely Slocum wrote the letter."

"You're telling me to stake my life on 'likely'?"

I looked to Nakayla for help.

She smiled. "This place serves an awesome breakfast, Sam."

Chapter Thirteen

The bedrooms in the Albemarle Inn all had distinctive names. We made arrangements with the innkeeper to take the Ribbons and Roses near the foot of the stairs. Ormandy would sleep in the vacant Royal Hideaway on the third floor. The other guests were not informed of our security role as we saw no reason to alarm them.

When Nakayla and I were in the car, I speed-dialed the mobile phone of my closest contact in the Asheville Police Department, veteran detective Curt Newland.

"What's up, Sam?"

"Where are you?"

"That's always a bad starting question. You going to dump a truckload of trouble on me?"

"Trying to keep it off both of us."

"Well, I was just headed out the station door. Are you going to keep me from my after-work pint at Pack's Tavern?"

The tavern was only a few blocks from the department. Cops were a good chunk of its clientele.

"No, I'm buying. See you in ten or fifteen. Bring four evidence bags and get a table where we can talk."

"Tuck's with me."

Tuck Efird was Newly's partner. Curt Newland's friends called him Newly and I felt privileged to be in that company. Police and private eyes were often at odds with one another, but I had solved the murder of Newly's previous partner. Now I was as close to the force as a civilian could be.

Despite Newly's approval, Tuck Efird had been slow to warm to me. Then Nakayla and I solved the murder of his ex-girlfriend. I needed to find a better way to make friends.

"Tuck's welcome. But if he decides to do shooters, the tab closes."

"Tuck? If he has two beers it's a special occasion."

I disconnected and asked Nakayla if she would drive from the tavern to the office to save time.

"Why four evidence bags?"

"One for the envelope and letter, two for the glasses with Ormandy's and the innkeeper's prints, and the fourth for a print from Slocum."

"What about the crow?"

"I'll leave it in the box."

"Sam, you can't take a dead animal into a restaurant."

"Why not? No one will see it. Besides, most of the menu is dead animals."

Beaten by my unassailable logic, Nakayla gave up the argument and moved on. "You think Slocum's just going to give you his prints?"

"If he's innocent, why not?"

"Are we sacrificing a glass of our own?"

"Something flatter should work fine. Maybe a kitchen knife."

Nakayla laughed. "You're asking the man to leave his prints on a potential weapon?"

She had a point.

"A spoon then?"

"I've got an old compact at the office I don't use. I'll wipe my prints. It has a smooth plastic case and a mirror, both good surfaces."

"Perfect. What about Blue? Should we leave him overnight at the office or the apartment?"

Nakayla pulled out her phone. "Let's see if I can catch somebody at Hewitt's office. One of them might take care of Blue while we're at the inn."

Nakayla reached Shirley who said Hewitt would be thrilled. She didn't bother to ask him, but that didn't matter. Hewitt would take him.

I double-parked in front of Pack's and got out carrying the tissue-wrapped envelope, glasses, and the resealed box containing one deceased crow.

Nakayla hopped in the driver's seat. "Want me to pick you up?"

"Nah, I'll walk."

"It's a tavern. Are you sure?"

"I'll stay sober as a judge."

Nakayla looked past me to the courthouse at the end of Pack Square. "If you mean the judges I know, then definitely hitch a ride with Newly." With a toot of the horn for punctuation, she drove off.

I found Newly and Tuck at a back table, a beer in front of each. When he saw my laden arms, Tuck used his foot to push out a chair for me.

"All hail, our patron saint." He eyed the items in my hands. "Look, Newly, he even brought us gifts. This must be the mother of all favors."

Newly scowled. "Should we pay for our own drinks?"

I set my burden in the chair beside me and shrugged. "If you feel lifting a few fingerprints is a breach of your ethical code, then by all means. If you want to unofficially expedite a matter to keep it from prematurely becoming a case with all the accompanying paperwork, then I'll spot you a few rounds while we discuss things."

"It doesn't hurt to listen to the man, Newly. Especially since we've already ordered the next round."

I removed the tissue from the envelope. "You're familiar with the Asheville Luminaries Festival?"

"That thing highlighting when Babe Ruth got sick?" Tuck asked.

"Yeah, but there's much more to it than that. They're also honoring a composer who wrote some of his famous pieces in Asheville. He died over seventy-five years ago. The star pianist booked to perform has roots here, but someone's not welcoming his participation." I held up the envelope by one corner. "He received a death threat this afternoon."

I set the envelope aside and unwrapped each drinking glass. "The pianist and the innkeeper where he's staying gave us prints for the purpose of elimination."

Newly stared at the glasses and then the envelope. "There's no address."

"It was on the box the letter came in."

Newly leaned over the table, studied the box, and eyed me suspiciously. "What else is in there?"

"Something that should stay in there till you're at the station unless you want the health department to shut this place down before your second round."

He eased back in his chair. "All right. We'll let that ride for the moment. Even if we're able to find a clean print, we'll still need to access all our databanks. Why the off-the-books route?"

"Because we think it's a hoax and bringing public attention is just what the perpetrator wants. Besides, I've got a strong person of interest."

I gave them a summary of the scene in the Lipinsky Hall auditorium between Ormandy and Slocum.

"So, what's your plan?" Newly asked. "Get him drinking a beer and then steal the glass?"

"I thought I'd ask him. That's why I wanted a fourth evidence bag. Look, if Slocum is innocent, then he won't want the public humiliation of being brought to the station for questioning. I'm sure the university frowns upon their professors issuing death threats."

Newly took a healthy swallow of beer while he weighed my reasoning. "And if he's guilty?"

"I tell him I'm reporting what I witnessed to the police, who will probably make a very public appearance on campus. I suspect he will admit it, claiming it was a joke that he had no intention of carrying out."

"Then you wouldn't need us," Tuck said.

"Not unless Ormandy wants to file a complaint. But that would raise the question of plagiarism, which casts suspicion on him."

"And everything fades away," Newly said. "If Slocum is guilty."

"If Slocum is guilty," I repeated. "Otherwise, the threat is still out there, and I'll advise Ormandy to come to you requesting an official investigation."

Newly reached into the outside pocket of his suit coat and extracted four sealable bags. He handed me one and then used the tissues to deposit the envelope and glasses in the other three. "When are you going to spring this little plan on Professor Slocum?"

"Tomorrow, if possible. Nakayla's checking the music department's website to see if his office hours are listed. We'll be right outside his door."

The conversation shifted to Ken Stokes and where the case stood. The inevitable cop-shop talk. I drank a Highland Gaelic Ale while Newly and Tuck finished their second round.

As we left, I handed Tuck the box. "It's your call what to do with this."

"Are you going to tell us what it is?"

"Maybe. If you want to wait for 'once upon a midnight dreary.'"

———

"I only fell down three times." I made the pronouncement as I opened the door to our office suite.

The clickety-clack of Nakayla's keyboard ceased.

"Pretty good for a man with an artificial leg," I added.

She got up from her desk. "Nothing artificial about you." Her kiss was soft and lingering.

"Hmm. I'll have to drink and walk more often."

"I was thinking more about our staying in a romantic spot like the Albemarle Inn." She glanced at Blue's empty cushion. "Now that our child is spending the night with Hewitt."

"Yes. It would be a shame to let the night slip away from us while doing something as mundane as guarding a man's life."

Nakayla stepped back. "There is that to consider. Maybe you should stay fully clothed."

I held up a hand. "Whoa, who says I'm not capable of multitasking?"

"Tasking?"

One would think with only one good foot I would keep it out of my mouth. I retreated into the hall, closed the door, and then reentered. "Hi, love of my life. I am so looking forward to getting you alone tonight. What say we lock Ormandy in his room and throw away the key?" I planted a loud kiss on her lips.

"What say we lock this door and I'll whisper Professor Norman Slocum's office hours in your ear."

The verbal equivalent of a cold shower.

———

We checked into the Albemarle Inn shortly before seven thirty. Nakayla and I each brought on overnight bag. She also carried her laptop, and I had the evidence bag with her compact for Slocum's prints. His posted office hours were nine thirty to eleven thirty the next morning.

Ormandy was still at the rehearsal for his Blue Ridge

Concerto, and I wondered if he'd added the part for the Minimoog. Paul Clarkson must have felt like a yo-yo, first in the piece, then out, and now in again.

Ted Kirkpatrick brought Ormandy safely back to the inn around nine. Both men were in good spirits so I deduced the rehearsal had gone well. Ted thanked Nakayla and me for staying the night and hoped we would soon get to the bottom of who was making the threat.

Ormandy proclaimed he had some tweaks to make on his score and would be in the Bartók room for a while. He promised to text me when he was ready to move so that I could be present in the third-floor hallway. To my dismay, he didn't quit till nearly one o'clock. Nakayla had long since fallen asleep. So much for multitasking.

———

Nakayla, Ormandy, and I enjoyed the awesome breakfast together. Fresh breads, berries, juices, and custom-prepared dishes ranging from pecan-topped baked French toast to an egg soufflé with fresh asparagus and parmesan. As I polished off the last of my frozen almond mousse coated with strawberry sauce, I lamented that the case of the threatening letter might be wrapping up by lunch. I could suffer through a few more mornings like this.

Ormandy drained his coffee cup and set it askew on the saucer. "You'll let me know immediately what you learn from Slocum. I've got to be out and about, and I don't want to be looking over my shoulder."

I dabbed the corners of my mouth with a linen napkin and then folded it beside my plate. "And if he admits it, do you want us to do anything? Bear in mind, his plagiarism claim will surface. Or you can turn this threat into leverage to keep him quiet, which might be smarter even if his accusation is baseless."

"You're right." Ormandy stood from the table. "I don't have time to get involved with his petty squabbles. Just let me know." He pivoted and strode briskly toward the stairs without so much as a thank you for our efforts.

I shook my head. "Just call me Ormandy whenever I get obnoxious and overbearing."

"Okay. Then it might be easier if you just legally changed your name."

I had to laugh because I should have known better than to give Nakayla such an easy setup line. "Clarkson was right. William Ormandy is trying to overcompensate for being Willie from East Tennessee."

"And I expect he's a lonely person," Nakayla observed. "He hides behind his music."

"Married?"

"Not that I saw on Wikipedia."

"Gay?"

"Maybe. But I still get the vibe that those score sheets are his identity and he doesn't know how to simply be himself. He's going through life playing a role as well as playing the piano."

I couldn't argue with her assessment. Nakayla had the gift of reading people. If she was trying to make me feel sorry for the guy, she was succeeding.

At nine fifteen, Nakayla and I waited outside Professor Norman Slocum's second-floor office in Lipinsky Hall. We'd tried to keep a low profile with our unscheduled visit, avoiding the main administrative office and casually conversing like we were patiently waiting for the professor's arrival. Students passed us without so much as a second glance.

A few minutes later, Slocum appeared carrying on old-style leather satchel. When he spotted us between him and his office door, his eyebrows knit together in the puzzled reaction of someone who fears he's forgotten some planned appointment.

"Are you waiting for me?" The question came with the inflection that he hoped the answer was no.

"Yes." Nakayla smiled and offered her hand. "I'm Nakayla Robertson and this is my partner Sam Blackman."

He was still perplexed. Our names meant nothing to him.

As I shook his hand, I added, "We just need a few minutes of your time. Nakayla and I are private detectives, and we're working in cooperation with the Asheville Police Department."

"Police?" The word rattled in his throat as he tried to suck in air and talk at the same time. "What do I have to do with the police?"

"Sir, if we could talk a few moments in your office—in private."

Slocum glanced around, checking to see who might have already been listening. "We're likely to be interrupted here. Students drop by. Let me put a note on the door, and we'll go down to one of the practice rooms."

He unlocked his door. I angled to one side where I could watch him. The interior looked like a tornado had roared through. Papers lay scattered across the top of his desk. Stacks rose from the floor. Sheets of music were pinned to a side wall of cork board. Slocum set his satchel down like a giant paperweight on the desktop, grabbed a sheet of white paper from a nearby printer tray, wrote a note, and taped it to his door. Then twisted his key in the lock.

"There," he said. "Follow me to the elevator."

I hesitated a moment, examining what Slocum had scribbled on the paper. "Back at 10." Six letters—five not counting the double a—and two numerals. The handwriting was block print, but the case was upper and lower, not just lower like the death threat. Had Slocum known why we were there and purposely altered his script?

We stood quietly in the elevator as it crept down two floors to the lowest level. Then he led us along a hall flanked by lockers on one side and small, modular rooms on the other. These must have been the practice rooms, some occupied, some empty. He opened the door to one containing two electric pianos.

"I'm sorry there aren't any chairs." He gestured to one of the two benches. "This will have to do." He closed the door.

The room felt airtight. It made for a good interrogation site. Newly might bear it in mind if they ever renovated the police department.

As Nakayla and I sat, Slocum pulled out his bench to get closer to us. "So, what's this all about?"

He'd regained his composure now that he was in his own element. He was the professor, and we were students. I decided to fire a broadside.

"Why did you send a death threat to William Ormandy?"

His head jerked back. His eyes gave life to the term bug-out. "What the hell are you talking about? I did no such thing!"

"What kind of shotgun do you own?"

He drew back like he thought I was going to physically attack him. "A shotgun? I detest all guns. Who told you I had a gun?"

"Professor Slocum, the night before last I witnessed your angry exchange with Ormandy. You made accusations against him that bordered on physical confrontation. The next afternoon a package arrived for Ormandy at the Albemarle Inn threatening his life if he played the concerto."

"Which concerto?"

"Why, the one you say he plagiarized."

He fixed me with a hard stare. "If you were here two nights ago, you know I never touched him. Yes, I was angry and I made threats to take him to court." He appealed to Nakayla, evidently giving up on convincing me. "And I listened from the wings to last night's rehearsal. He'd modified the score, and although I could still hear my basic structure, the piece is a less-obvious derivative of my work."

"Meaning what?" I asked.

"Meaning that proving his plagiarism will be harder, especially now that he's added a discordant section for the Moog synthesizer."

Ironic. What Ormandy had wanted to throw out might save him in court.

Nakayla slid forward on the bench. "Professor Slocum, can you think of anyone who might have a grudge against William Ormandy?"

"I haven't seen the man in over a decade. He was only here one year before going to the School of the Arts. I guess you'd have to consider whoever sent me the score. That must have been a symphony player or the conductor."

"How would they have been familiar with your piece?"

He thought a moment. "Maybe if they'd hung around Lipinsky Hall. I've had a couple of unofficial workshops, small gatherings of musicians who have been kind enough to play certain movements so I could hear whether the instrumentation had the impact I wanted."

Nakayla looked at me. "Sam says Ormandy claimed you'd been working on this for years."

"So? I won't premiere it until it's ready. It's a full symphony, the musical equivalent of a novel, if you will. Some authors publish a book once a decade. You don't turn creativity on and off like a spigot."

I'd read Jimmy Buffett said he wrote "Margaritaville" in five minutes, but somehow I didn't think Slocum would appreciate the comparison.

"I understand," I said. "What about Ormandy when he was a student here? Friends, enemies, was he a loner or a leader?"

Slocum shrugged. "I don't know. I only had him for a semester of composition theory. At first he showed promise, but then he got lazy. Started putting what time he did devote to his music into his performance pieces. I was disappointed because initially I thought he had talent." Slocum looked up at a corner of the small room as if a memory lodged there. "I think I asked one of his classmates about him. I got a one-word answer—girlfriend. Then I saw him on campus a few times with an attractive young woman and it was clear she had become his focus."

"Why did he leave the university?" Nakayla asked.

"The North Carolina School of the Arts has a, shall we say, a higher recognition in the musical world. He auditioned and got the acceptance."

Nakayla nodded. "And the girlfriend?"

"What about her?"

"I guess you don't know if they stayed together."

"If they did, it didn't last."

"Why would you say that?" I asked.

"Because I recognized her picture in the paper last week. You know with all this Festival publicity. She's married to Ted Kirkpatrick."

Nakayla and I exchanged a not-so-subtle glance of complete surprise. "Madison?" we said in unison.

"Is that her name? All I know is she must be young enough to be his daughter." Slocum looked nervous again. "Don't tell him I told you about his wife and Ormandy. Maybe he knows, maybe he doesn't, but I don't want him thinking I meant anything by it."

"We won't," I assured him. "It doesn't have anything to do with the letter to Ormandy. And we want to keep that letter from getting blown out of proportion. Not drag innocent people into an investigation. You can help us."

"How's that?"

Nakayla pulled her compact and the evidence bag from her purse. "Give us your fingerprints so we can rule you out."

"And then the police will quietly cross you off their list," I added, knowing full well I could make no such guarantee.

Chapter Fourteen

"Well, what do you think?" I asked Nakayla the question as we pulled out of university parking lot P17.

"I don't think he sent that package or else he wouldn't have so readily agreed to give us his prints."

"He could have worn gloves and feels confident that nothing will show up."

"Maybe," Nakayla agreed. "But to be on the safe side, I think we have to assume he didn't."

"Ormandy's not going to like that. Guess we'll just have to eat more breakfasts at the Albemarle Inn."

"The sacrifices you make for our clients," Nakayla said. "It's awe-inspiring."

"What do you make of the relationship between Ormandy and Madison Kirkpatrick?"

Nakayla hesitated. I didn't wait for her reply. "I mean, what are the odds they would know each other?"

"Pretty good, actually. If she was a student, even a year or two older, they could have met. The university's not that large. She was the one who recommended Ormandy, and Ted said she likes the symphony."

"But Luke said Clarkson recommended Ormandy."

"And there's no reason they can't be both right. Clarkson was in the department for Ormandy's freshman year. Madison was the girlfriend."

"So, Madison would also know Clarkson," I said. "This is like one of those overlapping Venn diagrams. John knows Suzy but doesn't know Ellen. Ellen knows Suzy and Suzy's boyfriend, Fred. Fred knows John who knows—"

"Who knows Kevin Bacon," Nakayla said laughingly. "Six degrees of separation. We're talking even fewer if the universe is restricted to the music department."

"Yeah. You know what's bugging me?"

"That a death threat carries more weight if it intersects with a murder?"

Her statement caught me up short. I hadn't seen any connection between the letter to Ormandy and the death of Ken Stokes. I still didn't see one, but maybe that's what was really gnawing at me. Some link I was missing. Maybe Nakayla was on to something. "How so?"

"Well, we have Ormandy arriving over an hour late for dinner with Ted Kirkpatrick. That means he doesn't have an alibi for the window of time when Ken died."

"That's what I was about to say."

"And don't you think it's odd that Ormandy would wait so long to notify Ted of the delay? He said he got a late start out of Cincinnati. It's a five-and-a-half-hour-drive. He should have known from the onset that he'd be late and not waited until an hour before the scheduled dinner to tell his host."

I hadn't thought about that point. "He's not the most considerate person on the planet."

"No, he's not. Still, I'd like to know his location during that time. And…" She left the thought hanging as if hesitant to complete it.

"And what?"

"And I'd like to know if Madison really was playing bridge that night."

I braked for the stoplight at Merrimon Avenue and turned to face my partner. "You cunning little fox. You think Ormandy was scoring more than his music?"

"I wouldn't put it quite so crudely. More like playing around."

"Then our most likely suspect is Ted Kirkpatrick himself. That makes no sense." I saw only one way forward. "The person in a position to subpoena phone records is Sheriff Cliff Hudson. Newly and Tuck don't have enough probable cause, but a murder investigation might garner more sympathy from a judge."

"You want to call Hudson from the car?" she asked.

"No. Let's get Slocum's prints to Newly, fill him in, and see if the lab managed to pull anything off the package and letter. If we don't have a match, then we'll let Ormandy know the bad news that the letter writer is still unidentified."

"We're not going to get a match, Sam."

"I know. Maybe I'll confess to sending the letter just to keep from hearing Ormandy whine."

Nakayla phoned Newly and arranged to meet him at City Bakery. We found him at a table, drinking coffee and munching a scone. He was all smiles. "Want something to eat?"

Nakayla shook her head. "Neither does Sam. We had a big breakfast."

The scone looked good, but Nakayla was right. I'd stuffed myself at the inn. Nice that someone was worried about my health. "I'll get us some coffee."

When I returned with two cups, I saw that Nakayla had pulled the evidence bag with the compact from her purse. Newly was looking at his watch and logging the time he took custody in a small notebook.

He set down his pen. "At least this isn't a dead animal. I've been flipped the bird before but that was a first."

"The crow yield any clues?"

"He was murdered by bird shot. Case closed. As for the letter, we aren't so lucky."

I handed Nakayla her coffee and slid into a chair. "No prints?"

"Nothing on the envelope or letter itself. Plenty on the outside. Probably the sender's are among them because I doubt he wore gloves in public. To have the local overnight delivery, it was sent from the main post office." Newly patted the evidence bag with Nakayla's compact. "But I'll check these prints against what clean prints we could lift. You say Slocum didn't protest?"

"No," Nakayla said. "That's why I doubt any prints are his. As soon as you confirm it, we'll contact Ormandy."

"If it's not him, do you have any other suspects?" Newly asked. "I'd like to make this official, in case, God forbid, something should happen to him."

I told Newly our unsubstantiated theory that Ormandy might have been in Asheville earlier than he claimed, but we felt Sheriff Hudson was the appropriate channel to pursue that inquiry.

"Then I'd better get these prints lifted and reviewed." Newly got to his feet. "And call Hudson. Ormandy's behavior sounds fishy to me. If I were the sheriff, I'd appreciate a heads-up."

"That's why you always take my calls, right?"

"Only because they might be from Nakayla." He pivoted and walked out of the café.

Nakayla took a sip of coffee, her brown eyes dancing over the rim.

"Go ahead," I said. "Say what a brilliant cop Newly is."

"Sam, did I ever say I loved you for your mind?"

"No. Not that I recall."

She leaned close and whispered, "That's because I can't snuggle up to your mind in that big four-poster bed at the Albemarle Inn." She gently stroked the back of my hand with her slender fingers.

———

"Where do we go next? Will you start sending me flowers?"

Sheriff Hudson and Newly must have been vying for comedic cop of the day.

I leaned back in my desk chair, the mobile phone on speaker so that Nakayla could hear. She sat opposite me. "What happened to a simple hello?"

"It doesn't express my joy at receiving yet another phone call from you."

"I live to make you happy. Nakayla's with me and we've had a development that may or may not have any bearing on Ken Stokes's murder. We wanted you to know about it."

"I'm listening."

Nakayla took the lead. "William Ormandy received a death threat yesterday. A dead crow and a letter warning him not to play."

"He's the guest pianist," Hudson confirmed. "The man who had dinner with Ted Kirkpatrick."

"Correct," Nakayla said. "And he was over an hour late for that dinner. But we've learned in investigating the death threat that Ormandy once dated Madison Kirkpatrick, Ted's new wife. He also knew Ken and Lynne Stokes. The relationships are more tangled than they first appeared. We're wondering if there was tension in that mix."

"The fact that they knew each other can simply explain how Ormandy came to be invited," Hudson argued.

"That's true," Nakayla agreed. "But we think it's odd if Ormandy claimed he was over an hour late because he got a late start from Cincinnati, then why did he wait so long to tell Ted?"

For a moment, Hudson said nothing. We let him digest the information.

"All I knew was that Ormandy was late and that Donaldson gave Ted Kirkpatrick an ironclad alibi," Hudson said. "I had no reason to suspect Ormandy."

"I know," I said. "Neither did we. But, to Nakayla's point

and this death threat aside, aren't you curious to know when Ormandy actually came to Asheville? And, given his history with Madison Kirkpatrick, shouldn't we confirm she actually played bridge that night? Maybe you already have."

"No. And I still don't see how an affair touches my case."

"What if Ken Stokes learned about it?" Nakayla said. "He was also friends with Ormandy from growing up in East Tennessee. Maybe Ormandy confided in him. Maybe Ken threatened to expose him for some reason. I admit it's a lot of maybes, but they're there just the same."

Again, Hudson was silent. Finally, he said, "Okay, I'll look into it, but quietly. Cell phone records will be the best start before we have any direct confrontations."

I lifted a piece of paper from my desk. "Good. Ormandy gave me his number." I read it to him twice.

"Are you two the only ones on it?"

"No. We've turned over what we've learned to the Asheville police. But they're being quiet about the threat. It's probably just a hoax by someone wanting publicity."

"Or it's tied into what you've told me about the relationships. If I do get confirmation that Ormandy lied about his where-abouts, I'd like to see the letter."

"I'm sure Curt Newland would be receptive, especially if you've got something to share."

Hudson laughed. "Everything's a deal, isn't it? So, to keep our good faith going, I got word that both the re-samples and the original samples arrived at the Raleigh lab this morning. Raleigh police are dusting for prints, and we're getting a rush on the analysis. I might have a preliminary report by the end of the day."

"Is the label on the first package handwritten?" Nakayla asked.

"Yes."

"Then you might want to go ahead and get a photocopy of the letter that came to Ormandy. You never know."

"Good call," I whispered.

"That's true," Hudson said. "Dismiss a lead, no matter how farfetched, at your own peril. Listen, Nakayla, if you ever get tired of working with Sam, I'll have a place for you."

"Thanks, but we share custody of a coonhound."

"Say no more. We have two. The wife would sooner be shed of me. I'll be back to you." With a chuckle, he hung up.

Nakayla smiled. "I think he's growing to like us."

"He's growing to like you. I'm just eye candy."

Before Nakayla could reply, my cell phone rang. "It's Newly." I accepted the call. "Newly, I've got you on speaker with Nakayla. What's up?"

"No matches, either with Slocum or our databases."

"It's what we expected. And you should expect a call from Sheriff Hudson." I told Newly the sheriff wanted to see the letter for a handwriting comparison to the sample shipment. "And he's going to take a closer look at Ormandy."

"All right," Newly said. "Are you following up with Ormandy about Slocum not matching the prints?"

"Yes. He and Ted both. I'll keep you posted."

When Newly rang off, I asked Nakayla, "What do we do now?"

"I think you make those calls to Ted and Ormandy. Prove you're not just eye candy on this case."

I had the good sense to contact Ted first. He was disappointed and asked if we could still stay close to Ormandy. He knew we were working Ken Stokes's murder, but any time we could spare would be appreciated. At least through the performance of the concertos. I agreed without telling him that his star pianist might soon be a person of interest in the Stokes's case, and the letter gave us an excuse to keep an eye on him.

Ormandy's first reaction when I informed him that the fingerprints weren't Professor Slocum's was, "Are you sure?"

"Yes. The good news is Slocum said he heard your Blue Ridge Concerto rehearsal and won't be taking any legal action."

"But we're no closer to knowing who sent the threat?"

"No, we're not. Are you sure you're not holding something back?"

The line went silent a moment. Then he said, "Nothing that has anything to do with the performance. Nothing at all."

I didn't press him. The call ended with my assurance that Nakayla and I would continue to stay at the inn.

We made arrangements for Blue to continue to stay with Hewitt. With both the death threat and Stokes's murder at a standstill, Nakayla and I swung by the construction site of her new home. Two panel vans with the words *Hamrick Flooring* on their sides were parked in the driveway. A white Ford F-150 pickup that I recognized as Ken Stokes's was tucked parallel to the curb.

"Walt must be here," Nakayla said. "Probably just checking on his subcontractors."

As we got out of the CR-V, the antique front door opened and Walt stepped out onto the porch. The tool belt around his waist told me he was doing more than supervising.

"Howdy." He forced a smile that had no heart behind it.

"Hi, Walt." I struggled for something more to say to the grieving father.

"How's Lynne?" Nakayla asked.

"As good as can be expected." He pulled a cell phone from his shirt pocket. "I've got the ringer up as loud as it goes. Don't want to miss a call if I'm running a saw or sander."

Nakayla stepped up on the porch. "Is she having contractions?"

"Just those Braxton Hicks things."

I joined her.

"Think of them as preliminaries," Nakayla told me, knowing my knowledge of the nuances of pregnancies was only slightly higher than my knowledge of nuclear physics.

"Will she have someone go through labor with her?" Nakayla asked.

"Some of her girlfriends have volunteered. I've got a list to go down when the time comes."

"Add my name to it if Lynne approves."

Walt's eyes teared. "I will. Any news?"

Nakayla looked to me to be the bearer of no news.

I tried to sound enthusiastic. "Sheriff Hudson's working some angles, one of which is the pending report on the water and soil samples that might have been collected from Kirkgate Paper. Maybe first of the week, after the funeral, we can get together and share whatever updates we have."

His lips tightened as he nodded. A moment passed and then he said, "Well, come inside. The flooring crew has laid down the front room and are now in the back bedrooms. Of course, the hardwoods need a final finish, and we'll do the kitchen floor after Sonny Jenkins installs the cabinets." He walked into the house with us behind him.

"I painted the window trim the other day. Now that it's dry I'm making sure they all open. Some need a thin spatula to break them free." He pointed to the windows on either side of the stone fireplace. Each was open at the top and bottom. An open toolbox sat on the hearth.

"And I'll do touch-up as necessary." Walt turned back to the entrance. "I also evened out the stain on the front door and greased the hinges. It's like pushing a feather. Kenny was really pleased you chose it, even though the measurements were wrong."

"I am too," Nakayla said. "I'm glad Ken pushed me."

His smile came more naturally. "Let me show you the light fixtures in the kitchen."

I walked over to one of the open windows, feigning interest in the manufacturer's sticker still fixed to one of the panes. As soon as Walt and Nakayla were out of the room, I moved to the toolbox. It contained more than tools. It contained a trove of Walt's fingerprints. Would he have reason to threaten Ormandy? I considered lifting a screwdriver.

"Sam, come see the progress," Nakayla shouted from the kitchen.

I stepped back and chastised myself. What did Walt care about a concert? And if he had any suspicions about Ormandy, why wouldn't he have told me? I realized I was losing focus. The case had reached the point where it was screwing with my head.

———

Nakayla and I decided to return to my apartment to pick up more clothes and then grab an early supper so we'd be at the Albemarle Inn when Ted Kirkpatrick dropped off Ormandy. Evidently, Ted had convinced Ormandy and Paul Clarkson to play a short excerpt from the Blue Ridge Concerto at the Wilma Dykeman lecture Saturday night, so they were squeezing in a late afternoon rehearsal.

Instead of going out to eat, Nakayla grilled ham and cheese sandwiches and poured the wine. I was just chewing my first bite when my cell phone rang.

"Newly," I mumbled. I washed the food down with a healthy gulp of Chardonnay and then activated the speaker function. "Any luck?"

"Nothing. Unless Slocum wore gloves or had his prints obliterated by the postal workers, he's in the clear."

"Thanks, Newly. For now let's keep Slocum in the mix." I disconnected.

I reached for my sandwich and my phone buzzed again. "Hudson," I told Nakayla, and again used the speaker.

"Sheriff, you've got Nakayla and me both."

"I'm making good on my promise. The sample reports came back. One set was clean, the other highly toxic."

"Just what we suspected," I said. "Someone substituted the clean for the dirty. That's the motive for Ken's murder."

"And our suspicions were one hundred percent wrong. The

clean sample was the one Eli Patterson took under my supervision. The dirty sample was the one left at the River Watchers office. Why would anyone from Kirkgate Paper doctor soil and water to trigger a pollution scare?"

"They wouldn't."

"Well, aren't you the great detective? And I now have neither a suspect nor a motive."

"Are you pulling phone records?"

"Yes. I've gotten Ken Stokes's and Luke and Ted Kirkpatrick's. The cell tower records match their stated locations. I just put in the Ormandy request so that will take a couple days."

"And Madison Kirkpatrick?"

"Yes, along with Ormandy. But I don't see the Kirkpatricks involved. It would mean at least one of them was trying to sabotage their own company."

Nakayla leaned closer to the phone. "What about Eli Patterson?"

"What about him?" Hudson asked.

"Does he or the River Watchers organization benefit from a rise in pollution? I mean donations, support from patrons and paper companies. Could their own success be putting them out of business? Patterson was the person who claimed he found the parcel. Now that we know it was doctored, something Kirkgate Paper surely wouldn't do, we have to look for a new motive. Could River Watchers benefit?"

Hudson laughed. "You sure you want to stay with Sam?"

"Goodbye, Sheriff." I ended the call.

This time I reached for my wine, but not quite fast enough. The phone's screen flashed. Ted Kirkpatrick. "Now what?" I muttered. I accepted the call and tried not to sound irritated. "Yes, Ted."

"I just got a call from a reporter at the *Asheville Citizen-Times*. He wants me to confirm we've had a massive pollution leak and that state officials are coming from Raleigh. Sam, what the hell's going on?"

Chapter Fifteen

I got up from the dinner table and starting pacing back and forth, holding the phone out in front of me in the palm of my hand. Nakayla slid back in her chair and watched. She knew that I thought better when I was moving.

"Look, Ted. I don't know where the reporter got his information, but call him back. Two sets of samples came to the lab. One clean, one dirty. The dirty one was dropped at River Watchers the night Ken Stokes died. The clean one was overseen by Sheriff Hudson. You and Luke are probably no longer suspects because why would you contaminate your own site? Hudson can verify this and keep the reporter from writing something they'll have to retract. And a retraction never undoes the initial damage."

"Which was probably the damned point! Go for the big headline and the correction comes in small print that nobody reads." Ted shouted so loudly I had to tighten my grip on the vibrating phone.

"I know you're upset and have a right to be, but if I can offer a word of advice—speak calmly and confidently to the reporter and tell him that Sheriff Hudson has the facts and there is no pollution spill. You have no idea how the erroneous story was started, but you'd appreciate the reporter following up for the truth before printing anything. You might work in a plug for the Luminaries Festival, saying your focus is on making that a success for the city and not getting distracted by what is obviously a lab mix-up."

Nakayla gave me a thumbs-up.

"Would you call him?" Ted asked. "I don't think I'd summarize the situation as well as you just did."

"No. I'll come across as a paid spokesman. I'll give you Sheriff Hudson's mobile number to pass along. Don't tell the reporter where you got it. And you might want to request your name be kept out of it as well. Hudson might push back wanting to know the reporter's sources." I pulled up my recent calls and repeated Hudson's number.

"Thanks, Sam. Are you and Nakayla investigating the sample tampering? It could be tied to Stokes's death somehow."

"We are, but it will be for Lynne and Walt. Any developments will first go to them. Where are you now?"

"Outside the auditorium at Lipinsky Hall. Ormandy and Clarkson are rehearsing the short piece they're playing before the Dykeman lecture. I should have Ormandy back at the inn around seven."

"Would you stay with him till we get there? And you can fill me in on your conversation with the reporter."

"How late will you be?"

I looked at the time on my phone. Ten after six. "Seven thirty, maybe eight. Shouldn't be any later."

"All right. Then I'll take Ormandy to dinner. Clarkson too. That should have us arriving at the inn about the same time."

The Moog player's name sparked a connection I needed to explore. "Would you pass along my number to Clarkson? Ask him to give me a call?"

Ted hesitated a moment. "Sure. Anything in particular?"

Ted was fishing, but I wasn't going to bite. "No. Just a

follow-up to a previous conversation. Nothing concerning you or Luke."

"Of course. I didn't mean to pry. And thanks for the advice." He disconnected.

"Who do you think leaked the lab results?" Nakayla asked.

"Someone who has it in for the Kirkpatricks. Probably whoever doctored those samples. And somehow there's a link to Ken Stokes. That's what we need to uncover."

Nakayla pointed to my half-eaten sandwich. "Finish your supper. I'll make the call."

"To whom?"

"Walt Stokes. I think he needs to know about those soil samples."

"Because?"

"Because he thinks Ken was killed by someone involved with Kirkgate Paper. At some point his grief will transform into rage, and he might do something he'll regret."

———

As we crossed the front room to the kitchen, our footsteps echoed off the new hardwood floor. Nakayla had requested Walt Stokes meet us at the house because she wanted to show him something. She assured him nothing was wrong but it was important to see him before construction progressed further. Our true intention was seeing him away from Lynne. I'd told Nakayla about my temptation to take one of Walt's tools for fingerprints and that her comment about grief transforming into rage made me concerned it might have already happened. I wanted to ask him straight to his face whether he sent the dead crow.

There was no place to sit, but the kitchen had the brightest overhead fixture, and as dusk settled outside, I wanted to clearly read Walt's face.

A rumble sounded from the street.

"That must be the Bronco," I said. "I'll meet him at the door."

I put on a big smile for my performance. Walt came up the sidewalk carrying a legal pad. He was ready for business.

"Good evening, Sam."

We shook hands.

"Nakayla's in the kitchen," I said. "Everything's looking good."

"That's Ken's doing. I'm just finishing up."

"Well, Nakayla's very happy." I gestured for him to precede me, a maneuver that would place him between us.

Nakayla stood next to where exposed pipes indicated the sink would be installed.

She didn't step forward to meet him. "Thanks for coming, Walt."

He nodded. "So, what creative idea has percolated up from your brain?"

She looked at me, and Walt turned around.

"Walt, no birdsongs."

"No what?" He looked at me like I was speaking in tongues.

"No birdsongs."

He turned to Nakayla. "Birdsongs? You want birdhouses? Feeders? Something to attract birds? I can make some, but it might be cheaper to buy them and let me place them for you."

Nakayla looked at me with relief. Walt was completely baffled.

"I think she's afraid I'll try to make them myself," I said.

Walt laughed. "I could do some bluebird houses. They're simple, can mount on a metal pole, and I could paint them to match the house. Also, a birdbath in the backyard would attract them."

I decided the charade had accomplished its goal. Walt clearly hadn't sent the crow. "Sounds good. The main reason we asked you here is to give you a case update that you can share with Lynne. We don't believe the Kirkpatricks were involved."

Walt's smile vanished. "Why?"

"The samples of soil and water that we thought Ken collected tested dangerously contaminated."

"See," he said, anger rising in his voice. "They didn't want the truth to come out."

"We have proof those samples were doctored," Nakayla said. "Eli Patterson and Sheriff Hudson retested the same spots. They were clean. Someone tried to make trouble for Kirkgate Paper."

Walt shook his head vigorously. "No! No! Kenny would never do that. Someone else must have intercepted those samples, if Kenny even took them in the first place. Kenny was very meticulous." His eyes widened. "Someone must have used Kenny. Had him fill out the paperwork and then substituted or contaminated the samples. I know my son. He would never willingly go along with such a scheme."

The word *willingly* leapt out. "Would someone have the leverage to force Ken to alter his samples?"

"You mean blackmail?"

"I mean anything that could pressure him."

"Nothing short of a gun to his head."

I knew the loyal father wasn't going to say anything that reflected badly on his son.

Walt studied our faces. "So what happens now?"

"We have to look beyond Kirkgate Paper," I said. "What's the history between Ken and William Ormandy?"

"William? I can't believe he'd have anything to do with Kenny's death. They knew each other in high school. Back in East Tennessee. After my wife died, Kenny and I moved here. That was in his senior year. I hated he had to transfer but Asheville was where the work was. He graduated from AC Reynolds High, worked with me, and took some courses at AB Tech. But between his love of the outdoors and our construction work, formal schooling wasn't his thing."

Nakayla circled around him to stand beside me. "And he's kept up with Ormandy all these years?"

Walt hesitated, and a touch of color flushed his cheeks. "Yes."

"But what?" I asked. "What is it you're not telling us?"

"Nothing. Just personal business."

I stepped closer to him. "Walt, there's nothing more personal than murder. Whatever you're hesitant to share pales in comparison."

He sighed. "Lynne and Kenny met when he transferred to her school. She was a year behind. They started dating. Kenny graduated and William Ormandy, or Willie as Kenny called him back then, came to UNC-Asheville. Lynne met him through Kenny and, well, she was smitten with him. She started going with him. That hurt my son, but Lynne was young and impressionable. Then Willie met another girl, an older student, and Lynne was out. I think Willie was so absorbed and into his music that he didn't realize the damage he'd done to his relationships with both Kenny and Lynne."

"Yet he played for their wedding," Nakayla said.

"Time passed. Like I said, William Ormandy was oblivious to other people's feelings. He came back to Asheville a couple of times and called Kenny. My son wasn't one to hold a grudge, and he and Lynne were back together by then."

I thought about the older student who was now Madison Kirkpatrick. "Do you know who the girl was?"

"Me?" He couldn't help but laugh. "I never knew what was going on with my son's romances. But everything worked out in the—" His breath caught. "Until now."

"Had Ormandy told Ken he was coming to play this concert?" I asked.

"No, but Kenny saw the publicity. He hoped they'd get together."

"Let me get one question behind us," I said. "And it has to be asked."

Without waiting, Walt said, "No, I didn't doctor those samples. I was home that night, right where you found me. No, I have no other corroboration before then, but if I'd been with Kenny, I wouldn't have left him."

"Did he usually collect his samples alone?"

"No. River Watchers tend do things in groups. It builds community."

"No particular names?" I pressed.

"His friend, Paul Clarkson. And sometimes he'd go with the director, Eli Patterson."

Clarkson had come looking for Ken the morning after he died. And he knew the combination to the storage chest. Eli Patterson claimed to have found the package, but he could have just said that it was on the chest to throw suspicion off any River Watchers, himself included.

"We've spoken with both of them," I said, and left it at that.

"You believe me, don't you? Neither Kenny nor I would doctor any samples."

Nakayla gave him a sympathetic smile. "We believe you. And I want you to finish the house Ken started." She stepped forward and hugged him.

Chapter Sixteen

We had just left Walt when my phone rang displaying a number I didn't recognize. I answered it anyway. "Hello."

"Is this Sam Blackman?"

The voice sounded familiar but I couldn't place it. "Yes. Who's speaking?"

"Paul Clarkson. Ted said you wanted to speak with me."

"Thanks for calling. Just a few follow-up questions. Are you someplace you can talk?"

"In my car. Alone. What's up?"

"First, let me put you on speaker. My partner Nakayla's with me." I handed her the phone so that I could drive hands free. She and Clarkson exchanged a brief greeting.

"We've learned something that's not for public release," I said.

"Yes?" He sounded curious.

"The Raleigh lab reports the samples we thought came from Kirkgate Paper's landfill had a dangerously high level of dioxin."

Clarkson gave a low whistle. "And it must be leaching into the Pigeon River again."

"That's the odd part. Sheriff Hudson and Eli Patterson conducted a retest. They found the site clean."

"Really? So there was some kind of lab mix-up?"

"That could have been the case, except before the information was made public, a newspaper reporter received an anonymous tip that the contamination had been discovered. Our suspicion is whoever doctored the original samples had wanted the results in bold headlines."

"You mean to embarrass the Kirkpatricks?"

"Can you think of another reason?"

The speaker phone went silent a few seconds, and then Clarkson offered an interesting supposition. "Well, it's no secret Kirkgate Paper wants to expand their mill. A competitor could benefit if that expansion were curtailed or delayed."

"What about an avid environmentalist?"

"Is that directed at me?" he snapped.

"No. You seem to get along fine with the Kirkpatricks. Also with Ken, right? Weren't you supposed to pick up the samples from him Monday morning?"

"That was the plan. I was going to package them, complete the paperwork, and get them to Eli Patterson for shipment. I was as surprised as anyone when Ken wasn't there. And then to learn he was dead." His voice trailed off.

"Do you have any leadership responsibilities with River Watchers?"

"Not really. I help schedule the volunteers and we often have guest speakers at our monthly meetings. I've arranged for a few of them. Ken was more active in the nuts and bolts of the organization."

"Do you know much about the funding for River Watchers?"

"Just that it relies upon donations. Like most nonprofits, money is always tight."

"And when contamination is found and made public?"

Again, the phone was silent a moment while Clarkson pondered the question. "Donations go up, including from the offending companies. You don't think Ken and Eli were involved in some kind of conspiracy?"

"No, I don't."

"But Eli alone?"

"We have no reason to think he didn't do exactly what he said. He found the shipping-ready parcel on the collection chest Monday morning and sent it off. Unless you know something different."

"No. All I know is that my friend is dead and I have no idea why."

I looked at Nakayla in the glow of the dashboard lights to see if she had any further questions. She shook her head.

"Well, that's what we're trying to find out," I said. "If you think of anything, let us know."

"Definitely. So is this contamination story going to be spread across the morning paper?"

"I doubt it. The reporter will have both test results before his deadline. It would be irresponsible to print that a spill had occurred. So, the good news is Kirkgate Paper won't be libeled by someone's vendetta. A vendetta that may have killed Ken Stokes."

"Yes," Clarkson agreed. "And I'm glad you and Nakayla are pushing for answers. Someone needs to even the score."

———

Nakayla and I found Ted Kirkpatrick engaged in conversation with an older couple in the sitting area of the inn's main room. We were hesitant to interrupt, but Ted waved us over.

"Sam, Nakayla, this is Linda and Mark Sawyer from Charlotte. They planned on staying here tonight only, but I've convinced them to extend their visit through Saturday and attend the Wilma Dykeman lecture."

"And listen to the sneak preview from Mr. Ormandy's Blue Ridge Concerto," gushed the woman. "It's so exciting to think that he's upstairs writing it as we speak."

I turned to Ted. "Is he?"

"Minor revisions. William shared some of his thinking with the Sawyers."

"I even suggested he work in a banjo part," the man added.

The woman frowned. "You'd want a banjo part written for 'Silent Night.'"

"Well, he said he'd consider it, didn't he?"

"He was just being polite." She grabbed her husband by the upper arm and led him toward the stairs. "Come on, Mark, let's let these people visit." She looked back over her shoulder. "Nice to meet you all. Maybe we'll see you Saturday night."

When they reached the first stair landing, Ted said, "Why don't we talk out on the veranda. No one's there."

We settled into three chairs at the far end. Dusk had deepened into night and the birds had been replaced by crickets. A cool breeze drifted across us bearing the faint smell of honeysuckle and the stars played peekaboo with wisps of fragmented clouds. It was an evening to remind me why I would never leave these ancient hills.

"So, any news?" Ted spoke barely above a whisper.

"Not really," Nakayla said. "No fingerprints on the envelope and letter. Too many on the package exterior. Professor Slocum might be the culprit, but only if he's a terrific actor."

"William's convinced it's Slocum," Ted said. "Maybe he'll also convince himself Slocum won't do anything now that you've confronted him." He started to rise from his chair.

"We have just a few more questions," I said.

Ted plopped back down with a sigh.

I leaned forward, elbows on knees. "Tell me what you can about your relationship with the River Watchers."

"There's not much to tell. The organization was formed in the aftermath of the PVP lawsuits in the 1990s. It benefited from funding promised as part of that settlement."

"Funding? What kind of funding are we talking about?"

"A grant that Eli Patterson applied for. He had the most detailed proposal—not only the water monitoring but educational programs for schoolchildren as well as adults. Boy Scouts, Girl Scouts, community colleges, all benefited from the River Watchers outreach programs."

"So, this grant carried through to operating expenses?"

"No. It paid for getting established as a nonprofit 501(c)(3) and about three years of operating expense. Eli and his board had to raise funds beyond that."

"And you've been financially supportive," I said.

"I've got no problem with their mission. Luke's closer to the finances as he heads up PR and our corporate donations, some of which come from a charitable trust that I hope will outlive the company, assuming our family sells it someday. As to our support, I believe we give at least a hundred thousand a year. I can't speak to what other support River Watchers might receive."

"And if toxic levels spiked, how would that affect donations?"

Ted thought a moment. "We'd go proactive. Probably give even more money."

I said nothing. We listened to the crickets.

"You don't think this was a scheme to get more donations, do you?"

I let the crickets answer him for a few seconds before saying, "I don't know, Ted. Maybe you should check on Kirkgate Paper's recent support."

When Ted had left, Nakayla and I returned to our room for a few minutes before checking on Ormandy.

She sat on the edge of the bed and kicked off her shoes. "Why did you ask Ted about his donations?"

"To get an idea of the dollars at play. Just because something is a nonprofit doesn't mean a lot of cash doesn't flow through it. Money, love, revenge. We might have one or all of these motives in this case."

"And what's your leading contender?"

"Why, love, of course… What else would you expect from a romantic guy like me?"

Nakayla laughed. "Certainly not subtlety. Why don't you go up and tell Beethoven he's safe while I slip into something more comfortable?"

"I'd love to."

Ormandy answered with an annoyed, "Come in," when I knocked on the door of Bartók's Retreat. I tried the knob. Unlocked.

Ormandy set down a score sheet. "Anything on the bird?"

"No. We're kind of at a dead end."

Ormandy shrugged. "It's Slocum. I don't care what he says. He won't do anything now that he knows we know."

"I'd still be cautious if I were you."

"Sure. I'm glad you and Nakayla are here."

"Then you'll keep locking your door?"

"Yeah. Sorry."

I decided to probe a little while he was talkative. "Have you spoken to Lynne?"

His cheeks flushed. "I…I haven't had the chance. I will. Yes. At the funeral Saturday. She's…she's a sweet girl. I feel so bad for her."

Ormandy's awkward stumbling made me feel I was finally witnessing some genuine sympathy from the man.

"Well, I'll let you get back to work."

He looked down at his score, his identity, and the aura of compassion disappeared. "Yes," he murmured.

I was no longer part of his world.

———

Nakayla and I left the Albemarle Inn after another delicious breakfast. The morning paper contained no mention of the toxic report from Raleigh. Evidently, responsible news judgment had prevailed after the reporter had followed up on Ted Kirkpatrick's suggestions to speak with Sheriff Hudson. I decided my first order of business upon reaching the office would be to brighten the sheriff's morning with a phone call.

"A warning," he grumbled. "I haven't had my quota of coffee."

"I just wanted you to know William Ormandy says he hasn't spoken to Lynne Stokes, and we're not any closer to uncovering who sent him the death threat."

"In other words, as far as the case goes, today is still yesterday."

"And what's your day?"

He laughed. "No better."

"Have you got a report on Ormandy's whereabouts before his dinner with Ted Kirkpatrick?"

"Not yet. I expect his GPS data from the cell towers later today. I did get the information on Ken Stokes's phone. Before the water destroyed it, he'd received one call in the afternoon from Paul Clarkson. Other than that just a few calls from his wife and his father."

"That fits. Clarkson said he spoke to Ken about getting the samples from him Monday morning. Any forensics on the doctored ones?"

"No prints. Either on the vials or the interior packaging. Plenty on the exterior carton where every UPS employee in North Carolina must have handled it." Hudson couldn't keep the frustration out of his voice. "And, of course, the shipping label was filled out in block letters that would bring first graders into the suspect pool."

"What about the nature of the toxic waste?"

"That's an interesting point," Hudson said. "Lab analysis shows the dioxin to be highly concentrated. The levels are above what even the mill would have turned out."

My knowledge of chemistry was limited to mixing baking soda and vinegar in my toy rockets when I was eight. "Any ideas on the source then?"

"Dioxin is most commonly formed by burning chlorine-based chemical compounds with hydrocarbons. That's the lab tech's explanation. I really don't understand it. But he said you can form dioxin by burning chlorine-rich waste in a backyard burn-barrel. The EPA warns the open burning of household waste in barrels is potentially one of the largest sources of airborne dioxin in the United States. The lab tech says it would be a fairly simple procedure to infuse those particles into water to purposely create a dioxin cocktail."

"And how many mountain households burn their trash?"

"Way too many. Between the barrel-burning mountaineers and the first graders, my suspect pool runneth over."

"Man, you've got my sympathy."

"I need more than your sympathy. Any ideas are welcome. Where are you going with your investigation?"

"Searching in the background till something jumps to the foreground. I'm interested in Kirkgate Paper's relationship to the River Watchers."

"We didn't find anything down that road. They seem to have a good relationship."

I was tempted to say that maybe he hadn't looked in the right spot, but I had no assurance we would fare any better. Still, the angle of a money motive should never be ruled out, so it wasn't a waste of time to cover the same territory.

"Let's just say I'm looking for more rocks to turn over, Sheriff."

"Good luck. Let me know what crawls out."

While I drove to the River Arts District, Nakayla searched the internet for any information on the River Watchers, whether from annual reports or public tax documents. I chose the more direct approach—a face-to-face with Executive Director Eli Patterson.

I realized he might not be in the office yet, but he'd mentioned the watchers were gathering tonight for a celebration of Ken's life. I suspected Patterson might be in early putting the finishing touches on the tribute video. I found him editing a montage of stills set to a simple instrumental melody of fiddle and banjo.

I stood behind Patterson as he played the last minute of poignant photographs of Ken on the mountain streams: in his kayak, fly fishing with friends, Ken and Lynne picnicking in Pisgah Forest, and closing with a close-up of Ken standing soaking wet in the middle of the Pigeon River. His grin a mile wide. I was struck by the irony. He died where he loved to live.

Patterson turned away from his keyboard, but not before wiping his eyes.

"Very nice," I said. "I hope you're giving a copy to Lynne and Walt."

"Oh, yes. Lynne was kind enough to share family photos." He took a deep breath and his shoulders slumped. "I can't believe he's gone." He pointed for me to take a neighboring chair. "What is it I can help you with?"

I eased slowly into the seat, thinking how I could begin my questions without sounding accusatory. "Have you spoken with Sheriff Hudson?"

"Not since he had me take the second set of samples from the river and the landfill. What's happened?"

"The samples you overnighted for the sheriff came back clean. The ones you found on your collection chest Monday morning were dangerously high in dioxin."

Patterson's mouth dropped open. I could almost hear the gears turning in his brain as he made sense of what occurred.

"That means someone deliberately delivered contaminated materials to us. They wanted to create a pollution scare."

I nodded. "That's the only conclusion I can come to. But who would benefit?"

"Someone who has a grudge against Kirkgate Paper," he said. "Or maybe Ted Kirkpatrick personally."

"A River Watcher?"

"One of our people? That's absurd. We work to keep our water pure so people can enjoy it and safely drink it. They'd be going against our whole reason for existing."

"Existing," I repeated. "You brought River Watchers into existence."

"Me and a lot of others. You don't know how serious the problem was. People were dying. Children were dying."

"And you got a grant, founded your organization, and even received funds from the paper mills."

His eyes narrowed. "And for almost thirty years we've run an aboveboard operation. If you're suggesting I'm in the pocket of the paper companies, then you're sadly mistaken."

"Not at all. The paper mills should have supported you. They clearly caused the problem. The deaths were on their hands. But now that the pollution levels have been greatly reduced and the river's been rejuvenated, are you getting the support, publicly and privately, that you once did?"

He thought a moment, a moment during which I tried to look as friendly and non-threatening as possible.

"No," he admitted. "We don't receive the funds we once did. At least not from the mills. They mainly come from environmental organizations or private citizens."

"And would you expect donations to go up or down if contamination was on the rise?"

"I would hope people would wake up and pony up. But I can't see one of our supporters resorting to such a deed simply to raise funds. And it would be short-lived once the sites were retested."

"But a certain amount of damage would have been done," I argued. "And money would probably be easier to raise."

Patterson rose from his chair and started pacing around the small room. "Then I'd be your prime suspect. But why the hell would I have killed Ken Stokes? Why would anyone? Everybody in River Watchers loved him."

"I don't know, but that's why I have to ask these questions."

He stopped and returned to his chair. "I understand. I hope you understand how upsetting this whole business has become."

"I do. And I just need to ask one more thing. You said the paper mills aren't contributing like they once did. Does that include Kirkgate Paper?"

"Sadly, it does. They used to be our lead donor. A hundred thousand. This year they cut it to fifty. Luke said they had to hold onto capital reserves to satisfy the bank requirements for their loans for the expansion."

"And that was from Luke, not Ted?"

Patterson threw up his hands. "He said it was a tough decision he and his father had to make. They hoped to return to their earlier levels once they increased production. So, we've had to tighten our belts and curtail some of our programs. Mainly our youth and educational offerings."

"And yet they're the lead sponsor for the Asheville Luminaries Festival."

"Yeah. It's a good event but it kind of hurts thinking those funds could have been ours."

I stood and extended my hand. "Thanks for letting me interrupt you. I hope everything goes well tonight."

Patterson rose and we shook. He glanced back at the close-up of Ken on the video monitor. "You know what the greatest challenge is?"

"No, sir."

He turned to me and I could see every year of his crusade etched into his face. "Trying to hope that somehow, some good comes out of this tragedy. When the lawsuits created the opportunity for River Watchers to be founded, I thought at least some good resulted from the deaths caused by the Pigeon River pollution. But what good can come from the death of a man, a father-to-be, like Ken?"

"I don't know."

"Then maybe that's your mission. To find that good."

Chapter Seventeen

"To find that good."

As I drove back to the office, Eli Patterson's words haunted me. I was on a quest for justice; good was even more elusive. Would putting someone in prison balance good against evil? How would that be good for Ken and Lynne's unborn child? What good ever comes from revenge?

Revenge. I'd lost a leg in Iraq, not to faceless jihadists, but fellow United States soldiers whose corrupt enterprise I threatened to expose. My leg was a pale loss compared to the loss of the lives of two members of my investigative team. I'd had my revenge, and the satisfaction was as short-lived as snow falling on a mountain stream.

Revenge. A motive every bit as strong as love or money. A relentless urge that once achieved often cools to sadness. What good is there in that? Sadness and bitterness.

"How'd it go?" Nakayla turned from her computer screen as I entered.

"Patterson seems forthcoming. He said that Kirkgate's donation to them has been cut from a hundred thousand to fifty, and it's having an impact on their mission. He admitted a pollution scare would probably help their fundraising."

"So, should we rule him out?"

"For being truthful? No, he was just stating what's obvious. And though he seemed genuinely torn up about Ken's death and Lynne's plight, I've dealt with suspects whose tears could earn an Oscar."

"Interesting about the budget impact," Nakayla said. "Guess who's their treasurer."

"Don't tell me it was Ken."

"Close. Lynne Stokes. Looking at last year's annual report, I learned she took that office around the time she'd have learned about her pregnancy. Prior to that she'd been a field monitor like Ken."

"One more point of friction between the Stokeses and Kirkpatricks. I assume Lynne felt the pressure of the budget shortfall. She'd have complained to Ken."

Nakayla nodded. "Which puts Ken back in the frame with a motive for doctoring the samples. Increase fundraising, if only short-term."

That possibility ran counter to every impression Ken had made on me. "Well, I'm not going to let this lie."

"What's your plan?"

I headed for my office. "I'm going to ask Ted why the funds were cut and why he told me otherwise."

But, in the few steps to my desk, I changed my mind. Ted said Luke was closer to the donations and PR functions of the company. He should be the person I asked. I walked down the hall to Hewitt's suite.

Shirley looked up from her computer. "Clarence Darrow is in court this morning."

"As a lawyer or a defendant?"

She flashed a broad grin. "I knew there was a reason I liked you."

"Good, because I came to ask you for a favor."

"I didn't say I liked you that much."

"Information is all." I explained why I needed to talk to Luke Kirkpatrick.

"What do you want? Phone numbers? Addresses?"

"I'd like to know where I'm likely to find him now."

"Come on, Sam. Do you know how many brewpubs there are in Asheville?"

I wasn't sure she was kidding. "Someone reached him somewhere to set up that initial interview."

"T'was I," she confessed. "I guess I could track him down for you."

"I'd prefer not to have him think I'm working for Hewitt in the conversation."

She eyed me suspiciously. "Found some dirt on our golden boy?" Nothing got past Shirley.

"Digging," was all I said.

"Well, as far as phones go, I have a mobile, a home landline, and two office numbers. Plus work and home addresses."

"Why two offices?"

"One's the mill. The other is the Marie Kirkpatrick Foundation, the charitable organization Ted started. He put Luke in charge of it."

"Who's Marie?"

"Luke's mother. Ted's first wife. And that foundation along with the PR efforts of Kirkgate Paper are run out of a separate office." She smiled. "An office in the Jackson Building. That's where I reached him."

She smiled because the Jackson Building was only a block away.

In 1924, this first skyscraper in Western North Carolina boasted fifteen stories, the tallest in the state. The neo-gothic style gave the building the distinctive flair of a bygone era. When it opened, a searchlight and telescope were housed on the top. Grotesque gargoyles leapt from the four upper corners and the pinnacle tower caught the eye of Hollywood. The climactic scene of the 1939 classic film *The Hunchback of Notre Dame* was shot atop the Jackson Building.

The office of the Marie Kirkpatrick Foundation bore no resemblance to the haunts of Quasimodo. I opened the unlocked door to a two-room suite on the seventh floor. The furniture looked like it had been shipped in from Ikea. A computer screen sat on a minimalist desk with no receptionist in the empty chair. Four gray leather chairs encircled a glass-top conference table near the window. An interior door on the left stood ajar, and Luke's voice carried through the crack. I froze, waiting to hear if someone was with him. It quickly became apparent he was on the phone.

"What time is his golf game?"

Silence.

"Then come by the house at two. Wear something easy to slip out of." He laughed. "We might not even make it to the pool."

It sounded like Luke was mixing his public relations with his private relations. Not wanting to create an awkward scene, I stepped back into the hall, planning to close the door and knock.

"Sure, Maddy, skinny-dipping works for me."

Too much information. I rapped my knuckles on the door-jamb. "Hello? Anybody home?"

"Gotta go. Someone's here."

I stayed on the threshold until Luke walked out of his office. He looked like he could have been walking up to the first tee. Casual Friday brought to you by Tommy Hilfiger.

He also looked stunned. "Sam, what are you doing here?"

"Not interrupting, I hope."

"No, no." He glanced around the office like he'd just wandered into it. "Cindy, my assistant, has Fridays off. I was just catching up on a few things before getting an early start on the weekend myself." He gestured to the table. "Please, sit. Has there been a break in the case?"

He sat and I took the chair opposite.

"Not really. I'm learning more about River Watchers from Eli Patterson and the role Ken played. Eli said Lynne Stokes was their treasurer."

"Really? I wasn't aware of that."

I glanced down through the glass top and saw Luke's right leg twitching. "Oh, I thought you supervise the donations for the company?"

"I do, but at the executive level. Eli is my contact, not his staff or volunteers."

"Was he upset when you cut back your level of funding?"

"Who said we cut back?"

"Eli. Fifty thousand rather than a hundred. One hundred is what your father told me Kirkgate Paper donated. But you must not see their work as important as he does."

The leg tremor increased. "No, no. It's strictly a bookkeeping change. River Watchers will get a hundred thousand this year. I now pay half of it from the foundation and half directly from the mill. It's what the accountants recommended. I just haven't written the foundation's check yet."

If Luke played poker, he held the title of world's worst bluffer. Something had definitely set him on edge.

"Why are you interested in the contributions to River Watchers?" he asked.

I weighed keeping Hudson's discovery a secret or breaking the news. I opted to push forward.

"Because the samples we first thought Ken might have taken tested toxic. But they might have been doctored and I don't believe Ken was responsible."

Luke's eyes widened. "Someone from River Watchers did it because they thought I'd halved the donation?"

I shrugged. "Maybe. You might want to make sure Eli Patterson knows that foundation gift is coming so that he can share it with his team. I'd better update your father on the misunderstanding."

"No!" The word exploded from his mouth. "I mean I can tell him. It's my fault there was the screwup. Besides, he's lunching at the club before a round of golf." He forced a smile. "You'd be wise not to upset him. It'll ruin his score."

I forced my own smile, though my stomach knotted. "No, I wouldn't want to ruin someone's score."

———

When Nakayla and I formed our detective agency, we'd agreed to steer clear of one type of investigation—the cheating spouse. We wouldn't be creeping around and shooting grainy photos through bedroom windows. Our first two cases, the murder of Nakayla's sister and the answer to why I'd been targeted in Iraq, netted us multiple millions of dollars that we kept in an offshore account. We could afford to be choosey.

As I sat in my CR-V a half block from Luke Kirkpatrick's home, I told myself a murder investigation trumped a cheating spouse any day of the week. And if that investigation meant shooting photos through a bedroom window, then so be it.

I'd driven by Luke's two-story house around one thirty. His black BMW SUV was parked on the apron of the driveway beside his two-car garage. The door was open, revealing a vintage Alpha Romeo convertible and another space large enough to accommodate a second vehicle. The Alpha's hood was up and a protective pad was draped over one fender. It looked like Luke's hobby was fixing classic automobiles. Beyond the garage, a six-foot-high privacy fence concealed what I assumed to be a swimming pool. A circulation pump sat on a concrete pad outside the fence. Rhododendron bushes had been planted in an effort to conceal it.

As the time neared two, I slid down in my seat, hoping to be unnoticed by anyone driving by. Two o'clock came and went. By two fifteen, I began to think I'd misunderstood Luke's end of the phone conversation. Then, in the side mirror, I saw a red Miata round the curve behind me. Its deep wax polish shone like a sparkling ruby. Almost as bright as the diamonds dangling from Madison Kirkpatrick's ears. Maddy.

I watched as she parked the Miata in the attached garage, emerged from the car, and flipped a wall switch as she entered the home's interior. The garage door descended. I pulled out my phone and opened an app that gave the camera a greater zoom range.

My options were limited. If I tried sneaking around the house, I didn't know which rooms were which. Odds were if any "afternoon delight" was occurring, it would be in an upper bedroom. I drew the line at climbing a drainpipe.

The overheard phone remark about the pool seemed to be my only avenue other than to wait for the garage door to open and maybe snap a photo of Luke kissing his stepmother in a manner that would make Oedipus blush. So, the rhododendrons hiding the filter system might also hide me.

The street was deserted, and I moved from the car at a walker's pace. If someone appeared, I'd simply keep walking. I circled back from a neighbor's yard to position the privacy fence between me and Luke's house until I could reach the shelter of the shrubbery. I crawled against the humming recirculating unit and crouched down. The lower part of a fence slat had been cut away to allow hoses to pass through, and the modification created about a three-inch gap. I went from crouching to lying on my stomach, not unlike when I was a boot camp recruit on a rifle range. My phone plugged the hole so that from the other side, the only thing visible was a black square unlikely to draw attention. I, however, had a view of the pool and pool house that ranged from wide angle to close up.

The ground surrounding the pump and bushes had been covered in pine needles. They weren't as annoying as the sands of Iraq, but after fifteen minutes of lying prone, my forearms began to itch. I feared I shared my location with an ant freeway.

I was on the verge of abandoning what was becoming a fool's adventure when a high-pitched giggle sounded from the pool house. I started the video record function a few seconds before Madison burst through the door. She gave new meaning to a two-piece bathing suit: two earrings. As my grandfather would have said, she was buck naked. Luke chased her, snapping a towel at her buttocks. He wore only sunglasses.

Madison dove into the water to escape. Luke tossed the towel and sunglasses onto a deck chair and jumped in after her.

I cut the recording, too embarrassed to capture any more because all I could think was how decent a man Ted Kirkpatrick seemed to be and that this was how his son and wife repaid his kindness.

I kept the phone in place blocking the hole until I rolled clear. The two illicit lovers were so engrossed in each other that I probably could have sat poolside and they wouldn't have noticed me.

I returned to my car and sat for a moment, processing what I'd just witnessed. If Madison hadn't been at her bridge club the night Ken died, her likely location would have been Luke's bed. No wonder he went out of his way to pick up his father when word came of Ken's death. But, I suffered misgivings about turning the video over to Sheriff Hudson. For one thing, I'd been trespassing. For another, I didn't want to be labeled as a sneaking, creeping, bedroom-peeking P.I. And, was what I'd witnessed even relevant to our case? If Ken had learned about the affair, then yes, Luke definitely had a motive to silence him. But that didn't explain the toxic samples. Maybe it didn't need to.

There seemed to be only one thing to do. I called Hewitt Donaldson.

Hewitt played the video on my phone for a third time. His face showed no sign of erotic voyeurism, simply disgust. He slid the offending instrument across the conference table to me.

We were the only ones in the room. I'd not even shared the clip with Nakayla. Yet.

Hewitt took a deep breath. "Well, this puts me in one hell of a bind."

"How so?"

"I reviewed Ted's prenup with Madison. There's a clause stipulating faithfulness that affects her share of the estate. I now know that clause should be triggered. Am I obligated to tell him? But her partner isn't some muscle-toned Casanova from a fitness gym. He's Ted's son, for God's sake. This video would destroy my friend."

"I can't advise you on that."

"I'm not asking for your advice," he snapped.

I said nothing.

Hewitt got up and began pacing around the table. "Sorry. You're only the messenger. But what were you doing there in the first place?"

I explained about my conversation with Eli Patterson and the discrepancy between the amount of the Kirkgate Paper donation and what Ted had told me. Ken Stokes would have been aware of the budget crunch and could have devised a plan to increase donations. "Confronting Luke about the issue brought me to his office where I overheard him talking with someone called Maddy. It didn't take a genius to suspect who Maddy might be."

Hewitt's eyes sharpened. "And what was Luke's response to your inquiry?"

"He said the second half of the funds was coming from the charitable foundation. It was a very convenient explanation, one that could have been contrived on the spur of the moment."

Hewitt stopped pacing. "I know the accountant who files the foundation's annual report. He not only reviews the foundation's investments but also its charitable donations. By law, a certain percentage needs to be bestowed to qualifying organizations each year. Transparency is part of the foundation's charter, so I shouldn't have any trouble getting specifics." He pointed to my phone. "Let's hold off on doing anything with the video until I have a chance to dig a little deeper."

His approach seemed reasonable.

"How did Ted meet Madison in the first place?"

Hewitt slid back into his chair. "She worked in member services at the country club. When Marie died, Madison reached out to him on behalf of the club. I think Ted was vulnerable to the attention of a younger woman. And they say there's no fool like an old fool. They started playing tennis together. She's quite good actually. Then she started accompanying him to functions and before I knew it, Ted approached me to review the prenup."

"And Luke?"

"Luke was still married at the time. Now whether he and Madison had already started their fling, who knows? That's not the point. It's what's happening now. And if I can find Luke's played fast and loose with the foundation's funds, then I have a less—how should I put it—a less revolting revelation to bring to Ted's attention. And we'll see where it goes from there. Meanwhile, I'm asking you to keep this strictly between us. Call me a prude, but it bothers me that Nakayla or Cory or Shirley would see this."

"All right. I'll pull this off my phone, but I'm keeping it on a secure disk and creating some stills. You never know what leverage we might need to get to the bottom of this whole mess."

"Thanks." Hewitt relaxed for the first time since viewing the video. "I'll see what I can learn this afternoon. What's your schedule for the weekend?"

"Ken Stokes's funeral and then the Wilma Dykeman lecture at the university."

Hewitt shook his head. "Ken's getting his wish. Recognition for Wilma. On the day of his burial."

Chapter Eighteen

Morning Star United Methodist Church sat atop a knoll overlooking a small valley. The age of the brick structure and the age of the grave markers in the adjacent cemetery testified that the surrounding mountain community had made the church a center of worship and fellowship for decades.

The sanctuary must have been the site of hundreds of funerals. Ken Stokes's had to be one of the saddest.

At ten thirty, Nakayla and I parked in the church lot. Even at that hour, the spring morning still held patches of fog that crept across the ground, carrying a dampness that drove attendees inside rather than lingering for outside conversation.

We found the small sanctuary already two-thirds full. My eyes immediately went to the wooden casket positioned in front of the chancel. Green bunting hid the wheeled pedestal upon which it rested. A sprig of lilac draped over its curved top.

I spotted Eli Patterson seated in a pew with a group I guessed to be Ken's fellow River Watchers. In front of them, Paul Clarkson and William Ormandy were together. Across the aisle sat Hewitt, Cory, and Shirley. Hewitt turned around and gave a beckoning wave for us to join them.

Ten minutes later the pews were filled, all except the front one reserved for family. An older woman stepped to the piano in the chancel and began playing a medley of hymns. What little whispering had existed now ceased, and a respectful silence fell upon the crowd.

As the final chord of "Amazing Grace" faded, a young minister entered from a door to the left of the chancel and signaled for all to rise. I was surprised that she was a woman somewhere in her thirties. In her black robe, she looked at home as much as a man, and I chastised myself for thinking this rural church wouldn't accept a female pastor.

Behind her came Lynne and Walt, a visible testament to how small their family had become. Walt's face was ashen; Lynne's eyes fixed on the floor as she followed her father-in-law to the empty pew.

The service was short but not shortchanged. The minister had obviously spent time with Lynne and Walt because she shared stories about how Ken's building of houses was a metaphor for his building of relationships. She wove in the theme of a river, acknowledging his work for water purity and saying how someday we must all cross over that river to the place Ken had gone. Cross over on a bridge built with love, love that would keep us always connected to Ken, love that touched even an unborn child.

We stood as the pallbearers wheeled the casket down the aisle with Lynne and Walt close behind. Then, in orderly fashion by pew, we dispersed and proceeded to the cemetery, walking down the slope through the wet grass to where a funeral tent sheltered the open grave. A few folding chairs had been placed at the edge for Walt, Lynne, and older, frailer attendees. Nakayla and I hung back, allowing others to move nearer.

The interment lasted about five minutes and finished with the Lord's Prayer, with some asking for forgiveness of debts, others for forgiveness of trespasses. During the petition to "deliver us from evil" someone's cell phone rang. I added a prayer that I'd switched mine to vibrate and cracked open my eyes to see who the offending culprit might be.

Hewitt Donaldson pawed at his suit pocket, trying to silence the incessant, melodic chirp. He muted it with the "Amen," and then the minister pronounced a benediction for we, the living.

Nakayla and I started back up the hill. I noticed that Hewitt had wandered off about thirty yards with the phone now to his ear.

Cory and Shirley caught up with us. "Wouldn't put it past him to have called himself," Shirley said. "Give the impression he's always in demand."

"You don't believe that, do you?" Nakayla asked.

"No. But funerals make me so depressed. I've got to have some way to lighten the mood."

"Chocolate," Cory said. "That's my remedy. Who's up for the French Broad Chocolate Lounge?"

Shirley clapped her hands. "Much better than making fun of Hewitt. You and Sam want to join us?"

"Did you ride with Hewitt?" I asked.

"No," Cory said. "Just Shirley and me. Hewitt said he needed some thinking time on the drive over."

I suspected Hewitt was still mulling over the mess we'd uncovered with Luke and Madison. As he'd told me, when you turn over rocks looking for one thing, you never know what else will come crawling out. "I want to talk to him a few minutes. Nakayla, you can go along with them if you like. It's a little early for me and chocolate."

Nakayla eyed me suspiciously. I'd never turned down chocolate in the past.

"Come on, girlfriend," Shirley urged. "I promise to curtail my snitty mood. Sam can find his way home. And if he can't, there'll still be the chocolate, an exceptional consolation prize."

Nakayla had to laugh. "All right." She gave me a peck on the cheek. "Try to be home by midafternoon to let Blue out."

"How much chocolate are you planning to eat?"

"Not that much. But Cory, Shirley, and I just might make a day of it." She turned to the two women. "Would you like to see how the house is coming along? Maybe give me some decorating ideas?"

They carried their conversation up the hill, leaving me with Hewitt and whatever thoughts he might share. The lawyer waved for me to come to him, the phone still at his ear. I stopped about six feet away to give him a little privacy, and then looked back at the new grave. Walt and Lynne were standing now. I saw Ormandy and Clarkson each give her a hug. The men were visibly upset.

I turned to Hewitt. He held up one finger signaling he'd be only a minute longer.

"Thanks, Vernon. Can you check that out first thing Monday morning? It's important we find out who set up the account." With those words, he disconnected.

I came closer. "What's up?"

"Let's take a little stroll." He began walking between the gravestones toward the rear of the church and away from the mourners. "That call that was so unpleasant during the prayer. It was from Vernon Fraser."

"Who's he?"

"Ted Kirkpatrick's personal accountant and the accountant for the Marie Kirkpatrick Foundation. He's also my accountant. Yesterday, I asked him to check out the payments made to River Watchers."

"Isn't he overstepping his bounds by sharing information about another client?"

"The charitable foundation has a policy of transparency. This includes not only grants it receives from Kirkgate Paper and other sources but also disbursements made to deserving nonprofits. Back in February, two payments were made to River Watchers, one for fifty thousand dollars and the other for a hundred thousand."

"Is that counting the one directly from Kirkgate Paper?"

"Vernon says that, other than the Luminaries Festival that's a company-sponsored promotion, Kirkgate's charitable giving now moves exclusively through the foundation. Vernon doesn't know why Luke told you otherwise because both checks came from the foundation."

"Right. Especially since more than the full amount was evidently paid. But why would Eli Patterson have lied to me?"

Hewitt stopped. "Why, indeed. Or maybe there's more going on than simple confusion over what funds came from where. Vernon Fraser has the clearance to review the foundation's bank account. This morning he logged in to make sure he was remembering accurately the issuance of the two payments. He found one on the first of February and one on the twenty-ninth. Interesting in itself since it's a leap year. Anyone searching transactions by date might not think to expand February beyond twenty-eight days."

"Or they write checks at the beginning and end of each month."

Hewitt shook his head. "Think, Sam. The end and beginning of adjacent months are consecutive days. And why not just write one check for a hundred and fifty thousand dollars?"

"Cash flow? Does your accountant have another answer?"

"He has an observation. He was able to call up the front and back images of the two checks. Not only were they deposited to different accounts, they were deposited to different banks. Luke had handwritten both checks. The smaller one was made out to River Watchers, the second had the payee's name scrunched closer together, but on close examination the 'ch' had been omitted."

"River Waters?"

"Yes. Someone reviewing the checks expecting to see River Watchers probably wouldn't catch the discrepancy. And if the actual deposit account was named River Waters, a teller would see it as legitimate."

I gave a soft whistle. "So, either Luke, or Luke in cahoots with Eli, could have siphoned off one hundred thousand dollars of foundation funds."

"It's a definite possibility. Still risky. Better to give the full amount to River Watchers, and then write the extra check beyond that. Then, if the beneficiary publicizes the contribution, the sum matches Ted's expectations. He'd have to go into the nuts and bolts of the financials to realize what happened."

"And if it's Luke, why wouldn't he do just that?"

"One word," Hewitt said. "Arrogance. The same reason he's sleeping with his father's wife. I think he enjoys the risk. Gets an adrenaline rush while thinking he's too clever by half." Hewitt's face tensed. "Well, we'll see about that. Vernon's going to check who's behind the River Waters account, and if it's Luke, then I'm going straight to Ted. I might hold back the pool video, but if Ted doesn't have a come-to-Jesus meeting with his son, then the little romp in the water is my trump card, and, by God, I'll play it."

His eyes bore into me, daring me to object.

"I've got no quarrel with that. Just keep me in the loop. I wouldn't want to be blindsided if Ted or Luke comes back to me. They'll suspect who spearheaded your inquiry, especially the pool footage." And I wanted a heads-up because I'd kept that incident from Nakayla at Hewitt's request. I should be the one to show it to her.

Hewitt relaxed. "So, see you tonight at the Dykeman lecture?"

"Nakayla and I will be there. Are you going to speak to Lynne and Walt now?"

"No. Someone might mention I interrupted a prayer to God. If it comes up, say my phone malfunctioned."

"I think they'll find operator error more believable."

Hewitt continued on around the rear of the church to the parking lot. I retraced my steps to where Lynne and Walt were still speaking to well-wishers. Then my eye caught someone purposefully heading me off. Sheriff Cliff Hudson in his dress uniform signaled for me to hold up.

"Hello, Sam. Let's stroll."

Strolling seemed to be the activity of the day.

"All right, Sheriff. Lead on." I fell in beside him.

"I wanted a few words alone." He headed farther down the cemetery's hill away from both the funeral tent and the church. "Anything I should know?" he asked softly.

His open-ended question had a number of answers, the two at the top involved sex and money.

"Working on some things."

"Do they involve William Ormandy and Madison Kirkpatrick?"

That question was even harder to sidestep. My mind raced. What did the sheriff know that I didn't? Was he testing to see how forthcoming I'd be? Had he uncovered Madison's affair? Was Ormandy a person of interest because he'd dated both Madison and Lynne?

I decided I had to give him something. "I know Ormandy and Madison were an item back in college, but I haven't been able to find any relevance to Ken Stokes's death."

"Did you know they are both liars?"

"How so?"

"We got the GPS tracking and voice calls from their cell phone accounts. Madison was supposed to be at her bridge club last Sunday night in the Montford area, but her phone was tied to a cell tower beyond that location. She placed two calls that put her in north Asheville—one at six fifteen to William Ormandy, the other at seven to Luke Kirkpatrick."

"What was Ormandy's location?"

"On I-40 about twenty miles west of here. That's from where he called Ted at six thirty."

I saw the implications. "So, he could have shown up for his dinner date on time."

"Yep," the sheriff confirmed. "The route was consistent with a drive from Cincinnati, but he lied as to when he arrived."

Had Ormandy met up with Madison? How many men was she involved with?

"Then did his location overlap Madison somewhere?"

"We don't know," the sheriff said. "He must have turned off his phone or gone into an area of no coverage. The next hit we got on a cell tower was in town just a few minutes before calling Ted Kirkpatrick to say he'd arrived."

"Eight fifteen," I said. "Ted told us that."

"Yes, which means we don't know where Ormandy was from six thirty to eight fifteen. A span that falls within the window of Ken's death. A last known location on I-40 close to the exit that would have brought him to the Pigeon River and the Kirkgate landfill."

I stopped and caught Hudson by the arm. "You don't honestly believe Ormandy had anything to do with Ken's death, do you?"

The sheriff shrugged. "I just follow the evidence. And there was one more phone call Ormandy made earlier when he was about two hours away in Knoxville."

"Do you know who to?"

The sheriff brushed his thick mustache with the back of his hand and turned to look up the hill at the few remaining mourners. "Yeah. Lynne Stokes."

It took me a second to recover from that totally unexpected name. "I'm sure there's a good reason for the call. They once dated."

"Well, Sam, I thought there'd be some connection. Ormandy wasn't just randomly dialing numbers. So I intend to question him again. But I like to have as much information ahead of time as I can gather. Which is why I'm standing in this cemetery talking to you. What else do you know?"

I couldn't see some conspiracy existing between Ormandy

and Lynne. The sheriff hadn't seen her face when we broke the news of Ken's death. But, Hudson was probably at a dead end otherwise. I felt our own inquiries offered more promise. Sex and money were at play in our investigation, and although I didn't know how the two tied into Ken's death, I had evidence in the form of video footage and check images. I decided despite what Hewitt might think, Hudson shouldn't be shut out completely.

"I don't know anything about Ormandy and Lynne, but did you find any overlap with Madison's cell phone?"

Hudson smiled. "What would you expect to find?"

"That it overlapped with Luke Kirkpatrick's."

He nodded. "From seven thirty till Ted called Luke with the word that I wanted them at the landfill. Any proof that they were together?"

"That night?" I hedged.

"Or any other night, damn it. You know where this is heading."

"I have no proof that they were together for any night." It wasn't a lie. I'd only seen them in the daytime. "But I have my suspicions. And there's something else." I started walking again, tracing the perimeter of the cemetery. "But I need you to sit on it until we know more about its implications."

"I won't hold back if I feel I need to move on something for the good of the case. Holding out could be obstruction of justice."

"Then I guess I'll have to spend the rest of the weekend or longer in your jail because I won't contribute to what could be a false accusation." I knew the sheriff thought I was withholding evidence, but I also knew I'd aroused his curiosity.

"How long are we talking about?"

"Tuesday. Wednesday at the latest."

"Okay," Hudson agreed.

"So, we're looking into banking records of River Watchers and Kirkgate donations. Lynne Stokes is the River Watchers treasurer, and she might have uncovered some sort of irregularity."

"What kind of irregularity?"

"She was having to deal with a shortfall in donations, a short-fall that might have been caused by money being diverted into another account. Whose account is yet to be determined."

"And Ken Stokes might have known this?"

"Or had his suspicions. But it could also be an honest mistake and we'd be casting aspersions on innocent people. The accountant needs to talk to the bank Monday morning. On the quiet."

"And you'll let me know something as soon as you hear?"

I looked Hudson straight in the eye. "I'm about seeking justice, not obstructing it. You'll know when I know."

Chapter Nineteen

I drove back to Asheville immersed in a swirl of thoughts. Sheriff Hudson had the data that showed Ormandy had called Lynne Stokes. The composer had then had a call from Madison, phoned Ted and lied about his location and estimated arrival, and then gone off the grid during the time Ken could have died. Had the calls to Madison and Lynne been related in some way? If Ormandy spoke to Lynne about Ken, could she have told him Ken might be at the Kirkgate landfill? Did he relay that information to Madison, who told Luke? Just because Luke's cell phone stayed overlapped with Madison's didn't mean one or both of them hadn't driven to meet Ormandy and left their phones behind.

But what possible motive could the three have shared? And who doctored the samples and delivered them to River Watchers? Conflicting motives created a muddied investigation. And just because, theoretically, Ormandy could have been at the landfill, didn't mean he was. I decided to leave that line of inquiry to Sheriff Hudson. Luke Kirkpatrick and his self-indulgent, self-destructive activities were enough to keep me busy.

———

Nakayla and I arrived early at UNC-Asheville to get a good parking space on campus. I didn't know how many attendees would be there for a lecture on Wilma Dykeman. The topic seemed rather esoteric.

Even though the program didn't begin until seven thirty, I was surprised to find the lobby fairly full at a little before seven. People clustered near the auditorium doors, waiting for them to open. I should have known an environmentally conscientious city like Asheville would support a tribute to one of their own. The crowd included a number of students who probably took courses in Environmental Studies, the lecturing professor's department.

I saw Eli Patterson and Walt Stokes talking to each other. I whispered to Nakayla, "I can't believe Walt's here on the day he buried his son."

"He knows this is what Ken argued for. He's going to see it through."

Beyond Walt and Eli stood Ted and Madison. He wore a dark blue suit; she, a white sequined dress more in keeping with a red-carpet appearance than a lecture in a college music building. I stared at her a moment as my mind involuntarily stripped away everything but her earrings. Ted was in animated conversation with a short, balding man. Whatever they were discussing caused Madison to clutch Ted's gesticulating hand in an effort to calm him down. He shook her away.

Luke Kirkpatrick had set up his baseball display tucked against the back left side of the lobby away from the main doors. Probably some fire marshal regulation. The layout appeared similar to what he'd used at last Saturday's game, although I saw only one security guard. Fifteen or twenty people stood in line to view his exhibit.

"Let's go see Luke's display," I told Nakayla.

"You saw it last weekend."

"I'd like a closer look."

"Better let me stand by the auditorium doors so I can get us good seats. I want to keep an eye on Ormandy."

When Nakayla had returned from her afternoon with Shirley and Cory, I'd brought her up to speed on the information Sheriff Hudson had shared as well as Hewitt's report from the accountant. Like me, she couldn't think of an overarching motive that explained everyone's actions.

"And I see Hewitt coming in," she added. "I'll ask if he'd like to sit with us." She moved away to intercept him.

As I crossed the lobby to the exhibition, Madison hurried ahead of me, cut through the line, and whispered something in Luke's ear. He gave a sharp shake of his head and nudged her away. She looked daggers at him and then retreated down an adjacent hall to the elevator. Evidently, whatever had upset her had disturbed her enough to seek a quieter retreat.

I joined the exhibit line. The older couple ahead of me turned around.

"Mr. Blackman. So we meet again."

I recognized Mark and Linda Sawyer, the vacationers who'd extended their stay at the Albemarle Inn.

"Yes. I'm glad you're able to be here. Looks like the program's going to be well attended."

"And I had no idea there'd be a baseball exhibit," Mr. Sawyer said.

His wife laughed. "We're lucky the Tourists aren't playing tonight or else we'd be at McCormick Field. Mark's idea of the perfect vacation is a week at Cooperstown hanging out in the Baseball Hall of Fame."

"America's game," he said defensively. "I'd trade the Panthers for a major league baseball team any day of the week and twice on Sundays."

"Well, this should be a treat for you," I said. "Autographed balls that Babe Ruth and Lou Gehrig hit for home runs here in 1931. And get the exhibitor to tell you the story of Babe Ruth's death in Asheville."

"I know it. 'The Bellyache Heard Round the World.'"

I patted him on the back. "You know your baseball history, sir."

We stepped up to the Plexiglas display case. Luke stood proudly beside it. I noticed a bat had been added to the balls.

"Hi, Sam," Luke said amiably.

"What's the story with the bat?"

"It's a vintage Louisville Slugger from the late 1920s. I have no proof Ruth or Gehrig used it, but they would have swung one like it."

Mark Sawyer leaned in closer. "Too bad it's not notched. The thing would be worth a fortune."

Luke bent to study the bat. "Notched?"

"Yeah. Ruth took to carving a notch in his bat for each home run. He started that during the second half of the 1927 season. A bat in the Hall of Fame has twenty-eight of them. That's the year he hit sixty home runs, a record that stood for thirty-four years." He sighed wistfully. "There'll never be another one like the Sultan of Swat."

"Interesting," Luke said. "But I do have an authentic signed baseball that Ruth hit out of McCormick Field in 1931."

Sawyer shifted his attention to the two autographed balls on their pedestals.

"1931?" the older man repeated.

"Yes, sir."

Sawyer shook his head. "I hate to tell you this, sonny, but someone sold you a bill of goods."

Luke's face reddened and his chest puffed out. "No, I've had both autographs authenticated."

"Maybe, but nobody hit these balls in 1931."

"Why not?"

"Because they didn't exist."

Luke stared at him in bewilderment.

"It's the stitching. It's red." Sawyer made the pronouncement like the argument was now irrefutably decided.

"So what?"

"So before 1934, the American League stitched its balls with red and blue thread and the National League used red and black thread. In 1934, baseballs were standardized for both leagues and sewn with red thread only." He pointed to the balls. "Like these." He smiled, trying to put Luke at ease. "But that doesn't mean you don't have a marvelous display and Asheville doesn't have a unique relationship with the Bambino."

"Thank you," Luke said flatly. He glared at me, as if daring me to comment.

I wasn't sure whether Luke had been caught out in a lie to inflate their value or been duped himself. "I didn't know the stitching history either," I admitted. "Maybe the previous owners had been told that same story."

Luke said nothing.

Mrs. Sawyer tugged at her husband's sleeve. "You're holding up the line, Mark. Let's go get our seats."

As I crossed the lobby to join Nakayla, Ted Kirkpatrick strode by me heading toward the baseball display.

"Good evening, Ted."

He stared right through me like I wasn't there. His face was frozen in a mask of fury, and I wondered if word of his son's embellishment of the baseball story had already reached him.

The auditorium doors opened as I joined Nakayla and Hewitt. The attorney looked like he was suffering his own bout of anger. A scowl seemed permanently etched in his forehead.

"What's going on?" I asked.

"That damn Vernon," Hewitt grumbled. "He just told Ted about the checks."

"Didn't you tell him to wait till you got more information on the River Waters account?"

"Of course I did. But he said Ted asked him if the planned donations were going well at the foundation. Vernon said he felt trapped. He admitted there was a possible deposit error and so Ted pressed him for details. When Vernon suggested they talk about it Monday, Ted said he wanted to see those checks for himself and he expected Vernon to bring copies to his house tonight, after the program."

"What did Ted say to you?"

"Nothing. Vernon at least had the good sense not to bring me into it. He told Ted it was something he caught this morning during a routine review."

I realized Vernon had to be the man I saw with Ted and Madison. "So, Vernon spoke to you?"

"Yes. And he made things worse by asking Eli about the checks. He was trying to cover his ass with everyone. Eli claims he never got a check from Kirkgate Paper, just one for fifty thousand from the foundation."

"Luke will close that account out first thing Monday," I said.

"Yeah, but he can't erase the trail. What he does have is time to concoct a story."

"For Monday," Nakayla said. "But right now his father's going to blindside him."

Hewitt and I followed her gaze to the display. Ted had pulled Luke away and was up in his son's face. Luke looked completely flustered. Ted turned away, but not before jamming his index finger into Luke's chest with one final point.

"You're right," Hewitt agreed. "Maybe this is a blessing in disguise. Ted might get to the bottom faster than we can. My job is to persuade him to tell us what he learns."

"How?" I asked.

"By threatening to go to the police. As an officer of the court, I have a responsibility to report a potential crime. Especially if Luke or Eli Patterson tries to cover it up."

"And if that doesn't work?" Nakayla asked.

"I'll find some other leverage." He shot me a quick glance, and I knew he meant the video. "But let's get settled and enjoy the evening. As a donor to the festival, I'm supposed to have reserved seats."

On the second row, we found four seats with signs reading "Hewitt Donaldson Law Firm" taped to the back. Hewitt took the one by the extra chair so he wouldn't have to fight for the armrest. I sat on the aisle where I could stretch my damaged leg.

The stage was set similarly to when I'd witnessed the blowup between Ormandy and Professor Slocum. In fact, the professor was in the seat across the aisle from me. I said, "Good evening," and he merely nodded.

The grand piano and Clarkson's array of Minimoogs had been placed farther upstage. A podium stood to the left where it wouldn't block the audience's view. Black curtains framed the backdrop and wings.

While we waited for the program to begin, I replayed the scene at the Babe Ruth exhibit in my mind. The more I thought about it, the more I became convinced that Luke had fabricated the story about the baseballs being home runs in Asheville.

A Ruth- or Gehrig-signed homer would be much more valuable than simply a ball some kid had asked the superstars to autograph. I pulled out my phone and did a quick search of memorabilia prices. A Babe Ruth autographed ball with a letter of authenticity—$20,000. Lou Gehrig—$6,000. Both pictured with blue and red stitching and identified as being from the 1932 season. It not only validated what Mark Sawyer had said about the threads, but the prices showed me that Luke could have purchased similar balls for under $30,000, and by claiming they were home runs in Asheville, inflated the value. For all that conniving, would Luke be so stupid as to construct a story that one fan so easily debunked? Yes. He was arrogant enough to make it up and too lazy to perform due diligence on whether the claim could be historically supported.

I set my phone to vibrate and dropped it in my sport coat pocket. I didn't want a replay of Hewitt's graveside debacle. A few minutes later, a distinguished-looking gentleman stood up from the front row and ascended the stairs to the stage. The audience hushed as he lightly tapped the podium microphone.

"Welcome. It's great see such a large turnout tonight. My name is Philip Derrick and I'm head of our continuing education program here at the university." He briefly promoted some upcoming events and then asked Ted Kirkpatrick to stand and be recognized for sponsoring tonight's lecture.

I would have expected Ted to be sitting down front with us, and that was where Mr. Derrick first looked. But after a few awkward seconds, as the audience swiveled in the seats trying to find him, Ted stood from the back row and gave an acknowledging wave. I didn't see Luke with him.

Derrick referred to his notes to explain the Asheville Luminaries Festival and then with that scripted segment out of the way, he broke into a broad grin. "And tonight we have a real treat. You've seen the baseball exhibit, now get ready for a taste of Blue Ridge and Bartók with composer William Ormandy on piano and our own music department graduate Paul Clarkson on the synthesizers."

An enthusiastic round of applause greeted the two men as they came from opposite wings. Both wore tuxedos, both looked relaxed and pleased to be there. Clarkson stood by his three Minimoogs, and Ormandy rested a hand upon the edge of the piano.

"Thank you," Ormandy said. "Paul and I are pleased to share a preview of next Friday's concert at the Thomas Wolfe Auditorium. We hope the excerpts we play tonight will encourage and not discourage you from attending."

Polite laughter rippled through the audience.

"Of course, that performance will feature the Asheville Symphony. Tonight, I'm afraid it's just Paul and me, although thanks to Robert Moog, Paul can make any sound from a violin to a jackhammer."

Clarkson smiled and flexed his fingers as if anxious to get his hands on a jackhammer.

"Don't worry," Ormandy said. "Neither I nor Bartók wrote for construction equipment."

The laughter was louder. To be such an obnoxious human being, Ormandy had a relaxed, warm stage presence.

"Our first piece will be taken from the second movement of Bartók's Third Piano Concerto. I know that's a lot of numbers to keep up with. Easier to say the birdsongs of his Asheville Concerto. It will be followed by a selection from my Blue Ridge Concerto that premieres next week. The motif pays tribute to our native Appalachian melodies. I'm sure you'll recognize a few."

He sat on the piano bench and turned to the keyboard. Clarkson took his place within the semicircle of his synthesizers. As they began to play, I recognized the trills I'd heard at the rehearsal. Clarkson laid in a soft bed of strings underneath the piano lead.

After about five minutes, the tone changed as Ormandy transitioned to his own composition. New birdsongs, not at all subtle, predominated. The distinctive whistle of the bobwhite became a brief call and response between the piano and the Minimoogs. A melody grew in the spaces between until I recognized the tune. Recognized it but couldn't recall its name.

"What is it?" I whispered to Nakayla.

"'Black Is the Color of My True Love's Hair.' The quintessential mountain ballad."

The melody swelled to a fullness, and then morphed into variations on the harmonies until the simpler tune again retreated. The piece ended with the bobwhite call growing softer until the lonesome, haunting sound faded away.

The applause was genuine and enthusiastic. I was surprised

that Professor Slocum stood up. A standing ovation? Then I realized he wasn't clapping as he stepped into the aisle and exited. Maybe he'd only come to check that his own composition hadn't been plagiarized.

Ormandy and Clarkson took bows and then exited via opposite wings. Philip Derrick returned to the podium.

"Wasn't that wonderful? Another round of applause, please."

Derrick then gave a brief bio of the speaker, Professor Ann Trammel, which included her work with River Watchers and cutting-edge research with the EPA. She bounded onto the stage with a physical energy I didn't expect in an academician. She couldn't have been more than thirty-five, and her tanned face evidenced more time in the outdoors than the university library.

"Wilma Dykeman," she practically shouted, as if pumping us up in a pep rally. "My hero. I'm so thrilled to tell you about her life, and more importantly, her legacy. Environmental pioneer, social and racial justice pioneer, she was the real deal." She snatched the wireless microphone out of the podium's holder and began to walk around the stage. No, it wasn't turning into a pep rally, it was a revival meeting.

"The woman was a true visionary, seeing the waste and ruin of our natural resources and calling us into action. Seeing the waste and ruin of marginalized people and pricking our conscience into facing our own complicity."

She stopped a second and coughed. I noticed a faint haze in the air. Then a bright glow erupted from each stage wing. Almost immediately a whooshing sound drowned out her voice followed by the blaring screech of a fire alarm. The professor wheeled around, looked into the wings, and then calmly spoke over the PA system, "Evacuate the building immediately and orderly. Do not push or shove. I repeat, do not push or shove."

A few people started screaming as flames became visible.

"You and Hewitt get out," I told Nakayla. "Help whomever you can."

"What about you?"

"I'll be right behind you." I said the words as I ran toward the stage, not away from it. Philip Derrick was already at the foot, helping the professor down.

"The drapes," she said. "The drapes are burning."

"Fire extinguishers?" I asked.

"I don't know where they are."

I looked to Derrick. The smoke was getting thicker and all three of us were coughing.

"I'm not familiar with this building," he managed to say. "Our priority should be to get everyone out."

He was right, but if the fire was confined to the curtains, a couple of fire extinguishers might keep it from spreading. I looked around the auditorium. The two aisles and dual sets of double doors meant people quickly made their way out without jamming the exits. The room was nearly clear. I followed Derrick and Professor Trammel into the lobby. No one had lingered. Everyone had moved on through to the outside quad.

I scanned the walls for a fire extinguisher. Nothing. Then I noticed Luke Kirkpatrick's Plexiglas case had been partially dismantled. He and the guard were gone but one of the baseballs was still on its pedestal. Surely they would have taken the bat and both balls with them. I ran to check.

Only Lou Gehrig was there. I didn't see Babe Ruth. I looked down the side hall toward the elevator. The thick end of the bat stuck out from around a corner. The wail of sirens suddenly filled the air. The firefighters would force me out of the building. I dropped the idea of finding an extinguisher and hurried for the bat.

I turned the corner and froze.

A pool of blood lay under my feet. I jumped back, from the blood, from the bat, and from the lifeless body of Luke Kirkpatrick.

Chapter Twenty

Homicide Detective Curt Newland entered the police interview room with two bottles of water. He handed one to me, then sat in a chair across the table and looked at me through red, bleary eyes. Whether it was because midnight had come and gone or because he'd suffered the sting of smoke while staying by the body until firefighters extinguished the blaze, I didn't know. Probably a combination of the two. And I figured I didn't look much better.

I'd speed-dialed his cell phone and then knelt beside Luke, ready to drag his body away if the fire drew nearer. Fortunately, Fire Station No. Seven had been only six minutes away, and the quick response meant the damage had been confined to the stage. In the side hall, I'd gone unnoticed long enough to be relieved by Newland. He'd told me to get the hell out or he'd have me arrested. Then he thanked me for preserving the crime scene.

"All right," he groaned. "Let's go through it in more official detail this time." He reached over and started an audio recording device, noting the date and time. "This is Curt Newland with Sam Blackman. Mr. Blackman, how did you, once again I might add, come to stumble over yet another dead body?"

Instead of answering, I asked, "Where's Nakayla?"

"Tuck drove her to your apartment. No use keeping everybody up all night."

I nodded my approval and then walked Newly through what I'd seen in Lipinsky Hall. The revelation that Luke's story about the baseballs wasn't true, the argument between Luke and his father, and the discrepancy in the checks written to River Watchers and how the accountant had told both Ted Kirkpatrick and Eli Patterson. Then I asked Newly if any of the others had contradicted my version of events.

"Well, Ted claims he and his son hadn't argued. He asked Luke to release the guard, pack up the exhibit, and come to his house immediately after the lecture."

"Sure looked like an argument to me."

Although we were being recorded, Newly leaned forward and lowered his voice. "Of course it was, but do you want to admit that your last conversation with your son was an argument? The man's in shock. His mind's probably denying there were any harsh words spoken."

"And why did he want Luke at his house?"

"That part fits the piece provided by the accountant, Vernon Fraser. Ted told me there was some simple mix-up with one of the foundation donations, and he wanted to clear it up before Monday."

"The simple mix-up was a hundred and fifty thousand dollars," I said.

"I know. I got Judge Wood out of bed to issue a court order freezing the foundation's assets. Tuck's already contacted the managers for both banks, one with the foundation's account and the other with whatever this River Waters might be."

"Do you know how the fire started?"

Newly held up his hand. "Who's supposed to be asking the questions here?"

"Sorry. Force of habit."

"We have a pretty good theory. You know the large trashcans on wheels the custodial staff uses to empty office waste bins?"

"Yeah."

"Two of them had been rolled behind the black curtains shielding each wing. They were both full of loose trash. The arson team's still running tests but the preliminary indication is the fires were both started with brake fluid and Pool Shock." Newly made the statement like I should immediately understand its significance.

I didn't. "I know what brake fluid is but what's Pool Shock?"

"A brand of swimming pool chlorine. Didn't you take high school chemistry? Mix it with brake fluid and it starts to smoke and then ignites through spontaneous combustion."

"We weren't into making bombs. Have you looked into Clarkson and Ormandy? They were both backstage."

"Yes, neither claimed to go behind the screening curtains, and they'd been seen at the back of the auditorium during the introduction of the professor. My question for you is who would want to kill Luke?"

"I think Walt still blames him for his son's death. Eli Patterson would be angry if he thought a donation had been pilfered."

"Could they have joined forces?"

"You mean one starts the fires while the other attacks Luke?" I shook my head. "The fires show premeditation. But how could they be sure Luke would be isolated?"

"They couldn't," Newly said. "But creating chaos creates opportunities." He rubbed his eyes. "Hell, I don't know. I'm reaching here. The most obvious suspect is Ted because of the alleged argument, but he was seated near the rear of the auditorium."

"Was his wife, Madison, with him?"

Newly cocked his head and eyed me suspiciously. "We haven't spoken with her. She was too distraught. Why do you ask?"

In my mind, I saw Madison whispering in Luke's ear. Then

him pushing her away. "Just that she might be the best person to have known if Ted stayed in the auditorium the whole time, not just when he stood and waved."

"We'll be talking to her, tomorrow at the latest."

"Have you contacted Sheriff Hudson?"

Newly sighed. "Sam, I haven't had time to go to the bathroom."

"Then call him from there. Multitask."

He couldn't help but smile. "Why the urgency?"

"Because Hudson shared some confidential information with me. If there's a link between the deaths of Ken and Luke, then you need to be working together off the same score sheet."

"Are you going to share it with me?"

"No." I said the word as I nodded yes and eyed the voice recorder.

"All right. Then we're done." He clicked off the machine.

I took a sip of water and cleared my throat. "Hudson sought and received cell phone records for individuals he thought might have a link to Ken's death or gave him dubious information." I shared what I'd learned about the locations and phone calls of Luke, Madison, and Ormandy.

"Interesting. What do you think was going on with Luke and Madison?"

"I don't know," I lied. "Maybe they were planning a surprise party for Ted."

"Oh, sounds like Ted would have been surprised, all right."

I let the remark go. The video of the nude swim would stay with me for now. Let Newly and Hudson find their own proof, if the affair had any bearing on the case. I wanted to keep it as leverage for my own interview with Madison. I wasn't above a little blackmail if it got me honest answers. And with Luke dead, Madison was the only person with whom I could play that pool card. Pool. Chlorine. Alpha Romeo. Brake fluid. Would Luke have sabotaged his father's event? Would Madison have done that on her own?

My thoughts were interrupted by a knock and then the opening door.

Tuck Efird stuck his head in. "You still recording?"

"No." Newly slid over and offered his partner the nearer seat. "Sam and I are just seeing who can concoct the wildest theories."

"Well, here's something to add to the confusion. The head of the arson team has ruled out any accelerant like gasoline or lighter fluid. Just the initial mix of brake fluid and chlorine."

"What's that tell us?" Newly asked.

"That the culprit wasn't serious about burning the place down."

"Did he give you a better estimate on how long it was from the time the chemicals were mixed to combustion?"

"Pouring the fluid on the crystals—a range of thirty seconds to two minutes."

"So someone went backstage after the professor started speaking."

Tuck shook his head. "Not necessarily. The new information is there might have been a planned delay with a third chemical. You have the Pool Shock, you have the brake fluid. You take a disposable plastic bowl and set it on the Pool Shock. You put the unopened brake fluid in the bowl. Most brands now come in plastic containers. Then pour acetone into the bowl so that it starts to eat away at both the bowl and the bottle. It might take five or ten minutes at most, depending upon the strength of the acetone, but eventually the brake fluid will flow unimpeded onto the Pool Shock. The arson team says the setup could have already been in place, and the arsonist simply added the acetone. He would have probably done some tests to get the best estimate as to time till combustion. Maybe put the brake fluid inside multilayered or thicker Styrofoam. Acetone dissolves that as well."

"How much acetone would be required?" Newly asked.

"Not much. Could have been concealed in a glass flask."

Newly looked at me. "What do you think?"

"Certainly broadens rather than narrows the field. Were the backstage doors locked?"

"No," Newly said. "Anyone could have had access."

"What about preliminary forensics where I found the body?"

"A verbal report only," Tuck said. "Looks like Luke was struck across the left temple with the thick end of the bat. His assailant was most likely right-handed or a damned good switch-hitter. The injury was probably fatal, but he suffered a second wound when the back of his head hit the floor."

"Prints?" Newly asked.

"That's the odd part. Nothing on the bat."

Newly arched an eyebrow. "Nothing at all?"

"Wiped clean. And we know there should have been Luke's prints at least."

"What about the baseballs?" I asked.

"Only the one you found," Tuck said. "The killer must have taken the other."

"Which was?" Newly asked.

"The Babe Ruth. The more valuable one."

I looked at Newly. "Robbery gone wrong?"

"Maybe. Maybe he thought the display would be abandoned during the evacuation, except Luke didn't leave. Tuck, what about the fire alarm? Where was that pulled?"

Tuck grinned. "I love it when my partner asks the right question. The triggered alarm was on the wall above the body. And guess what?"

"No prints on it either," I said.

Tuck made an invisible checkmark in the air. "Chalk one up for the amateur. Sam's right, Newly. The pulldown bar on the alarm had been wiped clean as well."

Newly wiped his brow with a handkerchief. The closed room had become stuffy. "Someone was either familiar with or had scouted the building. He knew the back doors and hallways to move through without being seen."

"Man or woman," I said.

Tuck frowned. "You think a woman could wield a bat with that strength?"

"Watch women's professional softball sometime," Newly said.

Or Serena Williams's tennis swing. My next move became crystal clear. Distraught or not, Madison Kirkpatrick was going to answer my questions.

Chapter Twenty-One

"Do you want to see it again?" I re-cued the swimming pool video that I'd transferred to my laptop.

Nakayla and I sat side by side at the small dining table in my apartment. After leaving Newly and Tuck, I'd come home Sunday morning exhausted and crashed for much-needed sleep.

I'd awakened a little after noon and told Nakayla about my Friday encounter with the frolicking Luke and Madison.

"Don't replay it," Nakayla said. "I've seen more than enough. Why are you just telling me about it now?"

"Because Hewitt asked me not to. He felt obliged to tell Ted, but he was working out how and when. I guess he wanted to honestly say only he and I had seen it."

"Then I'll repeat the question. Why are you telling me now?"

"Because I think you should call Madison and ask to meet. We need to find out what she said to Luke and what Ted might have said to her. Despite what Ted told the police, he and his son definitely had an argument."

"What if she refuses to meet with me?"

I pointed to the frontal nude freeze-frame of Madison running poolside. "Then we take off the kid gloves and everything else."

"Are you going to tell Hewitt what we're up to?"

"Not yet. Let's make sure we know what we're up to ourselves."

Nakayla reached out and closed the laptop. "Why do I get the feeling you're flying by the seat of your pants?"

I patted the computer. "At least I've got my pants on."

She tried to stifle a laugh. "So, do you have Madison's number?"

"Not yet. I'm expecting Newly to talk with Sheriff Hudson today and ask for any evidence that might link the two murders. Newly knows the sheriff has phone records, and if they're not offered voluntarily, he'll make a formal request." I glanced at my watch. "They should have connected by now."

I dialed the detective's cell phone. Newly picked up on the first ring. "I was just ready to hit the hay. What's up, Sam?"

"Did you talk to Hudson?"

"Yeah. We sang 'Kumbaya'. He's open to playing nice and sharing."

"Great. Feel like keeping the spirit going by giving me Madison Kirkpatrick's cell phone number?"

Silence.

"I'll share back. When I've got something to share."

"Does this have anything to do with the overlapping GPS locations for her and Luke?"

"Maybe. It's a little delicate."

"Delicate? Then I hope Nakayla doesn't let you within a mile of the woman."

"Newly, for once I'm taking your advice."

He laughed. "All right. I didn't memorize all the numbers. Let me call the station and have a duty officer relay the information to me. Back in five."

He was back in four. I repeated the ten digits so Nakayla could jot them down.

"We're going to speak with Ted and Madison this evening," Newly said. "After I get a few hours of sleep."

"Do me a favor. If you speak to Madison, don't tell her Nakayla and I want to talk to her. I need to keep us outside of any police involvement."

"You got that right. Who are you again?" He hung up.

Nakayla looked at the number. "When do you want me to do this?"

"Now. Text that it's urgent you meet with her as soon as possible."

"Okay." Nakayla entered the number and then typed the message so fast her thumbs were a blur. She hit *Send.* "What now?"

"Let's give her an hour. Then I want to call on Lynne Stokes and learn why Ormandy phoned her the afternoon Ken died."

"Why not ask Ormandy?"

"Because he's the one who lied to Ted. He lied to me when I asked him if he'd spoken to Lynne. And he also had backstage access last night. I'd rather collect as much additional information as we can before another confrontation. Meanwhile, I'll run Blue out for a quick walk."

When the coonhound and I returned, Nakayla held up her phone.

"Got a response. Read it yourself."

All caps.

YOU KNOW I JUST LOST MY STEPSON. TED AND I ARE DEVASTATED. HAVE THE COURTESY OF WAITING A WEEK.

I opened the laptop. "I'm not proud of myself, but Lynne lost her husband. I'll export this photo to a jpeg."

"It doesn't show Luke."

"I know. Let's start with only Madison in the frame. She knows Luke was there."

I sent the image to Nakayla's phone. "Forward it as a text

attachment. Just say 'See you at my office before noon tomorrow.' Then ignore any further texts from her."

"You're not going to confront her?" Nakayla asked.

"I would change the dynamics. This should play out woman-to-woman. At least initially."

Nakayla took one final look at the photo on her phone, shook her head with regret, and sent it on.

———

Ken's pickup was parked in the driveway when Nakayla and I slowly drove by the Stokeses' home. Walt's old Bronco wasn't there.

"Why don't you park a couple houses down?" Nakayla suggested. "No sense advertising our presence."

"What if neighbors are visiting her? They could have walked."

"We'll tell Lynne we wanted to give her an update, but we can come back later. She might ask any guests to leave."

Nakayla rang the bell, and we backed away so as not to crowd the door.

Just when we thought no one would answer, it cracked, and Lynne peered through. "It's Nakayla and Sam," she said. "I've got to go."

She dropped her cell phone from her ear and opened the door.

"I hope we're not interrupting," Nakayla said.

"No. That was just Walt. He's going to bring some clothes over in case he needs to spend the night. You know, in case the little one decides to put in an appearance." She stepped aside. "Come in."

We followed her into the living room and, strangely enough, took the seats we'd occupied when we brought Lynne the horrible news of her husband's death—the women on the sofa and I in the bentwood rocker. This time the air reeked of flowers in vases placed on every available surface. I glanced in the kitchen.

The counter was covered with casseroles, cakes, and pies. The new widow was overwhelmed with food.

"Thank you for coming to the service yesterday," she said.

"It was lovely," Nakayla said. "I hope you took comfort that so many people were there."

Lynne looked away, as if seeing our faces would cause her to cry. "It was. I didn't think I could get through it, but there must be some kind of spiritual strength we tap into. I did take comfort. Then. Now I keep expecting to hear Ken's truck pull up, or see him come through that door." She caught her breath and looked at us. "Here I am not offering you anything to eat or drink. Please. Folks have brought in enough food to feed Fort Bragg."

"Thank you," Nakayla said. "But Sam and I can't stay long. We wanted to talk with you in private about how our investigation is proceeding."

Lynne looked at me and then back to Nakayla. She slid a little closer to the edge of the sofa. "Have you discovered who killed Ken?"

"No," Nakayla said. "But we're trying to identify pieces of evidence that might give us a breakthrough. We need your help."

"Sure. Anything."

"Have you spoken with the police since yesterday?"

"No. Just a few words of condolence from Sheriff Hudson at the church."

"They're going to speak with you," Nakayla said.

"The sheriff?"

"Yes. And probably the Asheville Police."

Lynne studied our faces. "Is this about Luke somehow?"

Nakayla looked to me to answer.

"It might be. They're just being thorough with both investigations."

"I don't know anything about what happened last night."

"No one is saying otherwise," I said, trying to put her at ease.

"It's about a phone call you received from William Ormandy last Sunday."

"Yes. Did William say something about it?"

"No, he didn't. When I asked him if he'd spoken to you, he said he hadn't."

Vertical frown lines creased her forehead. "But he did call me."

"A little after four thirty?" I prompted.

"Yes."

"Do you mind telling us what he said?" Nakayla asked.

"That he was coming into town and he wanted to drop by."

"Did you know he was coming?"

"Ken and I had seen the publicity for his concert. We planned on going, but we hadn't made any special arrangements to see him. We thought we'd catch him afterwards."

"What did you tell him?" Nakayla asked.

"That Ken wasn't here. That I'd call back if Ken came in before it got too late, if he wanted to visit then. I told him I was pregnant and I didn't have much energy toward the end of the day."

Nakayla shifted uneasily, and I knew she was weighing how personal to take this interview.

"Were you uncomfortable seeing William alone?"

Lynne blushed. "It's not what you think. William and I dated for a while when he was a freshman at UNC-Asheville." She looked down at her distended abdomen. "It's silly, but I didn't want him to see me like this. Like I should be a balloon in the Macy's parade."

"And if Ken were here?"

"Then I wouldn't be the center of attention. They could talk about the old days when they were in high school together. And the River Watchers' work."

"William's involved with River Watchers?" I asked.

"He's not a volunteer, but everyone who grew up in the part

of East Tennessee that was polluted by the Pigeon River carries the memories. Ken said William contributed financially to the organization. Like Ken's mother, William's died of cancer. He's convinced it was because of the toxic water."

"Did you tell William where you thought Ken might be?"

"I said he was taking samples, but I wasn't exactly sure where."

William Ormandy had made that call before he passed close to the Kirkgate landfill. Then, after a call to Madison, his phone had gone dark.

I decided we needed to probe deeper. "How would you describe Ken's relationship with William?"

"They've known each other since grade school. Ken left early in his senior year when his father moved here." She hesitated, trying to find the right words. "There was some friction when William was at the university."

"What kind of friction?"

"You know, hurt feelings. Ken had introduced me to William. Ken and I had dated a few times, but then William asked me out. I was young and impressed that someone with his talent would be interested in me. But a few months later, he dumped me for Madison. She ran with a faster crowd. Ken and I reconnected. Then, when Madison broke up with William, he wanted us to get back together. He said he'd made a terrible mistake. By then, I'd seen Ken had so much more depth. It took a while for William to accept that. Eventually, fences were mended and now it's ancient history."

"Was yesterday at the funeral the first time you've spoken since the Sunday afternoon phone call?"

"Yes. But we're going to get together before he returns to Cincinnati. Probably after the concert. Paul Clarkson will join us." She dabbed her eyes with the back of her hand. "Both of them have been very sweet. Calling to see if I needed anything."

"Do you?" Nakayla asked.

Lynne bit her lower lip to keep it from trembling. Then she said, "All I want is what no one can give me. My husband."

Nakayla and I said nothing. Lynne sat with her hands in her lap, fingering her wedding band.

Suddenly, she looked up, her eyes bright and suspicious. "But you said you're looking at pieces of evidence. Does that include William's phone call?"

"It was just a loose end," Nakayla said. "Last Sunday, William was late for a meeting with Ted Kirkpatrick. The police are trying to verify his whereabouts."

"And where was he?"

"He said he was running late." Nakayla patted Lynne's arm. "We've no reason to doubt him. So, please don't mention it to him."

She squeezed Lynne's hand for reassurance.

"Because you have no reason to doubt him," Lynne repeated, her skepticism as thick as the flower-scented air.

Chapter Twenty-Two

The text from Madison came to Nakayla after ten o'clock Sunday night.

ELEVEN TOMORROW. ONLY YOU!

So, a few minutes before eleven, I closed my office door, sat in the guest chair without the squeaky springs, and quietly awaited Madison's arrival.

Nakayla and I had agreed she would tell Madison it was just the two of them. Technically, it was just the two of them—in that room.

Nakayla would use the photograph as leverage to get answers to our questions. If Madison proved uncooperative to the extent of physical violence, I would intervene. Should extreme measures be required, I had my Kimber semiautomatic in a desk drawer.

My cell phone rang. I'd forgotten to turn it off. Newly's name popped up on the screen.

"Hi," I whispered. "I might have to bail on you. What's up?"

"You want to call me later?"

"Only if something's left hanging. Did you get a bank report?"

"Yes. River Waters is an account opened last February by Luke Kirkpatrick. The original deposit was a hundred thousand dollars. One check was written for twenty-seven thousand to SHM."

"SHM? Never heard of them."

"It's an acronym for Sports Heroes Memorabilia."

"The baseballs. So Luke did divert money from River Watchers and make up the Asheville home runs story."

"Yes," Newly confirmed. "But it doesn't end there. He also set up an account labeled ASPGA."

"What's ASPGA?"

"A G rather than a C in ASPCA. The American Society for the Prevention of Cruelty to Animals. Another hundred thousand went into that account, and I bet Luke made some legitimate donation to ASPCA, like he did for River Watchers. He might have set up other accounts in the same way."

"What's your next step?"

"I'm afraid I've got to bring the bad news to Ted Kirkpatrick. His accountant plans to do a thorough audit and contact other charitable recipients to see if the amounts they were given match the checks written. In a year or two, Luke could have diverted as much as half a million dollars."

I remembered the argument between Ted and Luke. "You know the accountant told Ted about the check discrepancy Saturday night."

"But at that time no one knew that Luke was definitely behind it," Newly said. "And I've got other bad news for Ted. Luke listed Madison as a cosigner."

"On the diverted accounts?"

"Yes. Ted's going to learn his murdered son was not only a thief but his own wife was an accomplice. What did the guy do to deserve that?"

What indeed? Newly's question might have cut to the heart of the matter. "Have you spoken to Sheriff Hudson?"

"Yes. I told him what I've just told you. He reciprocated. The phone records put Luke and Madison at or near Luke's home at the time of Ken Stokes's death. Madison admits she was there and says she and Luke were planning a surprise party for Ted to celebrate a successful festival."

"Does Madison know you've discovered her connection to the River Waters account?"

"No. We talked to Ted and her last night."

I decided to move on from Madison before I felt I had to tell Newly she was about to arrive. "What about Ormandy?"

"He claims he forgot the car charger for his phone and cut it off to conserve his battery."

"Then where was he for almost two hours?"

"According to him, sitting in his car a half block from Ken Stokes's house waiting for Ken to come home."

"Lynne said she told Ormandy she'd call him when Ken was there."

"That fits with what Ormandy told me. He said he wanted to be close. Lynne was very special, and he'd just learned she was expecting. He wanted to congratulate them both."

"You believe him?"

"He's an odd duck with an artistic temperament that swings between arrogant and sentimental. I don't believe or disbelieve. The fact is he has no alibi because he has no corroborating witnesses. We're going to canvas the neighborhood to see if anyone remembers seeing his car."

"His license plate reads PIANOMAN. It might have caught someone's eye."

"Yeah, we got that. Any more useful sharing from you?"

I heard the hall door open. "Maybe," I whispered. "Gotta go." I disconnected and powered off the phone.

"Madison, come in," Nakayla said. "It's just the two of us. Would you like some coffee?"

"I'd like to know where you got that picture." Her voice was brittle, half angry, half fearful. "Are you working for Ted?"

My mind flashed back to our first meeting at the ball game. Ted introduced me as the famous detective he'd hire if he ever needed one. Madison had given me that strange look. Now she thought her husband had hired us.

"No," Nakayla assured her. "And we haven't spoken to Ted about this. Yet."

There was a muffled scrunch as Madison collapsed on the sofa. "So, is this blackmail? Because if it is, it won't work. I'll just tell Ted I'd gone over to Luke's pool to sunbathe when he wasn't there. That's the truth."

It was the answer we'd anticipated. I heard Nakayla set her laptop on the coffee table. A few seconds later, giggling and the snapping of a towel were followed by two splashes. Madison's gasp sounded like Nakayla had punched her in the solar plexus.

"Please, please," she moaned. "Don't do this."

"What we do with this depends," Nakayla said.

"Depends on what?"

"How truthfully you answer my questions. If I get the feeling you're spinning me lies, I'll call Sam and tell him to take his copy of the video straight to Ted."

"For God's sake, he's burying his son."

"And Walt Stokes just buried his, and an unborn baby has lost a father."

For a moment, the only noise I heard was Madison sobbing. Finally, she caught her breath enough to speak. "What do you want to know?"

"Where were you the night Ken Stokes died?"

"I already told the sheriff I was at Luke's planning a party."

Silence. I imagined Nakayla was simply staring at the woman.

"We were having an affair," Madison said, a haughtiness now in her voice.

"And why did you call William Ormandy at six fifteen that evening?"

"To see where he was. I knew he was traveling in and thought maybe we could grab a quick bite."

"You're telling me you didn't know your husband would be eating with him?"

"I meant a drink. Just a drink."

"What did he say?"

"That he didn't have time. We'd catch up later."

"So, when that rendezvous fell through, you went to Luke's."

Silence. I figured Madison was nodding the obvious answer.

"How did this affair start?" Nakayla asked.

"At a party. Last New Year's Eve. Ted and I had a gathering at our house for some of the company's key employees. Everyone left after the ball dropped, but Luke stayed behind to help clean up. He told Ted to go on up to bed. Luke and I had another drink. Maybe two. He'd flirted with me in the past, but I'd always laughed it off. This night he was more persistent. I could try and blame my willingness on the alcohol, but that only clouded my judgment, not my desire."

"But it wasn't just the once," Nakayla said.

"No. He said since I'd already broken my vows I had nothing more to lose. I reminded him of my prenup. I had a lot to lose. He said not to worry. He had a plan for sheltering money that would be in my name."

One or more of the bogus accounts, I thought. Then he'd used some of the funds to buy the baseballs. Was he planning on selling them at an inflated price and redepositing the money or was Madison being strung along?

"So, you kept this relationship going for the money?"

"No! Are you calling me a whore?"

"I'm not calling you anything. I'm just trying to understand why you continued to sleep with your husband's son."

"Because I cared for him. And I care for Ted." The sobs erupted again. "It will kill him if he sees that video."

"Yes, it probably will. But you're a survivor, aren't you, Madison?"

There was a pause, and then Madison spoke so softly I strained to hear her. "And you're black."

"Your point is?"

"My point is you're a survivor too. Don't tell me you haven't faced discrimination in these lily-white hills of backwoods mountaineers and snooty retirees. My maiden name was Hill, and we lived in those backwoods. In elementary school the kids called me Maddy Hillbilly. I wore hand-me-down clothes until I was fifteen, when my father died of alcoholism and we moved out of the mountains to the poor side of town. Between after-school jobs and studying for top grades, I proved myself as good as anyone. A scholarship to UNC-Asheville exposed me to an entirely different class of people."

"Like William Ormandy?"

Madison laughed. "Willie was just like me, someone who grew up poor and struggled to make it in the world of the privileged. He was blessed with musical talent. I had looks. For a while, we bonded, and I should never have broken up with him. But afterwards, it became clear to me his real love had been Lynne Stokes. I guess I cost him that relationship.

"We both made it to the world of the privileged. I took the job at the country club, learned tennis and social graces, and looked for Mr. Right. But, I was always the hired help. Someone to flirt with or proposition. I'll admit I made some bad choices. Then, when Ted's wife died, I genuinely felt sorry for him. He was like a lost little boy. We became friends, and, well, you know the rest." Her voice cracked. "Now I've thrown it all away."

As a trained investigator, I kept emotion out of analyzing evidence or interpreting a suspect's answers. However, I couldn't help but feel sorry for the woman. She was about to run into a buzz saw when Newly confronted her about the bank account. Hearing her now, I believed there was a good chance she was completely ignorant of the scam Luke was running. More likely, he added her to the accounts after they were established and the money deposited.

She probably didn't know the source. I was tempted to open the door and warn her, but I clearly would have violated Newly's investigation if he planned to surprise her with the information.

"Let's get back to Luke," Nakayla said. "I saw you talking to him in the lobby before the lecture. You seemed agitated."

"I was. Ted's accountant told me there was a problem with a check written from the charity. It had gone to an account named River Waters rather than River Watchers. River Waters was an account Luke set up for me. He claimed the name meant nothing. It was something generic that wouldn't directly tie back to me. But when I heard the name from the accountant, I knew we were in trouble."

"You went to tell Luke," Nakayla said.

"Yes, but he just brushed me off. He said he'd fix it and not to admit to anything. I realized he wasn't just talking about our affair, but something that could be a real crime."

"What did you do then?"

"I was too upset to go back into the auditorium. I knew the building from my student days so I stayed in one of the restrooms. Then the fire alarm sounded."

She doesn't have an alibi, I thought. She could have come back and confronted Luke after the program started. But then the fires made no sense. Those were premeditated before the accountant's revelation.

"Did you tell that to the police?" Nakayla asked.

"I told them I felt queasy and went to the ladies' room. That wasn't a lie. I did feel queasy."

"Did you know that the story of Babe Ruth and Lou Gehrig hitting those balls for home runs was a lie?"

"No. Luke told me he bought them from someone in Asheville who'd had them for years." Then she murmured, "That son of a bitch. He would have hung me out to dry, wouldn't he?"

Nakayla ignored her question. "And the old bat. Where did Luke get that?"

"From eBay. He thought it would complete the exhibit, even though Ruth and Gehrig never used it."

"Did William Ormandy know Luke?"

"Just through me. They had nothing in common."

"And Luke's relationship with Ken Stokes?"

"Antagonistic. Luke thought Ken was trying to undermine the company's expansion plans. Then, after Ken died and things continued to go wrong, he thought Ken's father was behind it. I said I didn't think so. Mr. Stokes is a decent man."

"And Luke's reaction?"

"He said maybe so but that Walt had better stay clear. He didn't care if the man's son had just died."

There was a long pause. Then Madison asked, "What are you going to do with that video? I've told you everything I know."

"For now? Nothing. You need to be there for Ted. But Madison, if Luke tied you to checking accounts, the police are going to have questions, and you'd better have some honest answers."

Madison said nothing.

The rustle of clothing told me both women had stood. Footsteps headed toward the door. The latch clicked open.

"Yes, I'm black," Nakayla said. "Yes, I've faced discrimination. But I've never let those people define who I am or the principles that I live by. You should have done the same."

The door closed.

Chapter Twenty-Three

"I don't think we need to do anything more with the video." Hewitt Donaldson shook his head and sighed. "Once Ted buries his son, I'll have a heart-to-heart with Madison. I know the terms of her prenup and might have leverage with what course of action ensues. This joint checking account scam might bring things to a head anyway, without getting into the other sordid details."

Nakayla and I were in Hewitt's conference room where he was joined by Shirley and Cory. I'd phoned him as soon as Madison left, and he decided to share the situation with his team. I'd not realized Hewitt had such a prudish outlook, and he actually blushed while describing the pool scene. I have to admit I was glad he was doing the play-by-play and not me.

"How was her tan?" Shirley asked me.

"What the hell does that have to do with anything?" Hewitt growled. "All you need to know is she was in the buff."

"Right. And in case you hadn't noticed, it's only mid-April. How many people do you know who lay out in the sun at this time of year? And the pool must be heated or Mr. Macho's equipment would have deflated like a pricked balloon, pun intended."

Hewitt gaped at her.

"Not that I'm speaking from personal experience," Shirley added. "Just that her sunbathing story has as much chance of being believed as my levitating out of this chair."

"Probably less of a chance," I said.

"My thoughts exactly." Shirley turned to Hewitt. "So, as far as hot water's concerned, Madison's goose is cooked. I agree with you. The video's superfluous, and if she's working on a tan, with her money she'd be using a salon, not bopping over to her stepson's."

"She didn't have a tan," I said. "Not even a tan line."

Shirley shrugged. "So, Hewitt, I doubt she'll change her story from what she admitted to Nakayla. It's your call as to how much you want to get involved between her and her husband."

Hewitt clasped his hands together on top of his legal pad and smiled. "I acknowledge your insights, Shirley, and you can consider your employment secure for the rest of the afternoon. But let's set aside the role of dallying wife for the moment. It's Madison's potential to be a murderous lover I'm more concerned with. Where was she when Luke was killed?"

"She told me she was in the ladies' restroom," Nakayla said. "Learning about the true purpose of the bank accounts had upset her. And Luke had done nothing to allay her fears."

Cory DeMille, Hewitt's paralegal, stopped scribbling in her notepad. "Could she have worked herself into such a rage that she hit Luke with that bat? Maybe she didn't mean to kill him."

"I don't know," I said. "Possibly. But here's what's bothering me. We have a string of incidents from Ken Stokes's death to Luke's murder with our suspects harboring varying motives." I stood up from the table, pacing as I laid out my thoughts.

"Let's start with Ken. He has an argument with Luke. He then is in the Pigeon River the next afternoon and evening, allegedly taking water samples. But soil samples are also taken. Samples that prove to be toxic. Our likely suspect for Ken's death is Luke, but his tryst with his stepmother gives him an alibi unless she's covering for him. But why would he turn in contaminated samples? Enter Eli Patterson whose River Watchers' budget has been cut. Was he in cahoots with Ken to make trouble for Kirkgate Paper, or did Ken find Eli doctoring the samples and a fatal argument resulted? Or was River Watcher Paul Clarkson involved as well? He admitted he'd called Ken in the afternoon and offered to pick up the samples the next day. That fits both with phone records and because he came by the construction site Monday morning looking for Ken."

I walked to where Nakayla sat and placed a hand on her shoulder. "What reaction was triggered by Ken's death? Walt Stokes and Ken's wife approached Nakayla and me to investigate. But maybe Walt didn't want to wait. He works in construction, he must have at least a rudimentary knowledge of chemicals, and he could have rigged those waste bins to catch fire."

Nakayla turned in her chair to look up at me. "But why attack the Dykeman lecture? That was the event Ken advocated."

I started pacing again. "I know. And I don't have an answer. I do find it interesting that the fire didn't start until after Ormandy and Clarkson had played their excerpts. Could Ormandy have thought the Kirkpatricks were behind Ken's death? Ormandy said he supported River Watchers financially, as he'd grown up with the aftermath of the Pigeon River's toxicity. Maybe he was insuring he got paid per his contract while secretly undermining other aspects of the festival. From what we've learned, he and Lynne Stokes were close at one time. So Ken could have either been a rival or the accepted husband of someone he cared about, and he genuinely felt sorry for her loss."

Hewitt interrupted me. "Which puts him in the frame for either confronting Ken or sabotaging the Kirkpatricks. It can't be both."

"Correct. But both possibilities are still in play until we can eliminate one."

"What about Ted and Luke?" Shirley asked. "Could Ted have lost his temper with his son?"

"He had lost his temper," I said. "I witnessed Ted get up in Luke's face, but then he walked away. I think the moment of rage had passed. And he wouldn't have started those fires."

"But they could have been separate incidents," Shirley argued.

"They could have," I admitted. "But Luke's body was found beneath the pulled fire alarm. The flames weren't visible outside of the auditorium when the alarm sounded. If it were Madison, would she have had the presence of mind to bludgeon Luke and then wipe down both the bat and the alarm?"

"Unlikely," Hewitt said. "Which brings me back to Walt if you're looking for the person with a motive that covers more of the incidents."

I nodded. "And that motive is?"

The four answered in unison. "Revenge."

"Revenge," I repeated. "And Walt goes back to East Tennessee where his wife died amid the toxic discharge of the paper mills."

"But why now?" Cory asked. "There's no evidence the Kirkpatricks killed Ken, if you're saying that's the trigger."

"I'm saying if revenge is the motive, then we have to recognize that Walt Stokes doesn't hold a patent on it." I smiled at Nakayla. "In our brief career as detectives, our major cases have revolved around some crime in the past rippling through with consequences for the present."

"'The past is never dead,'" Hewitt said. "'It's not even past.' Not my words, William Faulkner's. And he was an author with great insights into human nature."

I returned to my chair. "So, maybe we look back to those dark days. Is there a list of the families who lost loved ones attributed to the pollution?"

"I could get on that," Cory volunteered.

"All right," I said. "Any other prospects?"

Nakayla leaned forward. "What about the trial?"

"What trial?" I asked.

"The man who killed the executive with the baseball bat."

Shirley gasped. "Talk about bad karma. Ted Kirkpatrick testifies and then years later Luke meets the same fate."

"Leroy Mock," Nakayla said. "I looked him up in doing background research on the lawsuits. He just died a few months ago."

Hewitt's eyebrows arched. "Really?"

"Yes," Nakayla said. "Did you know him?"

"No. But I followed the trial, and I knew Ted back then. I believe after the conviction and life sentence, Mock's wife divorced him. I think she had a child who couldn't have been very old. The whole thing was tragic. Losing twin boys and then cut off from his one remaining child." Hewitt nodded to Cory. "Mock bears looking into. Those East Tennessee hill people can be clannish, the kind of folk who have long memories."

"Leroy Mock may have had visitors," I said. "Someone must have claimed the body."

"I'll check it out," Nakayla said. "Maybe the best step is to call the warden at Central Prison."

"As a defense attorney, I'm not the ideal candidate," Hewitt said. "Mock wasn't my client. His original lawyer, a public defender, is also dead. And if you approach them asking for medical information, HIPAA laws apply for fifty years after death."

"Why would we need that?" Nakayla asked.

"Because not only Mock's death but his specific illness could have triggered something."

Hewitt made a good point, one that I took a step further. "I'm concerned if we ask for official records of either health information or relatives, the prison might reach out to the family for permission. I'd like to pursue this under the radar for as long as we can."

"A cellmate, then," Nakayla suggested. "Either from the blocks or the long-term care facility."

The rest of us voiced our approval.

"I could be a reporter," she said. "Doing a follow-up on the history of pollution in our rivers."

Hewitt pointed his finger at Nakayla. "That might work. And believe it or not, I have a few clients serving time there. I would have standing to speak with them, at least as an initial inquiry to see if they can provide a lead to who might have known Mock well."

I felt energized. At least we were creating an action plan. "How soon can you set that in motion?"

Hewitt laughed. "As soon as you stop talking. Cory, go ahead and research any pollution-attributed deaths, if such records exist. Shirley, pull the files on our Raleigh inmates. This is the only time you'll hear me say I wish we had more." He stood and made shooing motions with his hands. "Nakayla and Sam, go back to whatever it is that you do. We've got this."

Chapter Twenty-Four

Hewitt's instructions had given everyone but me an immediate assignment: Cory researching deaths attributable to the Pigeon River pollution, Shirley researching Central Prison inmates tied to Hewitt, and Nakayla formulating her identity as a journalist if she had the opportunity to question a prisoner who'd been close to Leroy Mock.

I was sitting at my desk trying to convince myself that Walt Stokes wasn't our leading suspect when Nakayla slipped into my guest chair.

"If Hewitt is able to connect with someone who knew Leroy Mock, then I want to be careful how I present myself."

"What do you mean? I think your idea to be a journalist is a good one."

"But I'm not," she protested. "What if they ask for identification? I can't say I'm with *The Asheville Citizen-Times* or one of the area's small-town weekly newspapers. I'm sure there's some kind of law against gaining entrance to a state penal institution under false pretenses."

"Probably. But if you're caught, it's convenient that you'll already be in prison."

She groaned. "Sam, I'm serious. It seemed like a good idea in Hewitt's conference room, but now I'm not so sure."

I understood her point. It's one thing to lie to a suspect and another to lie to a government official. "What if you're a freelance journalist? Print up some business cards with that title, our office address, and your cell phone number. Better yet, add a headshot so it looks like a photo ID and laminate it. Everything will match the information on your driver's license."

Nakayla gave me a thumbs-up. "I like it. I could say I'm writing an article for a magazine like *Our State* or *WNC*. If they press me, I can say it's on spec." She got up. "I can design the layout online and send it to a printer for a quick turnaround. If Hewitt arranges an interview, I'll drive to Raleigh as soon as the cards are finished."

"Even if you don't use them this time, I can see them being a good cover for investigations in the future." I pulled out my phone. "Let's step into the hall, and I'll take your photo with that beige background."

———

Leaving Nakayla busy on her computer and Blue sleeping on his cushion, I decided to check in on the progress the workers might be making on Nakayla's house. Walt's old Bronco was parked at the curb and a van with the logo proclaiming *Junior's Ever-Clean Gutters and Downspouts* sat in the driveway. A team of men, some on ladders, some crouched on the edge of the roof, were focused on attaching gutters to the eaves. I didn't see Walt, so I skirted the gutter activity by walking around the house to enter from the rear.

In the backyard, I found Walt measuring a plank of wood stretched across two sawhorses. He marked a cut spot and then measured again.

"Measure twice, cut once," I said.

He looked up and managed a smile. "Hi, Sam. Nice day to be outside. I thought I'd work on the flooring for the back deck.

What do you think about enlarging it a little so if you grill outside you're farther away from the house?"

"I'll check with Nakayla, but I doubt she'll object to anything that reduces the risk of another fire."

He laid his carpenter's pencil on the board and walked around the sawhorses to greet me. We shook hands, and then his face turned grim. The man looked like he'd aged ten years in the week since I'd first met him.

"Fire," he said. "That was something Saturday night. You know I was there."

"Yes. I saw you talking with Eli Patterson in the lobby before the doors opened."

"Well, I've had my differences with the Kirkpatricks, but I sure as hell didn't wish this to happen."

"You know it was arson and murder."

He made a clicking sound with his tongue and nodded. "I'm sure some folks think I'm happy about it, like it evened some score. But nothing could be further from the truth. I wouldn't wish my pain on anyone. Ted's got to be hurting."

And he'll keep on hurting as Luke's actions come to light.

"Part of me wants to reach out to him," Walt said. "Part of me thinks he probably doesn't want anything to do with me. He may think I killed his son."

Walt didn't sound like someone who was a potential suspect. His glistening eyes and raspy whisper bore witness to an emotional turmoil he couldn't mask.

"But somebody did, Walt. Any idea who that could have been?"

"No, and since Saturday night I can't help but wonder if the same person killed both Ken and Luke. But for the life of me I can't figure out a connection."

I decided to probe for more information, even though I could be tipping Walt off to our line of inquiry.

"Did you know Leroy Mock?"

"The man who killed that paper mill executive?"

"Yes, back when the pollution was at its worst."

"I knew who he was. I'd see him in town sometimes. His family lived closer to the river." Walt moistened his dry lips. "None of that should ever have happened. Neither the pollution nor the killing. When Mock lost them babies, I guess he just snapped."

"Did you know a lot of people who lost relatives?"

His jaw tightened. "Know 'em? I am one. I'm sure the contamination caused my wife's cancer. I feel like all of us from that part of East Tennessee are living under a death sentence." He paused. "You think someone from those days is responsible for Luke's murder? Then why would they kill Kenny?"

"I don't know. Like you, I can't see a connection."

My cell phone rang. I glanced at the screen. Hewitt.

"Sorry, Walt. I'd better take this."

"Go ahead. And I'll give what you said some thought." He turned back to his work.

I answered Hewitt's call as I hustled to my car. "What's up?"

"Where are you?"

"At Nakayla's house. I just had a little informal chat with Walt. I don't think he's our guy for Luke's murder."

"Neither do I," Hewitt agreed. "I got through to an inmate whom I defended back in the 1990s."

"Does he have a lead for us?"

"He is the lead. He went inside about the same time as Leroy Mock. They served twenty-five years together."

"Cellmates?"

"Same cell block. Mock wasn't much of a talker, but he did tell my guy that he had a wife and a son. The wife remarried and later died of cancer. He didn't see his child for years. The son started visiting once he was old enough to be on his own. Mock said it was some consolation for what the paper mills had stolen from him. Then he was diagnosed. Of course it was cancer. He'd go in and out of the prison hospital for treatment.

My client worked as a prison orderly there, and he'd drop in to see Mock. He met the son once. When Mock got into the final stages, he went to the prison's long-term care facility. My client also worked that unit. He never saw the son again, but Mock told him things would be set right. My client thought he meant with God. Maybe not."

"Does he have a name for the son?"

"Just a first. Willie."

Paul Clarkson's words rang in my head. *I knew him when he was a pimply-faced kid named Willie from East Tennessee.*

"Hewitt, it's William Ormandy. He used to be called Willie."

"Then Ormandy may be a stage name. Eugene Ormandy was a famous classical conductor."

My mind raced. "Ted had publicity pamphlets and posters printed for the festival. Could you fax one with Ormandy's picture to Central Prison and request they show it to your client? Check Nakayla. She might have one."

"Okay. What are you going to do?"

"Find Ormandy. From now on I want to know where he is at all times."

I checked my watch. Four o'clock. Ormandy might be rehearsing somewhere. The fire eliminated Lipinsky Hall as an option but there must have been other pianos on campus—or elsewhere in Asheville, for that matter. I didn't want to call him because I had nothing to say over the phone. In person, I could ask a few questions about Saturday night and observe his body language. My other choice was to call Newly and tell him my suspicions. But I had no proof. A confirmation from Hewitt's inmate would change all that.

The logical place to start looking for Ormandy was the Albemarle Inn. If he wasn't there, he might have mentioned to the innkeeper where he was going.

I pulled into the side parking lot. The Ohio PIANOMAN license plate tagged the only other vehicle. Someone could have picked Ormandy up, but I gambled he was in Bartók's Retreat. *Lair* more aptly described it if he was the culprit.

Rather than confront him, I decided to park halfway down the block where I could put him under surveillance. I'd just turned around when Ormandy came out the door. He waved. There was no way I could evade talking to him.

I backed the CR-V beside his car and got out.

"Sam, what are you doing here?"

"I, uh, I dropped by to pick up Nakayla's hairbrush. She left it here. How are you doing?"

He stepped forward, blocking me in between our two vehicles. "Still kind of shaken. The police came by earlier. I'm afraid they think I was involved somehow."

"They just have to rule everyone out. You and Paul Clarkson had been on stage before the fire."

"Yeah, but why would I kill Luke? I hardly knew him."

"You knew his stepmother, right?"

"We dated a while. That was years ago. I've talked to her a few times since I got the festival gig. I seem to have attracted police suspicions because I turned off my phone the night Ken died. I told them I was just trying to save the battery."

"But you got to Asheville earlier than you claimed."

His eyes squinted and his body stiffened. "Who told you that?"

I shrugged. "I'm a detective. It's my business to know."

He looked down and scuffed the gravel with the sole of his shoe. "I wanted to see Lynne, congratulate her on the baby, but I was waiting for Ken to come home."

At least he was being consistent with his story.

"Do you think Walt killed Luke?" he asked. "It would kill Lynne if her father-in-law went to jail."

"No. I don't. It could be a broader motive than Ken's death."

His eyes darted back to me. "Like what?"

"I don't know. You're from East Tennessee. Wasn't there a lot of animosity against the paper mills and the owners?"

"That's before my time. I was just a toddler when that went down."

"And it didn't affect your family?"

"No. We were lucky. But plenty of others suffered. Like Ken's mother." He stopped. "Are you sure about Walt? I could see him blaming the Kirkpatricks for both deaths."

"I am sure. He understands he needs to be here for Lynne. You understand that too."

He blushed. "She's special. I didn't see that once." He took a deep breath. "Well, I've got one more rehearsal to get to."

"So the concert's still on?"

Ormandy backed up and crossed in front of his car to the driver's door. "Yes. Ted said no way was a murderer going to stop the festival finale. But this rehearsal's for Luke's funeral. It's this Saturday, the morning after the concert. A sad way for everything to end."

"Has Lipinski Hall reopened already?"

Ormandy looked over the car roof. "No. Ted's a member at First Presbyterian. That's where we're meeting." He smiled. "Just the piano. No Moog for once." He opened the door and ducked his head under but then popped back up. "Your theory about a motive from the past. That doesn't work for Ken's death."

"I know. It doesn't fit with any theory."

"Like my score."

"Your Blue Ridge Concerto?"

"Yes. Someone tried to make trouble by copying and giving it to Slocum. That wasn't Walt."

I watched him go, knowing where I could find him later, wondering if his score comment held a significance I'd missed.

Chapter Twenty-Five

I sat in my car, unsure what to do next. Until Hewitt received confirmation that Ormandy was Leroy Mock's son, I was stuck on pause, the doubts about his guilt ebbing and flowing as facts and suppositions cycled through my head. Lynne and Paul Clarkson knew him from his freshman year at UNC-Asheville. Would he have used a stage name then? Then I remembered that Leroy Mock's wife was said to have divorced him and remarried. Their first-born child was so young he could have taken his stepfather's name. And the background fit. Ormandy was from Hartford, Tennessee, aka Widowville, ground zero for the impact of the Pigeon River's deadly pollutants. That fact fortified the possibility that Ormandy was our man. He warranted continuous surveillance.

I phoned Nakayla as I drove to the church.

"Where are you?" she asked.

"Keeping tabs on Ormandy. He's playing for Luke's funeral and rehearsing at First Presbyterian."

"Doesn't sound like the actions of someone who hates the Kirkpatricks."

"Maybe that's the point. Throw us off. This whole case has been one of conflicting actions. Like pieces from multiple puzzles dumped from the same box."

"Or extra pieces created to blur the picture," she said.

"One thing we need to clear up is Ormandy's name. If he's Mock's son then he's either changed his name or was adopted by his stepfather. Can you research Tennessee records? Or maybe Lynne or Clarkson would know."

"Sure. I'll get on it right away. But maybe a positive ID from Hewitt's client in Central Prison will save us the trouble."

"We can hope," I said. "Keep me posted."

I pulled into the church's parking lot. Late afternoon it was all but deserted. I saw Ormandy's PIANOMAN license plate and Ted Kirkpatrick's festival bumper sticker. I guessed Ted was there to talk to the minister and confirm Ormandy's musical contribution. How betrayed would he feel if the pianist turned out to be his son's murderer?

I circled around and parked in a far corner where I could be ready to tail Ormandy without drawing attention to myself. My cell rang. Ormandy's number.

"William?"

"Sorry to bother you about what's probably nothing. I was supposed to meet Ted at the church."

"Right. You said First Presbyterian."

"Yes, and I'm waiting in the sanctuary. His car's in the lot but I can't find him in the church."

"Maybe he parked and walked uptown for something."

"Maybe. But he's always been prompt for every other meeting. And he has my cell number. I'm worried, Sam."

So was I. "Have you tried calling him?"

"Yes. I went straight to voicemail."

Could Ormandy have done something to Ted? Is he covering his tracks? Not that much time had elapsed since he left me at the inn. "Sit tight, William. I'll try his office. Call me if he shows up."

I disconnected with no intention of calling Ted's office. I drove across the parking lot to his Lexus and hurried to the driver's door. It was slightly ajar. A set of keys, one with a Lexus logo, lay on the pavement beside the front tire. I opened the door wider. My pulse jumped at the sight of blood smeared on the driver's headrest. I looked across to the passenger's seat. A black purse had spilled some of its contents onto the floor. Madison had been with him.

I placed my palm on the hood. No difference in temp from the air. I moved two spaces to Ormandy's car. The hood was warm. Ted had gotten there first and something bad had happened.

My cell rang. Nakayla.

"Sam. It's not Ormandy. The inmate looked at the photograph. Mock's son had long black hair and a thinner face."

"Damn it. Can't we get a name from the prison hospital?"

"We can, but Hewitt has to make an official request. Privacy rules protect the identities of a prisoner's family so that no vigilantes can seek retribution beyond what the justice system imposed. I've also hit a dead end with Mock's wife. She left East Tennessee shortly after her husband's conviction, and there's no re-marriage record in the state."

I clutched the phone tighter with frustration. "Ted's missing. And I think so is Madison." I quickly briefed her on what I'd found.

"If not Ormandy, then who?"

My mind snapped back to Slocum and the confrontation. I was missing something about the score. If Slocum had been telling the truth about someone anonymously giving him a copy, then that person could have been more deeply tied into the effort to sabotage the concert. Slocum claimed it was probably one of the symphony players familiar with his composition.

But somebody else had the score early. Paul Clarkson. He said he wasn't taking water samples with Ken because he'd been reviewing Ormandy's score. He would have known Slocum, known how to slide a copy under his office door. But Clarkson had been Ken's friend. He'd calmed Ken down when Luke had shoved him. What had he really told him? That he had a way to get even?

The tingle started at the back of my neck.

"Sam, you there?" Nakayla's anxiety infused the question.

"Yes. And I know where we screwed up. We dismissed Clarkson because he'd come looking for samples the morning after Ken's death."

"Clarkson? It's Clarkson?"

"We'd dismissed him because he knew the combination and the doctored samples hadn't been put in the collection chest. Both those actions drew attention away from him and took the focus off any River Watchers who would have known how to open the chest's lock. Clarkson said he'd called Ken to say he couldn't join him for sample collections. We had no one's word but Clarkson's. Had he arranged to meet Ken at the Kirkgate landfill? Or had he just asked Ken where he was taking samples? Clarkson had a foot in both camps—the River Watchers and the Luminaries Festival. And he had Ormandy's score that he could copy and anonymously pass along to Slocum."

"You need to tell Newly."

"We need to find Ted and Madison. Call the Moog factory and see if Clarkson's at work. If not, then you get to Newly. Urge him to pull the plate number and description of Clarkson's car and put out a BOLO. Share it with Sheriff Hudson so they can also be on the lookout."

"But our evidence is circumstantial. Newly might balk."

"He won't," I argued. "Not when you tell him I said it's now life or death. Then see if you can find a picture of Paul Clarkson."

"Why?"

"To have Hewitt forward it to Central Prison and his inmate who met Leroy Mock's son."

"And what will you be doing?"

"Going back to where this all started. The river."

Chapter Twenty-Six

In my heart I knew it came back to the river. Ted and his family couldn't step free of the long shadow cast by the paper mills' wanton disregard for the lives—animal and human—poisoned by their toxic waste.

Whether that river was the literal ending or only the beginning of this painful and tragic saga, I didn't know. But if Clarkson had Ted and Madison with him, I felt an inexplicable urge to return to the site of Ken's death as a way of closing off a possible destination. Newly and the Asheville Police could cover Clarkson's house and alert patrols to be on the lookout for his vehicle. Sheriff Hudson didn't have jurisdiction over Luke's murder, but his deputies could monitor his county roads. There was nothing I could do officially. Except wait at the river where a final reckoning might go down.

I turned onto the narrow dirt road leading to the kayak put-in where we'd found Ken's pickup. The closeness of the forest brought dusk early to what had been a sunny afternoon. I doubted at this weekday hour either kayakers or anglers would be venturing out. Upstream lay the mills that river enthusiasts avoided.

My phone rang. I felt reassured that at least I had a signal.

Nakayla spoke breathlessly before I had a chance to even say hello.

"Clarkson didn't show up for work today."

"He might have been tailing Ted, looking for an opportunity to confront him."

"Newly's issued a BOLO."

That meant Newly had a model and plate number.

"What's Clarkson driving?"

"A red 2018 Kia Sportage. That's a compact SUV. And it's registered to Paul William Clarkson."

"William?"

"Yes. Like Ormandy, Paul could have been called Willie as a child."

"I bet you're right. Is Newly overseeing things from the station?"

"No," Nakayla said. "He and Tuck are headed to Clarkson's house near Woodfin."

I knew Woodfin. It was a working-class community north of Asheville.

"Where are you?" Nakayla asked.

"On that dirt road to the river. I'll hang here till you have some news."

"And you call me if you see only a flash of that red Kia. I mean it, Sam. Be careful for once."

"I know. Hey, love you."

"Then you'll take me seriously." She paused. "And I love you too."

I connected the phone to the car charger and dropped it on the seat beside me where I could quickly retrieve it. The road's surface became a washboard that bounced me around like a carnival ride. Although I'd only been on it in the dark, I remembered from the sudden bone-jarring condition that the river was getting close.

The road curved left and there it was, the access clearing

bordering the Pigeon River. Looking at the reflected golden surface sparkles of the late afternoon sun, it was hard to believe the clear, rippling waterway had carried so much death. But my eyes and thoughts didn't linger there. Both lasered onto a red Kia, parked facing outward.

I steered my CR-V into a broadside stop, blocking the single lane exit. The Kia appeared to be empty. I reached for the phone only after I first reached for my Kimber in the glovebox. If Clarkson had Ted and Madison, then odds were he was armed.

I called Nakayla. "The Kia's here," I whispered. "No sign of anyone." As I spoke, I eased out and softly closed the door.

"I'll call Hudson." Her voice trembled. "Do you think he's taken them to the landfill?"

I walked to the Kia and placed my hand palm-down on the hood. "His engine's still warm. I drove like a maniac and couldn't be too far behind them."

"Good. If they're walking to the landfill, then they might still be on the way, assuming Clarkson wants to get there to…" Her voice trailed off, unable to speak what we both dreaded.

I peered into the Kia. Blood splotches were visible on the front passenger's seat. Clarkson must have struck Ted as he was getting out of his Lexus and then forced him into the Kia. Madison would have been put in the back seat. If Clarkson enabled the childproof locks, she would have been trapped there. And if Ted were injured, the walk to the landfill would be going slowly.

I started moving along the river. I could see freshly trampled ferns and smashed mushrooms. "Tell Hudson to bring bolt cutters if he needs to get in through the company road that comes directly to the landfill. And tell him he'd better bring an ambulance in tow. I need to go. Don't worry." I disconnected, avoiding a second emotional goodbye, and made sure the ringer was off.

I followed the trail so clearly laid before me and wondered if Ted and Madison were shuffling along at gunpoint. At two spots, I found shreds of soft fabric dangling from the thorns of blackberry bushes. The remnants had to have been torn from Madison's blouse and reassured me I was on the right path.

I moved as quickly and quietly as I could, hoping to overtake them. Without thinking, my military-training mode of search and stalk kicked into gear. In Iraq, patrols had been conducted in a barren, arid landscape. Now I navigated through forest vegetation but with the same adrenaline rush.

My eyes, ears, nose, and even skin ramped into hypersensitivity. Buzzing and darting dragonflies moved with me. Even though a cool breeze came off the water, sweat dripped from my forehead and pooled against the pistol tucked in the small of my back.

Confronting Clarkson with a gun in my hand would instantly escalate the situation. So brazen an action as kidnapping made it clear he'd reach a point of desperation, and I feared he was beyond rational negotiation. Still, it was better at least to appear unarmed and foster the possibility of a defusing dialogue.

Light grew brighter as trees thinned. Stepping into the clearing, I saw Clarkson, Madison, and Ted about thirty yards ahead. Clarkson walked behind them, pushing Ted in the back with his left hand while holding a pistol in his right. Ted seemed to be on the verge of stumbling, either dizzy from his head wound or the fact that his hands were tied behind him. Madison's were also. Beyond them, fluttering in the breeze, danced strips of the crime scene tape that had marked the site of Ken's death and the sample soil holes.

Clarkson steered them closer to the river and then pushed them to their knees. A chill ran through me. I was about to witness an execution.

"Clarkson!"

His head whipped around. "Back off, Blackman." He waved the pistol in the air. "This is between me and the Kirkpatricks."

"I know all about you and the Kirkpatricks." I gambled my

theory was right. "And about your father, Leroy Mock." I held my empty hands out to my side. "About the cancer that decimated your family. But murder is no answer."

I spoke slowly, lowering my volume as I cautiously approached. De-escalate—the immediate goal. Patiently take one step at a time. I had a small window to calm things down before Sheriff Hudson and his deputies arrived with sirens wailing and lights flashing.

"You've gotten the world's attention, Paul." I switched to his given name desperately trying to reinforce any bond, no matter how tenuous.

"I don't want the world's attention. I want justice, something the world is incapable of giving because the world listens only to money and power."

Keep him talking. I was now thirty feet away. "Money and power? How does Ken Stokes fit with money and power?"

Clarkson's lower lip trembled. "That was an accident. I told him I had a way to even the score with the Kirkpatricks. A way for Ken to get payback for Luke's assaulting him at the ball game. But he refused to agree. Tried to stop me. Destroy my samples." He glanced down at the ground. "Standing right here." His breath caught. "I pushed him away." Another quick glance, this time to the river beside him.

I could see it all. Clarkson's flare-up at Ken for not embracing the plan. Maybe Ken even threatened to report Clarkson's scheme. Physically shoving Ken away and onto the river rocks.

"No one was supposed to die." Clarkson whined the words. "Certainly not Ken. I only wanted to embarrass the Kirkpatricks. Maybe stop the expansion of the mill. I promised my father I'd bring them down a notch or two." He bent down and yelled at Ted. "But your son and his stupid display. He saw me pull the fire alarm. Came over with that bat. How ironic. Him confronting me with a baseball bat. I wrestled it away. I did what I had to."

"And now?" I asked.

He gave a cold smile. "I'm where I should be. It's my fate." He glanced down at the couple kneeling before him. "Our fate. We're tied together in life and death."

"And Madison? Like Ken, she bears no guilt."

"When you find a cancer, you cut it out along with everything it touches." He brought the pistol down to Madison's head.

Ted shouted angrily. "You murdered my son. You will not murder my wife." He twisted his body around and headbutted Clarkson on his knee.

Ted couldn't strike hard, but, for a split second, Clarkson was thrown off-balance. I snatched my Kimber from my waistband and rushed to cover the ten yards between us. Ted struggled to stand. Clarkson raised the pistol to him.

"No!" I aimed as Uncle Sam taught me—for body mass.

The shots fired in one synchronous boom.

Ted stumbled backwards, teetered on the riverbank, and then tumbled in with a splash. Clarkson flew through the air like he was hurled by a giant, invisible fist. His pistol spun free as his grip instantly loosened.

Without breaking stride, I kicked his gun away, registering it as a .38-caliber revolver. Tucking my Kimber back in my waistband, I jumped into the Pigeon River. Ted drifted in the current faceup, his hands still bound behind him. Swirling pink tendrils flowed from beneath him, darkening to red as I struggled across slick rocks and through the knee-high flowing water.

With an eye on the motionless Clarkson, I grabbed Ted by the belt and pulled him to shore. The blood appeared to be streaming from his right shoulder. Applied pressure could help staunch the bleeding and the cold mountain water would constrict his blood vessels. His eyes fluttered and I suspected he was going into shock.

"Stay with me, Ted. I'm going to get you up on the bank."

"You mean my damn landfill," he rasped.

I managed to get both arms under him, lift, and slide him onto the grass. I rolled him over enough to untie his hands and then ripped off my soaked shirt and folded it as a compress. Taking Ted's left arm, I placed his hand on top of the fabric. "Press down as best you're able. I need to free Madison and secure Clarkson."

"I'm here." Madison had managed to stumble to us.

I quickly untied her and showed her where to apply pressure. Then I ran to where the powerful impact of a .45-caliber slug had felled Clarkson. He lay on his back, his face ghostly pale. The bullet wound in his right chest bled profusely. His labored breathing gurgled in his throat. Frightened eyes looked up at me.

"An ambulance is on the way." I tried to sound confident.

Clarkson struggled to form words. I placed my ear a few inches from his lips.

"It went so wrong," he whispered. "Not what I meant. But the Kirkpatricks were responsible for everything. Even Ken. Had to pay."

"Don't talk." I pressed my palms down on the open wound. Unlike Ted's, Clarkson's blood continued to flow unabated.

"I'm cold," he murmured. "Am I in the river? The water's so cold."

His eyes closed. His breathing stopped. The river had carried him away.

Chapter Twenty-Seven

Nakayla and I sat in a sterile conference room in the Asheville Police Department. It was nine thirty the morning after the terrible events by the Pigeon River. We were joined by Newly, Tuck, and Sheriff Cliff Hudson. Newly had requested that we gather to share information on the two cases—the murder of Luke Kirkpatrick and the death of Ken Stokes.

I'd been at the Haywood County Sheriff's Department until two in the morning as Hudson debriefed me on what had transpired in his jurisdiction. Then I made and signed a formal statement. Nakayla had brought me a change for my wet, bloody clothes and then driven me home for a few hours of restless sleep.

All of us had cups of coffee sitting on the table in front of us, not for the flavor but for the caffeine.

Newly took a sip and cleared his throat. "Well, thank you all for coming in after what's been a long night. I won't keep you any longer than necessary and, Sheriff, I appreciate your sharing Sam's statement so that he doesn't have to do it again."

Hudson wiped coffee from his mustache and nodded.

Newly glanced at the notepad in front of him. "Ted Kirkpatrick is still in intensive care but his surgeons are optimistic for his recovery from the gunshot. Fortunately, the head wound where Clarkson struck him in the parking lot wasn't serious. I haven't interviewed Madison yet, but she should be able to back up everything Clarkson told Sam, at least everything except his dying words."

"We're ready to close the Ken Stokes case," Hudson said. "From what Clarkson told Sam, we'd have probably charged him with manslaughter. Our DA might have taken a plea of involuntary. But, it sounds like Stokes's death pushed him over the edge."

"Our DA wouldn't have gone so easy," Tuck said. "Clarkson lived in a small farmhouse north of Woodfin. We found a recently fired shotgun in his bedroom."

"The crow?" I asked.

"That's my guess. We saw some in a neighboring field. Also we found the Babe Ruth baseball hidden in his sock drawer. In a shed he had acetone, Pool Shock, and brake fluid—all the elements used in the fire."

"And he had burn-barrels for trash," Newly said. "They could have created the dioxins for the doctored samples."

Hudson shook his head. "So much hate."

"So much death." The words caught in my throat as I stared at my hands folded in front of me, hands that had held the gun that killed him. "Hewitt's inmate confirmed Clarkson was the man who visited Leroy Mock. Clarkson lost twin brothers, his mother, and finally his incarcerated father. I can't tell you their deaths were because of the river pollution, but no one could tell him otherwise."

Newly leaned forward. "Sam, you did what you had to. I'm convinced you prevented a double murder and a suicide because it sounds to me that Clarkson would have killed himself. Despite the history, Ted is a man who is trying to do the right thing. Remember what he's lost. Clarkson took his only son from him."

I glanced at Nakayla and bit my tongue. Some son. Bedding his father's wife. I let the moment pass.

"And Clarkson's hate had been building for years," Tuck said. "I tracked down his stepfather earlier this morning. He lives in Bristol, Virginia. He said that despite the fact their marriage was over the moment their twins died, his wife never let go of her believe Leroy Mock had been railroaded. Clearly, he'd been distraught and stricken with grief. And Ted Kirkpatrick, the man who testified against him, only paid a fine. The stepfather said although she'd moved away physically, she couldn't move on emotionally, and they divorced after three years. Paul William Clarkson, known as Willie as a kid, kept his stepfather's name, but they hadn't spoken in eight years. About the time he reconnected with Leroy Mock."

"And I pity him for it," I said. "None of them could escape the river."

———

Later that afternoon, Nakayla and I sat at a different conference table. We were waiting in Hewitt's office for the attorney to make an appearance. Shirley had phoned inquiring whether we could meet him at two. When we'd arrived, the usually teasing office manager simply asked us to wait in the conference room.

We sat for ten minutes, hardly speaking to each other. Nakayla and I were talked out. I thought about the multiple Paul Clarksons I had known: the distraught and vengeful man pointing the revolver at Madison and Ted, the calculating Clarkson who widened the suspect pool by leaving the doctored samples atop the collection chest, the deceitful Clarkson who threw us off by showing up at Ken's construction site looking for him.

And then there was Clarkson, the maestro of the Moog, who creatively married virtuoso keyboard talent with technical engineering skills. In his own way, he rivaled William Ormandy for musical proficiency. Had his life gone differently, would he have been an Asheville Luminary of the future?

The door opened. I turned, expecting to see Hewitt. Madison Kirkpatrick entered. Hewitt followed a few steps behind.

She looked a mess. Her blond hair hung in unbrushed tangles. Her face was devoid of makeup, exposing blemished, sallow skin. Her puffy eyes were red from crying. Gone were the flashy earrings and glitzy necklaces. She was the plain mountain girl who'd struggled to rise above her roots.

I stood and offered my hand. She looked at me with surprise and managed a thin smile.

"Thank you," she whispered.

"Please, sit." Hewitt pulled out a chair for her. After taking his own seat, he said, "I saw Madison at the hospital this morning. She'd been there all night with Ted. He's regained consciousness and is out of danger."

"That's good news," Nakayla said.

"We spoke briefly, and she asked to meet with me here. She wants to come to some resolution regarding the video. I told her any conversation about it needs to involve you two." Hewitt eased back from the table. "I'll let her speak for herself."

Madison clasped and unclasped her hands nervously. "I committed a terrible wrong. I betrayed my husband. I betrayed myself. I make no excuses. You need to believe that I love Ted. If he saw or heard about the video and the affair, he'd be destroyed. He's lost his son. He would then forever have a tainted memory of him. I can't risk that happening." She looked at Hewitt. "I've told Mr. Donaldson that as soon as Ted has recovered sufficiently, I'll file for divorce. I'll make no claim on Ted's assets, and we'll craft a reason that doesn't reflect badly on him. In exchange, I ask for your word that you'll destroy that awful footage so that there's no way it could ever be made public." Her pleading eyes focused on each of us in turn. "Please."

Nakayla and I looked at each other. I gave a small nod.

Nakayla reached out and lightly touched Madison's hand. "Do you want to leave him?"

"No," she sobbed. "But better to leave him than destroy him."

"The video will be erased," I said. "Go back to your husband for good."

———

On the first Saturday in June, Nakayla threw an open house party. She and I had spent the previous two days supervising the delivery of new furniture and home accessories. Pictures were hung. Kitchen drawers filled. Groceries purchased. Even Blue got a new bed. In short, the house became a home, and Nakayla undertook each task with undisguised joy. It was contagious, and I was happy for her.

The gathering was small. Hewitt, Cory, and Shirley were there. Lynne and Walt, of course. Women from Nakayla's book club. I tended bar in the kitchen, at least for the first round of drinks. Then everyone was told to get his or her own refills.

Although the house was supposed to be the center of admiration, it fell a distant second to the adoration bestowed upon our youngest guest. Kenneth Walter Stokes made his social debut in the home of his father's last project. I knew it had to be a bittersweet occasion for Lynne and her father-in-law, but little K.W., as he was called, interjected a joyful note into what had been a sorrow-filled score. And I noticed no one was more smitten with the little fellow than Nakayla.

Hewitt stepped near me. "Can you talk a moment on the back deck?"

I followed him outside.

He leaned against the railing. "I spoke with Ted yesterday. He's been released by his doctors, and, although weak, he should have no long-term complications from the wound."

"That's good news. And Madison?"

"She's been devoted to him. That's a large part of why he's had such a successful recuperation. And I've asked Vernon Fraser not to tell Ted she was on those fraudulent accounts. I'm convinced she was unaware of what Luke was doing."

"I'm glad someone could be redeemed out of this whole sordid mess."

"Yes. And Ted's come to a decision. He's setting up an ESOP."

"What's that?"

"An employee stock option plan. He has the goal of gradually selling his company to his employees. Aside from Madison, they're his only family now. Them and the trust he's setting up."

"Trust for whom?"

Hewitt smiled. "Why, little K.W. It will be anonymous, but the legal work is already underway."

"That's kind of him."

"I told you he was a good man." He moved from the railing and offered his hand. "And so are you. Ted says he owes you his life, and he's anxious to repay you somehow."

"The trust for K.W. is payment enough."

"That's what I told him. But he insisted on doing something, so I made a suggestion. We've set up a mini-trust."

"For what?"

"For you and Nakayla to have home plate season tickets to the Asheville Tourists. For life." He clapped me on the back. "Who knows? Maybe you'll witness a home run by a future Babe Ruth."

Later, Nakayla and I sat on her new sofa, each enjoying a glass of white wine. Blue lay on his cushion in front of the dormant fireplace.

"I think that went well," I said. "The house looks great. Your personality's infused throughout."

"I'm glad you like it." She set her glass on an end table. "Come. I have something to show you."

"Can I bring my wine?"

"Yes. Follow me." She led me to the guest bedroom and the closed, sliding closet doors. "I got a new house, and Blue got a new cushion. It's only fair you get something new." She slid back one of the doors to reveal shirts and pants hanging from a wardrobe rod. Then she gestured to a set of dresser drawers. "And there's socks, underwear, and T-shirts as well." She opened the top drawer and retrieved a key. She pressed it into my hand. "I want you to know my vintage door, locked or not, is always open for you."

I looked at the closet and then the dresser. "What? No pajamas?"

She raised up on tiptoes to kiss me. "Who needs them?"

AUTHOR'S NOTE

Although this book is a work of fiction, many of its elements are based upon historical facts. Babe Ruth and Lou Gehrig played exhibition games in Asheville, North Carolina, where Ruth was mistakenly reported "dead" from his gastrointestinal inflammation that became known as "the bellyache heard 'round the world."

Internationally renowned composer Béla Bartók stayed in Asheville for his health December 1943 to April 1944, composed his *Sonata for Solo Violin,* and began work on his Third Piano Concerto, also known as The Asheville Concerto because of the Asheville birdsongs incorporated in the slow second movement. During his time in Asheville, Bartók stayed at the Albemarle Inn, a wonderful B and B still operating today.

Robert Moog, inventor of the Moog synthesizer, spent the latter years of his life in Asheville, teaching at UNC-Asheville, and resurrecting his Moog Music company. The Moog factory still produces a line of synthesizers, and, like Sam Blackman, visitors can sign up for a fascinating tour of the facility.

Wilma Dykeman was a pioneering environmentalist and social justice advocate ahead of her time. She fought for clean water and her seminal book of 1955, *The French Broad,* brought water pollution to national attention. She particularly challenged the paper companies of the Asheville area for their toxic dumping into the mountain waterways.

The resulting pollution described in the story is also true. Wanton dumping of chemical waste turned the Pigeon River into the "Dead River." Tennessee residents were the downstream victims and the town of Hartford became known as "Widowville" because of the number of deaths attributed to the dioxin poison penetrating the environment. Old paper mill landfills still exist today and the leaching of the waste back into the water is an ongoing concern, exacerbated by the relaxation of EPA and Clean Water Act standards.

Linking all of these separate historical occurrences into a story required the creation of the Asheville Luminaries Festival, a wholly fictional event. But, given Asheville's rich legacy of artistic and innovative individuals, it is an event that could easily exist.

ACKNOWLEDGMENTS

Special thanks to the innkeepers of the Albemarle Inn, Rosemary and Fabrizio Chiariello, for sharing their inn's marvelous history.

I'm grateful to Poisoned Pen Press, especially my editor Barbara Peters, for making Sam and Nakayla's adventures possible. Also to my family, Linda, Melissa, Pete, Charlie, Lindsay, Jordan, and Sawyer for being in my life.

In writing a story that deals with deadly environmental disasters of the recent past, I've become more aware of dangers in the immediate future as standards relax and climate conditions challenge the world. I appreciate all efforts being made to ensure Spaceship Earth receives our protection and our care.

ABOUT THE AUTHOR

by Linda de Castrique

Mark de Castrique was born in Hendersonville, North Carolina, near Asheville. He went straight from the hospital to the funeral home, where his father was the funeral director and the family lived upstairs. The unusual setting sparked his popular Buryin' Barry series and launched his mystery-writing career.

Mark is the author of twenty novels—seven set in the fictional North Carolina mountain town of Gainesboro, eight set in Asheville, two in Washington DC, one science thriller in the year 2030, and two mysteries written for middle-graders and set in the Charlotte region.

His novels have received Starred Reviews from *Publishers Weekly*, *Library Journal*, and *Booklist*. The *Chicago Tribune* wrote, "As important and as impressive as the author's narrative skills are the subtle ways he captures the geography—both physical and human—of a unique part of the American South."

Mark is a veteran of the broadcast and film production

business. In Washington DC, he directed numerous news and public affairs programs and received an Emmy Award for his documentary film work. Through his company, MARK et al., he writes and produces videos for corporate and broadcast clients.

His years in Washington inspired his DC thrillers, *The 13th Target*, involving a terrorist plot against the Federal Reserve, and *The Singularity Race*, a winner-take-all quest for Artificial Intelligence.

Mark lives in Charlotte, but he and his wife, Linda, can be often found in the North Carolina mountains or the nation's capital.